MATTHEW RIEF

BETRAYED IN THE KEYS
A Logan Dodge Adventure

Florida Keys Adventure Series
Volume 4

Logan Dodge Adventures

Gold in the Keys
(Florida Keys Adventure Series Book 1)

Hunted in the Keys
(Florida Keys Adventure Series Book 2)

Revenge in the Keys
(Florida Keys Adventure Series Book 3)

Betrayed in the Keys
(Florida Keys Adventure Series Book 4)

If you're interested in receiving my newsletter for updates on my upcoming books, you can sign up on my website:

matthewrief.com

MAP

PROLOGUE

Florida Bay
1672

A strong gust of warm sea air brushed against the man's scruffy face, causing him to shield it with his hand and look over his right shoulder. His deep brown eyes grew wide, then he blinked a few times, unable to believe what he was seeing. Less than half a mile from where he sat perched atop the mainmast of his ship, the dark outline of a second ship appeared like a demon through a veil of dense morning fog.

"Captain!" he yelled as loudly as he could. He held tightly to the upper portions of the main ratlines as he leaned over, casting his gaze towards the quarterdeck.

Captain John Shadow, the notoriously ruthless pirate, stood beside the port gunwale. He was an imposing sight, standing at well over six feet tall,

5

with the strong frame of a man who'd spent a lifetime undergoing the harsh conditions at sea. He had midnight-black hair that he kept short and a full beard with sideburns like stirrups. His roughly chiseled face and piercing brown eyes struck fear into his adversaries. He wore a leather tricorn hat that was tattered from years at sea, a white button-up shirt, black pants, and tall leather boots. Attached to his waistband were a pair of gold-hilted cutlasses along with a dagger and a loaded flintlock, weapons that rarely left his body.

His left arm rested against the main boom as he looked out over the bow and the white-covered horizon. Hearing the call from above, he gazed towards the lookout post atop the mainmast. In the waters of Florida Bay and along the stretch of islands off Southern Florida, it was important to station a watch to keep an eye out for shallow reefs and ledges. Though charts were used, they were far from perfect, and oftentimes mistakes were made.

Seeing that the lookout was pointing over the stern, Shadow turned around, and his eyes grew wide when he saw the approaching ship. Instinctively, he reached into his trousers' front pocket and pulled out a brass spyglass.

"How are they sailing in such shallow waters, Blackwood?" Shadow asked his first mate, but as he focused through his scope at the oncoming ship, he realized that it wasn't an ordinary warship. "That's a sloop," he added, pulling his spyglass away and handing it to his first mate.

Nash Blackwood looked through the lens at the ship. Unlike his captain, Blackwood was short and stocky, but he was as strong as an ox.

After a few seconds, he nodded. "Yes, Captain.

She's a sloop alright."

Peering through the scope, they could see the first union flag, one similar to the Union Jack aside from its lack of Irish diagonal stripes, as it waved gently at the peak of the mainmast.

For nearly five years, Shadow and his buccaneers had sailed unencumbered throughout the waters surrounding the southern islands off Florida. They called the islands by their Spanish name of Los Martires, meaning *the martyrs*, a name which had been given to them by Ponce de León as he'd searched for the Fountain of Youth. During their years of piracy, Shadow and his crew had picked off their prey, one by one, with deadly precision. Their shallow draft, unparallel speed, and knowledge of their domain allowed them to catch many unsuspecting Spanish galleons and English merchant ships off guard.

For the first time since Shadow and his crew had committed mutiny, taken over the *Crescent* and turned to piracy, they'd become the hunted.

On the approaching ship, the Royal Navy sailors rigged their sails to catch all of the tropical wind as they zeroed in on the pirates. Though sloops were primarily merchant vessels, many English higher-ups saw the value in a warship that could track down its enemies faster and in shallower waters. What the *Valiant* lacked in firepower, it made up for in maneuverability.

Most of its hull was copper-clad, preventing barnacles and other sea growth from attaching themselves and causing drag. The hull design was streamlined for efficiency, its masts, sails, and rigging the best that royal money could buy. It was crewed by some of the most seasoned and well-trained sailors in the Royal Navy. And William Gray, a British officer who was well known for his ability to track down and courageously engage pirates, was its captain.

"Load the bow cannon," Gray yelled. "Prepare to fire a warning shot."

Back on the *Crescent*, Shadow glanced down at his compass, which was mounted in a gimbal in order to be less affected by the motion of the ship. The thin slice of magnetic ore oriented itself in its naturally drawn north-south direction, giving Shadow an indication of north in relation to the course they were heading.

"Check our speed, Blackwood," Shadow said.

His first mate nodded and brought two men up from the main deck. One of them grabbed a small coil of rope with a flat wooden triangle attached on all three corners at the end. The rope was marked at intervals by uniformly spaced knots, and the other end was coiled around a wooden reel. With a nod of his head, the buccaneer dropped the triangle into the sea from the stern. The friction of the water against the wood caused the line to pay out from the reel. The ship's speed would be estimated by timing the paying out of the knots using a sandglass.

As the last of the fine sand tumbled to the bottom of the glass, Blackwood looked up and said, "Nine knots, Captain."

Shadow had his chart table and map rule laid out on an upturned barrel that was a quarter of the way filled with freshwater. A quick calculation revealed that it would take just under three hours for his ship to reach their shoreline fortifications to the southeast, and that was if the wind stayed true. It would be less if he could sail straight, but the fourteen-knot headwind blowing in from the east forced the captain to tack his schooner back and forth, making it take longer to travel from one place to another. Trying to reach his fortifications was out of the question.

A moment later, the sounds of waves crashing against the hull were overtaken by a loud explosion from far behind them. Shadow turned around just in time to see a cannonball splash into the water a few hundred feet from the *Crescent*'s starboard side. It was a warning shot, and Shadow knew that he'd have to give the English warship an answer soon.

As he did before any engagement, Shadow ran through scenarios in his mind. Since he couldn't outrun his enemy, he only had two options: fight or surrender. But even if he threw up a makeshift white flag, signaling surrender, he knew that the Royal Navy sailors would show no mercy. He along with his crew would be hanged in Port Royal in front of hundreds of angry spectators. Shadow had seen it many times before. No, there would be no surrender. If they went down, they'd do so sword in hand and with freedom in their lungs.

Shadow decided in an instant to take on the approaching ship like he had every other problem in his life, head-on. After having Blackwood gather the crew on the main deck, he stepped onto the railing just forward of the helm and grabbed the mainsheet with his left hand for support.

"Warriors of the seas," Shadow yelled, standing with his chest out, "for years I've fought alongside you. Countless times have we battled and spilt blood together. Now, this beast that lurks in the fog demands our surrender. It demands that we resign our fate to the gallows and die as prisoners." He paused a moment, then added with an even stronger tone, "I cannot speak for you men, but as for myself, as long as I have breath in my lungs and blood coursing through my veins, I will fight with all that I am. I will not go down until every trace of life has left me. I will fight, and fight on until I have nothing left." He paused for a moment to catch his breath. Then, snatching one of his rapiers with his right hand, he continued, "This beast demands our lives. But if it wants them, it's gonna have to come and bloody get them!"

Shadow lifted his sword high above his head and gave a loud battle cry. As his men joined in the intimidating chorus, Shadow leapt back onto the quarterdeck. Striding towards the stern, he aimed his sword towards the *Valiant* and yelled once more, this time directing his barbaric voice towards his enemies.

As his newly energized men prepared for battle, Shadow took another look at the ship behind them and cursed it under his breath. A young man with tanned skin and dirty blond hair ran up beside him. He handed his captain a leather sash with four loaded flintlocks holstered in a row, which Shadow secured across his chest. Then he handed Shadow two loaded muskets, which he propped against the gunwale beside him.

"Thank you, Ulysses," Shadow said. He placed a hand on the young man's shoulder, looked into his eyes, and added, "Be courageous, and get to your post."

The young man nodded and strode down the steps towards the third cannon from the stern. Shadow watched as his crew jumped into action, taking charge of their roles and completing actions as they had hundreds of times before. They grabbed muskets, powder kegs, and cannonballs, staged boarding lines with metal hooks attached, and moved the cannons into position.

Though the ship's ten guns below deck were essentially locked in place, the five up on the main deck were easily mobile, allowing them to be moved back and forth depending on their enemy's location. Shadow watched as the main deck gun crews rolled their cannons into place and secured them.

When his men were almost finished preparing, Shadow gave out another loud battle cry and grabbed hold of the helm himself. With strong movements, he rotated it as fast as he could to port, causing the rudder to angle and the ship to undergo a sweeping turn. As the *Crescent* completed its turn and the approaching English ship came into view, the main boom slammed into the rigging and the mainsail caught all of the wind, accelerating them towards their enemy.

As the two ships closed in on each other, a loud explosion rattled the air, followed by a plume of white smoke as the *Valiant* again fired its bow cannon. This time it was clear that the English captain was no longer interested in sending warning shots. The heavy ball of lead rocketed toward them, spinning and slicing through the air before splashing into the water less than fifty feet from the *Crescent*'s port bow. Shadow smiled as a large spray of seawater rose into the air.

When the two ships were less than a quarter of a mile from each other, Shadow turned sharply to port, wanting to take the English on his starboard side. Twenty of his men gathered at the starboard bow, loading their muskets and preparing to fire. As the gun teams loaded their cannons and muscled the barrels through the starboard portholes, Shadow ordered his men at the bow to take aim.

Closing the distance to just a few hundred feet, Shadow ordered the main and fore sail sheets to be loosened until the massive sails flapped in the wind. With the wind spilling out of the sails, the *Crescent* slowed as the two bows crossed each other. Shadow didn't hesitate.

"Fire muskets!" he yelled.

Less than a second later, the starboard bow of the *Crescent* exploded to life as a loud symphony of gunpowder ignited. Plumes of white smoke appeared as the line of musket balls tore through the air. The sailors aboard the *Valiant* took cover, but a handful were struck by the ferocious balls of lead, some dying on impact and some losing limbs as the force ripped them from their bodies.

With the two ships sailing alongside each other, Shadow turned his attention to his gun teams. They would engage in the most common and brutal configuration of Naval warfare in the age of sail: broadside to broadside. Shadow could see the *Valiant* sailors moving about on the deck, their blue uniforms unmistakable and the officers' golden buttons reflecting off what little light bled through the surrounding fog.

Shadow grabbed one of his rapiers with his right hand and held it high over his head.

"Fire!" he yelled, his voice booming and filled with rage.

With careful and practiced timing, the cannons along the starboard side of the *Crescent* thundered to life two at a time. There was reason behind every action, regardless of how chaotic it seemed. Firing all ten cannons along the starboard side at the same time would create a combined recoil force that the *Crescent*'s inner hull wouldn't be able to withstand.

In a loud haze of yellow flame and white-gray smoke, the six-pound balls of lead exploded out of the cannons' mouths. Screaming through the air at over seven hundred miles per hour, the heavy projectiles crashed through the *Valiant*'s hull, sending hundreds of sharp splinters spraying like shrapnel into anything and anyone in their path.

Within seconds, the English ship retaliated. A wave of cannon and musket balls crashed back at the *Crescent*, shattering its hull and sending many of its crew to a painful death. With his ship sailing to a stop alongside the *Valiant*, Shadow took cover, then rose and ordered his men to fire at will. His musket team of twenty had moved beside him and were taking aim once more. Shadow grabbed his musket and aimed over the gunwale at an English officer manning the helm. Having spent his entire life shooting, Shadow pulled the trigger and sent the ball into the officer's chest with expert precision.

The battle waged on in a loud and violent haze, Shadow watched as handfuls of his men screamed and fell to the deck around him, wailing in pools of blood. His resolve and the resolve of those still alive only strengthened as they continued to pick off sailors aboard the *Valiant*. But Shadow could see that they were losing. They were outnumbered, outtrained, and outgunned.

In a seemingly foolish act of desperation, he ordered his men to board the English warship. If they couldn't defeat their opponents from afar, maybe they could up close and in their faces. The pirate way. Ropes with metal hooks were tossed and pulled taut until the two ships pressed against each other. Shadow gathered what remained of his crew, gave out a barbaric yell, and pressed his right leg up onto the gunwale. With all of his strength, he hurled himself through the air and landed on the deck of the *Valiant*.

With his men right on his heels, Shadow snatched two flintlocks from across his chest, raised them at a cluster of sailors closing in on him, and fired them both. The deck of the *Valiant* transformed into a brutal symphony of exploding gunpowder, clanking swords, and agonizing screams. As Shadow dropped the flintlocks and grabbed two more, he headed towards the *Valiant*'s quarterdeck.

Aiming forward, he took down two more sailors, then dropped his guns and slid both rapiers free from their sheaths. As he and his men stormed up the stairs, heading for the stern, a musket ball grazed Shadow's side, tearing off a chunk of flesh and sending a burning pain through his body. The pirate captain twisted sideways and grunted but kept moving through the pain up onto the quarterdeck.

With strong, calculated strikes, Shadow sliced through his opponents in flashes of movement. His adrenaline surged as he cut down his attackers with reckless abandon. But even with the incredible success of his strike on the *Valiant*, his men were still outnumbered. Glancing over his shoulder at the battle waging on the main deck, Shadow could see that his force of over a hundred pirates had dwindled down to just thirty.

Shadow shifted his gaze back towards the helm just in time to see the *Valiant*'s captain, William Gray, move towards him. Though not as big as Shadow, Gray was imposing nonetheless and had fought many successful battles at sea. Holding a silver-hilted sabre that had been passed down for three generations in his right hand, he stabbed it through Blackwood with a strong motion. The blade penetrated to the other side, blood dripping from its tip as Blackwood wailed. Gray pulled the blade free, and Shadow's first mate fell hard to the deck.

Shadow gazed into the English captain's eyes, rage overtaking his face.

Shadow lunged towards Gray and hit him with a series of strong rapier attacks, slicing his swords through the air with incredible dexterity, only to be deflected at the last second. Equally matched in skill and experience, the two engaged in an epic sword fight at the stern, dueling amongst the sounds of exploding gunpowder and dying men.

Glancing to his right, Shadow spotted an English officer zeroing in on one of his men from behind. Shoving Gray aside, he grabbed his last remaining flintlock, took aim, and pulled the trigger just as the officer was about to stab his sword through the air. The bullet struck him in the chest, blood spraying out his back as he collapsed to the deck.

Shadow had saved the man's life, but not without cost. As he turned back to engage Gray, the *Valiant*'s captain swung his sword violently through the air, slicing a gash across Shadow's chest. Shadow's body twisted and he fell to the deck, the pain being too much to bear.

Gray stepped towards him and, calling upon all of his remaining strength, Shadow grabbed his rapier from the deck. Slicing it as hard as he could through the air, Shadow caught Gray off guard and cut a deep gash in the captain's left leg just below the knee. Gray let out a loud and powerful scream as he fell on top of Shadow, blood gushing out of his leg.

Still holding tight to his sword, Gray held it up against Shadow's neck and looked deep into his eyes.

"You and your crew are dead," Gray said. "You

have been defeated."

Shadow's face shifted away from anger in an instant, and the pirate captain laughed maniacally.

"Even if you kill me," Shadow said, "you will never find my treasure."

The English captain grunted, then reared back and swung his sword as hard as he could towards Shadow. At the last second, Shadow gripped the dagger from his waistband and blocked the blow, the two blades colliding with an ear-shattering clank. The two captains' faces were only inches apart as they scowled at each other.

"You could search for ten lifetimes," Shadow said, "and you would never find it."

A deafening explosion rattled the air and shook the deck beneath them. Their eyes gravitated towards the *Crescent*, where the explosion had come from. The hundred-foot schooner had been torn to shreds by cannon fire, and the explosion had come from below its decks and nearly split the ship in two. Water flowed into its hull from all sides, and it was clear that the ocean would claim it in a matter of seconds.

Shadow knew what had happened. With the pirates on the verge of defeat, one of his men had lit the powder kegs, creating a massive explosion that had destroyed the *Crescent* from the inside. It was a last-ditch effort to keep their ship out of enemy hands.

The explosion infuriated Gray, even though the pirates were down to their last men. The battle was over, but Gray wasn't just interested in taking them down. No, he wanted their ship, and above all else, he wanted their treasure.

Casting his gaze back down towards a bleeding Shadow, Gray brought his sword back and swung it down as hard as he could. Shadow tried to deflect the blow again with his dagger, but the force was too great and it knocked his only weapon out of his hands. As the dagger tumbled over the gunwale and splashed into the water below, Gray yelled another curse and stabbed Shadow through the heart without a moment's hesitation.

Air burst from Shadow's lungs, and his eyes grew wide. Death was upon him. He could feel the life draining from his body with every passing second. Tilting his head to the right, he watched as his ship was swallowed by the sea. He felt a stiff breeze against his face, then his head dropped and his eyes closed, never to open again.

ONE

Key West
February 2009

I spent hours examining the old dagger, admiring its craftsmanship and condition long after the orange sun sank into the Gulf of Mexico. The blade was dull, and I slid my hands over its intricate details, from its worn tip down to its golden hilt. Sitting on the sunbed of my forty-eight-foot Baia Flash, I took in a deep breath of fresh tropical air and set the dagger on the ivory-colored cushion beside me.

The moon was nearly full, and it cast a silvery polish over the still waters of Conch Harbor Marina and the open ocean beyond. Countless questions filled my mind, the most prominent one being, who was Beatrice Taylor—the woman whose name was elegantly carved into the dagger's hilt? I'd been told that it had been found by accident by a local shrimper, and I couldn't help but wonder what else might be resting at the bottom at the location where it had been discovered.

"Are you gonna stare at that all night?" Angelina said, appearing from inside the salon and snapping me from my thoughts.

Angelina Fox was tall, athletic, and stunningly beautiful. She had long blond hair, smooth tanned skin, and blue eyes that seemed to pull you in and capture you in their spell. But despite her supermodel looks, she was also a highly trained fighter and one of the deadliest snipers in the world.

I glanced over my shoulder and smiled at her. "I guess I have stared at it long enough, haven't I?"

"If I didn't know any better, I'd guess you were trying to summon a genie."

She moved alongside the sunbed, her bare feet seeming to hover over the deck as she plopped down beside me and grabbed the dagger. She was wearing a colorful sundress instead of her typical denim shorts and tee shirt.

"Where did Chris say he found it?" she asked while looking it over.

"He didn't find it. It was his uncle. And he wasn't very specific, unfortunately."

Chris Hale was a friend of mine who I'd met under unfortunate circumstances during Tropical Storm Fay. His family's yacht had crashed into Loggerhead Key in Dry Tortugas, and I'd spent two days on the island, protecting his family from a Cuban gang leader hell-bent on murdering them. I hadn't seen Chris or his wife and daughters for half a year, until they'd pulled into the marina and moored just down the dock from me earlier today. By way of thanking me for saving them, Chris had given me the dagger and told me it had been found by his uncle and given to him as part of his inheritance.

A second later, Ange slid off the sunbed and jumped to her feet. Holding the dagger in her right hand, she swung it through the air like a buccaneer, then brought her eyes over to meet mine.

"Don't tell me that you'd rather sit and stare at this knife all night than take me out on the town," she said, exaggeratedly fluttering her eyelashes at me.

I shook my head, then slid my bare feet onto the deck, stood tall, and pulled her in close. "Wouldn't even think about it."

I placed my hand against her cheek and kissed her softly. A few minutes later, I'd changed into a fresh tee shirt, along with socks and a pair of black Converse low-tops. I locked up the Baia and turned on the security system, and we headed down the dock towards the waterfront.

I usually didn't like to go out on the town when there was a cruise ship moored. It wasn't that I didn't enjoy good nightlife. In fact, one of the reasons I'd chosen Key West as opposed to other towns I loved in the Keys was its notorious crazy side. But when a cruise ship pulled in and thousands of tourists came ashore, they clashed with the thousands of tourists who'd driven down from the mainland and made it difficult to get a table or order a drink at many of the local joints, especially along the waterfront and on the famous Duval Street. But Ange really wanted to try out a place called Tipsy Turvy, a local bar she'd read about in some magazine that apparently had a really good vibe.

It was a Friday night, and the wild tropical paradise was buzzing with life. Just a few blocks from the marina, we were met with crowds of tourists that filled the sidewalks and intermixed with everyone from human statues to acrobatic dancers and a few guys dressed up and walking around on stilts. Live music played from every street corner and almost every restaurant, creating a blended symphony of Buffett, the Beach Boys, and Jack Johnson.

Most tourists come down in the winter months, primarily December through February, to escape the northern cold. While much of the country is dealing with snow-covered driveways and iced-over windshields, the Keys boast an average high of seventy-five degrees. Throw in beautiful white sandy beaches, incredible fishing, and some of the best seafood around, and you get thousands hopping on a plane or driving hours to feel the lower-latitude sunshine.

Less than five minutes after leaving the marina, we spotted a lively bar with the name Tipsy Turvy in bright red neon letters hanging over the entrance. People were overflowing out both the street entrance and the entrance along the waterfront, but that didn't dissuade Ange in the slightest.

"Buy me a drink, sailor?" she said, shooting me a captivating smile.

My hand clasped hers as I smiled back, stepping up onto the old maple hardwood floor and into the cluster of people. We found a pair of open stools near the end of the bar and plopped down onto the blue cushions. The bartender, a purple-haired woman with tattoos up both arms, asked us what we'd be having, and a few minutes later, she set our drinks on the rustic counter.

"You sure you don't want to sit on one of those?" Ange asked, a childlike grin on her face as she nodded at a few stools down the bar from us. They were the embarrassing kind you usually see in tropical tourist destinations around the world, with plastic bikini butt cheeks sticking out the back, complete with chipped paint and all.

"A man like me can only handle so much," I said. I grabbed my mojito and chimed the glass against the rim of Ange's mai tai. After we both took a long pull, my eyes focused on a shirtless beer bellied drunk guy wearing a green Dr. Seuss–style hat.

Ange laughed when she saw my expression and said, "Well, thank you for humoring me tonight. I realize this isn't your typical scene."

I kissed her on the cheek, then took a few glances around the room and spotted a dark-haired young girl with freckles sitting at a table with three preppy-looking guys wearing polo and button-up shirts. They were sitting on the far side of the room, and my view was constantly being obstructed by passing people, but something about the way that they interacted seemed off.

"You'd better get to drinking if you're gonna keep up with me tonight," Ange said.

I shook myself from my thoughts, turned to look at her and saw that her glass, which had been full only seconds earlier, was now empty. She looked at the bartender and added, "I'll have another, please."

"I think I'm gonna take it easy tonight," I said, nursing my favorite drink.

Ange chuckled. "You? Take it easy? I'll believe that when I see it. What's on your mind, anyway? Thinking about that old dagger?"

"Yeah. And what else we might find down there. I feel like there's a whole story here just waiting to be told."

The waitress returned with another mai tai, and Ange wrapped her right hand around it, raised it in the air beside me, and said, "To the ocean's booty."

I laughed, grabbed my mojito and chimed the glass against hers.

"That's not the only booty I'll drink to."

I killed the rest of it with one long pull, then set it back on the counter. Uncontrollably, my eyes gravitated back towards the young woman and the three guys at the other side of the bar. I got the overwhelming sense that something wasn't right. It came from years of working in dangerous situations around the world. Whether I wanted it to or not, every time I stepped into a public place, my mind went to work, sizing up the place and everyone in it.

The girl, though smiling at times, had a faint look of fear in her eyes. And the three guys were so loud and obnoxious that I could hear a few of their words over the crowd between us. I glanced over a few times over the next half hour, observing them carefully. Just as I finished my second mojito, I noticed one of the guys reach into his pocket. Like the other guys, he had a clean-cut look to him. He had short brown hair and was wearing a light blue polo shirt.

I continued to watch as the intoxicated young woman looked the other way and the guy who'd reached for his pocket snatched her drink from the table. His action was blocked by a passing group of retirees, but I knew what he did. The look on his face after he set the drink back in front of the young woman, urging her to drink, said it all.

I turned back towards the bar, shook my head slightly and glanced at Ange, who was about to finish her fourth drink.

"Something seems off about that group," she said. Then she turned, looked across the room and added, "There were three girls with them when we walked in."

I nodded, and when our eyes met, Ange saw the fire burning within mine.

"That guy with the polo shirt just slipped her something," I said.

Ange's face went from curious to hell-hath-no-fury rage in a microsecond. Without a moment's hesitation, her eyes narrowed like a mama bear watching some stranger mess with her cubs, and she sprang from the barstool, causing it to tilt over and rattle onto the floor.

I stood beside her and placed a hand on her shoulder. Ange had kept me in check many times before, but now it was my turn to be the reasonable one. Something about seeing a helpless young woman being taken advantage of by a group of guys tipped her off the deep end in a hurry. I felt a surge of rage burning within me as well but managed to keep my head level.

"Wait," I said, but she brushed it off.

"Screw that," she said. "Those punks will be lucky if they can still stand when I'm through with them."

"Not here," I said, raising my voice. She stopped and sighed, and I continued, "One of them has a switchblade, and who knows what else they might have?" She gave me a who-the-hell-cares look, and I scanned around the bar. "We can't risk anyone else getting hurt."

I knew that there was only a microscopic chance that the punks could pose even the slightest challenge for Ange and me, but we didn't know them and, more importantly, we didn't know if they were armed with something a little more dangerous than a knife. Killing someone with a gun from point-blank range doesn't exactly require a lot of skill. And even though Ange and I were both armed, I didn't want to give them any sort of fighting chance.

She shrugged, the ripples around her eyes relaxing a little. "What do you want to do? Just take them out back and lay into them?"

"Exactly. Just like that time in Bogotá."

She paused for a moment as she remembered the incident a few years back.

"Okay," she said. "But this time, we strike first."

We stared at the group intently, watching as the three guys rose to their feet. They brought the young woman up by lifting under her arms and laughed amongst themselves as they ushered her through the cluster of people, tables, and chairs.

"Okay," I said, moving past Ange. "Time to put an end to this."

TWO

As I suspected, the group of guys were leading the intoxicated and drugged young woman to the side door. I headed for the back, moving swiftly through a sea of tables, chairs, waitresses, and people standing and watching a soccer game and golf highlights on the flat-screens. Near the back, I moved past two rows of crowded pool tables and out a pair of back doors that were propped open with a flowerpot.

The bar had a few outdoor tables, and there was an intense game of cornhole taking place just outside the doors. Less than fifty feet from the back of the bar was the dark ocean, and I could hear the soft crashing of waves against the boardwalk. Just a short walk down the waterfront was the Mallory Square Pier, where a large cruise ship was moored.

I hooked a sharp left, moving towards the side of the bar, where the group of guys were leading the woman. The side door led out to a small open space between the bar and the restaurant beside it, and the space was filled with dumpsters and a few chairs for people to take their smoke breaks. It was quieter over there, but I wasn't standing for very long before the muffled sounds from inside the bar instantly grew louder as the old metal door creaked open in front of me.

The big guy came through first, carrying a large glass of half-drunk beer in one hand, a sick smile plastered across his face. Next came the two other guys, who moved on either side of the young girl, practically carrying her as her feet dragged loosely and took the occasional struggled attempt at a step.

The big guy's smile vanished in an instant as he looked up and saw me standing in front of them. I stared back into his cocky, predatorial eyes, letting him see the rage burning within me.

"Let her go," I said, my voice low and powerful.

The group stopped and looked me over with their mostly intoxicated eyes.

"Piss off," the fat one said.

They took a step towards me and I placed a hand in the air.

"Look," I said. "You three are gonna let her go one way or another. That's a fact. The only question is how many broken bones you're each gonna have by the time you do."

The guys froze for a moment, then looked at each other and laughed. Then the fat one took a step towards me and said, "Maybe you didn't hear me, dumbass. But I told you to piss off."

As his blood started to boil, I kept a calm, stern voice and said, "I'm betting on close to ten broken bones between the three of you. What do you think, Ange?"

27

Ange, who had exited right behind the group without the guys noticing, was standing against the wall beside the door.

"That's way too low," she said loudly, causing the three guys to turn around like spooked deer. She moved away from the wall towards the group and added, "I'm gonna break over five of this little preppy punk's alone. I'd say closer to twenty."

The startled guys looked back and forth between myself and Ange, the two in the back keeping the girl held up.

"On second thought," the tall, skinny guy said, speaking for the first time, "just you piss off, asshole." He pointed at me, then turned back to look at Ange. "Your girlfriend can stay. In fact, I think I'd like to get her a drink."

I took a big stride towards the group, having had enough of their crap.

"Alright," I said. "This is your last chance. Either you guys let her go, or you'll be spending the next few weeks in a hospital."

The fat guy laughed, then moved towards me and put a finger in my face. "Hey, who in the hell do you think you—"

Before he'd even realized what was happening, I grabbed hold of his finger with a tight grip and twisted his arm forcefully in a direction it wasn't intended to go. His finger cracked audibly as I hyperextended his arm and bent his elbow back. Stepping behind him, I brought his arm over my shoulder, bent my knees down and hurled him over my body.

He groaned as his heavy frame did an unwanted front flip and his back slammed hard onto the pavement. When I looked up, Ange already had

Skinny on the ground as well. She'd hit him with a roundhouse kick to his face, and blood flowed out from his nostrils as he rocked back and forth, his hands pressed to either side of his nose.

That left only Polo Shirt standing, and as Ange and I closed in on him, he threw the girl to the ground and reached for something tucked into the back of his waistband. His left hand gripped a silver Springfield compact pistol, and just as he pulled it out, I tackled him hard to the ground, causing the handgun to rattle onto the pavement beside us. I threw a few solid punches into his face to teach him a lesson, then rose to my feet and grabbed his handgun from the ground.

"You fucking asshole," Polo Shirt said as he struggled to his feet. He wiped the blood from his face with the top of his hand, then grunted as he lunged towards me.

Ange jumped in, hitting him with a strong side kick to his gut that caused him to gag and lurch forward. Wrapping her arms around his neck, she slammed him to the ground and put him in a reverse chin lock. Before the guy knew what was happening, a deep and powerful pain radiated across his body as Ange pulled him back, squeezing tightly with her arms forced into his neck. He wailed in pain as Ange turned over, knocked him unconscious, and rose to her feet.

With all three guys on the ground and immobilized, I told Ange to help the girl while I checked the guys for any more weapons. After searching their clothes, the only other thing I found was a switchblade in the fat guy's pocket, which I tossed into the ocean along with Polo Shirt's Springfield.

I moved over to Ange, who was cradling the

woman, her forehead bleeding from being thrown to the ground. I crouched down beside the woman and gazed into her wide-open hazel eyes.

"Can you hear me?" I asked, placing my hand softly against hers.

Her body shook, and she breathed heavily.

"She's in shock," Ange said.

I moved in closer and said, "You're safe now."

After a few quick breaths, she blinked twice and said, "They... they said they would kill me if I screamed."

Ange held the girl tighter and motioned towards the three bodies sprawled out in awkward positions beside us.

"Don't worry," Ange said softly. "They're not gonna hurt anyone anytime soon. What's your name?"

The woman slowed her breathing slightly and said, "Candace. I'm... I'm on the cruise ship *Princess Louisa*. I came ashore with my friends and those guys got us all drunk."

I stared deeply into her eyes. "Candace, everything's going to be okay. We're gonna take you safely back to your ship, but we need you to call your friends and let them know what happened. We need to make sure that they're okay and didn't get taken away as well."

She sat for a moment and her eyes grew wide. Clearly, she hadn't thought that there might be more bad guys around. Reaching around her, she said, "My purse—it's not here. I must have left it inside."

I rose to my feet. "What's it look like?" I asked, and when she told me that it was small and light pink, I told Ange to wait with her while I went inside to get it.

Fortunately, I managed to find both Candace's purse and her friends within a few minutes and I explained the situation to them. Ange and I walked all four of them along the waterfront and down the pier towards the gangway to the *Princess Louisa*. After the cruise attendant had checked their tickets and effects, Candace turned to Ange and me.

"Thank you," she said, her face having become wet with tears after realizing how close she'd just come to being raped.

Ange stepped towards her, wiped away a streak of dripping mascara from her face, and said, "I'm glad we were there to stop it."

When she looked to me, I added, "Be careful. There are islands in the Caribbean where this sort of thing is far more common. Enjoy yourselves, but just be aware that this kind of thing happens, so you need to be cautious."

She nodded, then Ange and I hugged her and she headed across the gangway onto the cruise ship beside her friends. Ange and I stood beside each other on the pier, watching as they disappeared from view. It was almost 1100, so the pier was bustling with people heading back to their floating resort, some of them barely sober enough to stay on their feet.

Ange turned to me and smiled. "Can't we just have one normal night out together?"

I laughed. "You and me? I wouldn't bet on it."

We walked along the waterfront, heading north towards Conch Harbor Marina. The night was dying down a little, and Mallory Square was no longer filled with the loud, bustling crowd that it had been earlier.

We decided not to call the police on the three guys who'd drugged Candace. For one, we both hated dealing with law enforcement, though in the months

31

I'd lived in Key West, I'd had no choice but to work alongside them a few times. And secondly, we both agreed that the beating we'd given them would be punishment enough and would hopefully dissuade them from such behavior in the future.

When we arrived back at the dock and stepped aboard the Baia, I grabbed a coconut water from my fridge, along with the old dagger, and sat out on the sunbed. It was one of my favorite places to just sit, relax, and stare out over the water.

I stared at the dagger in my hands, reading the inscription once more and wondering what its story was. For hundreds of years, it had been resting beneath the waves, and now it was in my hands. I think the romanticism more than anything else is what draws me to treasure hunting.

"Well?" Ange said. She moved beside me and stared down at the dagger, her sandy-colored eyebrows rising over her tropical-blue eyes.

I laughed. "Well, what?"

"Are we gonna find the rest of this girl's treasure or what?"

I nodded and grabbed the coconut water resting beside me, feeling the condensation on the ice-cold can as I brought it to my lips and took a few long pulls.

"Good," she said. "Then you and I can buy a big yacht and sail off into the sunset together."

I shook my head. "I thought you liked living in the Keys."

She frowned at me jokingly. "It's a metaphor, Logan."

"Well, I'm sorry to burst your bubble, but anything we find in US waters is gonna be confiscated by Uncle Sam. And then Spain or

32

whatever country feels entitled to it will step in and try to take it all. We got lucky with the Aztec treasure, even though we only got a one percent finder's fee, but I wouldn't count on it again."

She sat back down beside me, snatched the coconut water from my hands, tilted her head back and killed the rest of the liquid. Wiping her lips, she said, "You never know. We might get more than you expect."

I smiled. "Ever the optimist," I said, then swung my feet onto the deck beside Ange and rose to my feet.

Moving over to the console, I opened a small storage compartment and pulled out a few rolled-up maps. Unfurling them on the outdoor dinette beside me and keeping them down with a few mugs and my monocular, I focused on the area where Chris said his uncle had found the dagger.

Ange moved beside me, and we spent an hour plotting out a grid to search the area.

"He said his uncle had the net in the water for roughly twenty minutes," I said. "And he was trawling at fifteen knots along this line here." I hovered a pencil above the map. "That leaves us with a five-mile stretch, and I'd say roughly a quarter of a mile girth to play it safe."

"One and a quarter square miles," Ange said. "That's eight hundred acres for you Americans."

I grinned. Though Ange had lived in many countries, she was born and raised in Sweden. After her parents had been killed, she had run away and had lived on her own ever since. We'd had an on-again, off-again relationship for a few years now, our jobs working as mercenaries making it hard to form a serious relationship. But for the past five months,

33

she'd lived with me in Key West, and I'd loved every minute of it.

"We should take it to Professor Murchison," she said. "I'm sure he can help us figure out who this Beatrice was and what ship she was on."

I nodded. "And, Pete. Let's head over to his restaurant tomorrow for lunch. See what he thinks."

Grabbing my iPhone, I sent a message to the professor containing a quick explanation of how the dagger had been found, along with a few pictures. Professor Murchison taught at Key West Community College and was probably the most overqualified guy on campus. He was incredibly smart, and he had been immensely helpful in the search and identification of U-3546, a lost German U-boat my dad had found off the coast of Islamorada the night he'd been murdered.

We spent a few more hours looking over charts, conducting internet searches and letting our imaginations run wild. We both downed a few beers, and by one in the morning, we fell asleep on the sunbed, the gentle breeze off the ocean keeping us relatively cool and fending off the bugs.

THREE

I woke up naturally the next morning to a beautiful sunrise. Ange's body was draped over mine, and I did my best not to disturb her as I crawled out from under a colorful thin cotton blanket and onto the damp fiberglass deck. I moved barefoot down into the salon and whipped up my usual breakfast, consisting of freshly sliced mango, banana, and a warm pot of Colombian medium roast. Feeling hungrier than usual, I warmed up some leftover lobster and made a few rolls using a baguette Ange had bought from a bakery just down the waterfront.

We sat together, propped against the cushions and enjoying a delicious breakfast that was made even better by the artistically painted sky, which elegantly displayed every color on the spectrum between yellow and red.

While eating, I heard footsteps approaching our position from just down the dock. Glancing up, I saw

Benjamin Kincaid striding towards us in his short-sleeved dark blue police uniform. Ben was a young deputy who was about my height and had short blond hair and blue eyes. Though we'd disliked each other at first, a friendship had grown between us, mainly due to our shared love of guns, and we went shooting over at the Big Coppitt Gun Club a few times a month. He also owned a pair of top-of-the-line jet skis and would invite me to go racing around the islands every now and then.

I was surprised to see him down at the marina in his uniform, as he usually only came by when he was off duty.

"Morning, Logan," he said with more of a serious tone than usual.

"Hey, Ben," I said. "What brings you by this early?"

He paused a moment, then glanced at Ange and said, "Good to see you, Angelina. You two mind if I come aboard and talk to you for a few minutes?"

"Not at all," I said.

"Are you thirsty or hungry?" Ange asked. "We've got some good lobster rolls here."

"For breakfast?" He stepped onto the swim platform, then sat across from us near the helm. "You two are becoming more conch like every time I see you."

I laughed. "Says the guy from Miami." I paused for a moment, then handed him a coconut water and added, "What's up?"

He grabbed it, popped it open, then looked off into the distance through a pair of dark sunglasses. After taking a sip, he glanced back at us.

"Look," he said, "I got a call last night while on patrol downtown. It was a 911 call from a guy just outside of Tipsy Turvy. He said there was a fight and a lot of guys were injured. But by the time I got there, the alley was empty." He paused for a moment and took a drink of coconut water. Ange and I looked at each other, then back at Ben. "Look, there's a security camera outside the bar, so I know you guys did it. What happened? What was the deal with the woman?"

"They were planning to rape her," Ange snapped. "They'd drugged her in the bar. She was barely coherent when we took her and her friends back to their cruise ship."

Ben nodded, listening intently.

"I figured as much," he said. "That's what I assumed when I saw the footage. I just wanted to stop by and let you guys know that I've got your backs if anything comes of it."

"What do you mean?" I said.

"Well, there haven't been any charges filed yet, but don't be surprised if those guys do eventually."

"They were trying to rape that girl," Ange said.

Ben raised his hands in the air. "Look, I just want you to be ready just in case. But I'm confident that with the footage, and if we can track down the girl, they wouldn't have a case. But I'm not working on it anymore. As far as I'm concerned, it's a closed case."

Ange and I both nodded.

"Thanks for letting us know, Ben," I said.

He took another drink, patted his knee and rose to his feet.

"Well, I best be getting going," he said. "Thanks for the drink." After stepping onto the dock, he added, "And thank you both for protecting that woman."

"We didn't have a choice," I said, stepping towards him and shaking his hand.

"I'll see you guys later," he said, then disappeared down the dock.

I moved back to the dinette and sat beside Ange.

"It's nice to see we've earned the complete trust of the law here," she said. "Those guys are just lucky we left them in such great shape."

I grinned. She was right. In other parts of the world, I'd seen the limits of Ange's mercy when it came to dealing with scum. Usually, Ange wouldn't leave a rapist breathing.

"Well, let's not worry about it," I said. "It's a beautiful day in paradise."

Once we were finished, we decided to cruise over to the area where the dagger had been found. It wasn't quite 0700 yet, and the ocean was as smooth as glass, without a whitecap in sight as far as we could see. There were only a few sporadic clouds on the horizon as well, and the weather report called for sunny with a high of seventy-eight degrees.

We took a quick shower and, after drying off, I slipped into a pair of black swim trunks and a gray tee shirt. I filled a silver thermos with what remained of the coffee, put on a pair of Oakley sunglasses, then moved back into the cockpit and started up the twin six-hundred-horsepower engines. Ange appeared a second later, wearing a white bikini bottom and a maroon tank top.

I handed her the helm, then jumped onto the dock and disconnected the power line and freshwater hose and untied the nylon ropes securing the Baia to the cleats. Hopping aboard, I gave her the okay and watched as she expertly brought us away from the dock. A few minutes later, just after we'd cruised out of the marina and between Wisteria Island and Sunset Key, Ange glanced over her shoulder at me and grinned.

"You ready for this, Dodge?" she asked, her eyebrows raised behind a pair of silver-rimmed aviator sunglasses.

Before I replied, she punched the throttles, roaring the massive engines to life and accelerating the Baia with a powerful jolt. I gripped the corner of the hardtop just beside Ange, and she laughed as our wake grew from a small cluster of bubbles into a large cloudy vortex in a matter of seconds. I watched the odometer just over her shoulder as she crept our speed up over fifty knots, shooting us through the calm water. We flew through the Northwest Channel and around Calda Bank, Ange putting us on a course due northeast and bypassing the Lower Keys.

The surface was a little bit choppier in the open waters of the Gulf, but it was no match for the Baia. It wasn't until halfway to our destination, while we were passing Big Pine Key far in the distance over the starboard bow, that Ange eased her down to her cruising speed of thirty knots. We both glanced back and forth from the surface ahead of us to the GPS screen displaying our destination. By 0830, we'd reached the spot where Chris's uncle had pulled up his net and found the dagger, and Ange slowed the Baia to an idle.

The water around us was crystal clear and only about ten feet deep, allowing us to see the bottom easily. We decided to make the one-and-a-quarter-mile run using only the depth gauge, the fish finder, and our eyes, just to see if there were any distinctly unique formations. Ange kept the Baia steady at four knots, and I stood up on the bow, staring down into the ocean below and feeling an overwhelming sense of excitement. I knew that the waters we were searching weren't exactly remote, and if there was anything to be spotted by the naked eye it would have already been found, but I couldn't help it. After finding the *Intrepid* and the Aztec treasure she'd carried, and after finding the lost U-boat, I guess you could say I've got the bug.

"Stop!" I said, raising a hand in the air as I bent over the bow and peered down into the clear water below.

Ange eased back on the throttle.

"Did you find something?" she asked, her voice overflowing with excitement.

"Yeah. Can you hand me my mask?"

With the Baia in an idle, she stepped across the cockpit, hinged open a storage door and pulled out my frameless Cressi dive mask.

As she grabbed it, I added, "And my gloves and tickle stick."

She paused and looked up at me. I grinned and she just shook her head, then reached back into the compartment.

"I'm gonna get you back for that," she said. "Just so you know."

I laughed as she grabbed the gear I'd requested and handed it to me around the starboard edge of the windscreen.

"Hey, you wanna eat, don't you?"

She smiled as I slid the mask over my face, then put on the gloves. Reading my mind, Ange had also given me a small net, which I strapped to my left wrist. Holding the tickle stick in my right hand, I thanked Ange, then turned around, took a long powerful stride and launched facefirst into the warm air. A second later, I splashed into the water and sank like a torpedo all the way to the bottom. The water felt good on my body, which had felt the wrath of the hot Southern Florida sun all morning. I've always loved being in the water and often found myself looking for any excuse I could find to take a dip.

At the bottom, I zeroed in on my quarry. Under a small outcropping of rocks, I spotted three long pairs of antennas sticking out. One of the best things about living in the Keys is the seemingly endless supply of great-tasting fresh seafood. And there was no bounty from the ocean that I enjoyed more than the Florida spiny-tailed lobster. With the end of the season only a month away, most of the lobster had vacated their shallow dwellings for safer, deeper waters. The last thing I wanted was to pass on a good opportunity.

Holding the net in my left hand and the tickle stick in my right, I finned right over the trio of lobsters and used the tip of the stick to prod them out one by one. These lobster swim fastest backward, so by situating the net behind them and tapping the front of them, you send them swimming back right into the net and they trap themselves. After being down just a few minutes, I had my limit of six bugs that were each easily above the regulation size of three inches carapace length.

Pressing my bare feet against the ocean floor, I pushed myself up and broke free of the surface. Ange was standing on the port side of the Baia, staring down at me as I held the full net up in the air. I kicked for the stern, climbed up onto the swim platform and handed them to her.

"Well, it isn't exactly the kind of treasure we're looking for," she said, smiling from ear to ear. "But I can't complain."

I sat on the transom and toweled off as Ange opened the live well and dropped the lobsters inside.

We spent a few more hours cruising along the line, recording depth readings and notable underwater formations. By 1100, we'd finished the course and had a pretty good lay of the ocean.

"It'll take weeks to survey all of this," I said, looking out over the blue water. "Maybe longer than that."

Ange nodded. "There are far worse places to spend your time. Heard anything back from the professor?"

I shook my head. "Not yet. But I told Pete I'd be at the restaurant around one o'clock. Let's start heading back to Key West."

It was a perfectly clear day, so as Ange started up the engines, I stared off into the horizon in all directions. To the north, I could see all the way to the Everglades, and to the south, the Seven Mile Bridge and glimpses of the Atlantic beyond it. In less than a minute, Ange had us turned around and cruising at thirty knots, heading west through the Gulf along the Lower Keys.

FOUR

When we arrived back at Conch Harbor Marina, I noticed that Jack's forty-five-foot Sea Ray named *Calypso* had returned and was moored in its usual spot at slip forty-seven. Jack Rubio is the owner and operator of Rubio Charters, a fishing and diving charter that has been running for almost a hundred years in Key West. We'd first met back in '98 when I was eleven years old and my dad, a Navy diver, had been stationed at Naval Station Key West. We met on a dive charter and had been friends ever since. A third-generation conch, Jack was one of the best divers I knew, and he knew every island, reef, bank, cut, and ledge in the Keys as well as anyone alive.

Ange eased the Baia against the white fenders, and I jumped onto the dock and tied her off. Glancing down towards the *Calypso*, I spotted a group of four guys and two women walking towards me, carrying two massive blackfin tuna and a sailfish between

43

them. Judging by their pale complexions, which had turned painfully red from a long morning out on the water, I knew that they were tourists.

They laughed and talked loudly as they shuffled their heavyset frames past me. I watched as they continued on towards the side door of the Greasy Pelican, the marina's restaurant that sat right over the water and offered clean-and-cook service for freshly caught fish.

After locking up the Baia, I tucked the leather-bound dagger into my waistband beside my Sig, then Ange and I headed over to the *Calypso*, spotting Jack out on the deck with a black plastic garbage bag in his hands. His beautiful boat was a mess, with empty beer cans all over the place, fish guts and blood on the transom, and three tangled fishing poles resting against the starboard gunwale.

"They look like they had fun," I said, glancing over at Jack as he threw an aluminum can into the half-full garbage bag, causing it to chime in a symphony of tings against a pile of others.

Jack was all wiry muscle. At six feet, he was a few inches shorter than me and probably tipped the scale at only a buck seventy. He had curly blond hair, blue eyes, and rarely wore anything more than a pair of boardshorts. To the naked eye, he looked like a typical island beach bum, but the truth was he was a savvy businessman and always worked hard at whatever he did.

"Oh yeah," he said, sarcastically. "Those landlubbers had the time of their lives."

Ange and I stepped over the transom and helped Jack clean up, wiping down the fiberglass with rags, picking up trash and helping him untangle the fishing poles. Even from across the marina, we could hear the group talking obnoxiously over by the Pelican. They took pictures with their phones, dropped the fish on the dock and used more profanities than even I'm used to, and I was in the Navy for eight years.

Jack looked at them and shook his head. "A lot of these people don't give a damn about the romance of it all, bro," he said. "They think it's all about the noise and the damn photos that they can show and brag to their friends about. But fishing here is much more than that. It's an art, and those beauties we caught deserved better than those clowns."

As we finished up, I turned to Jack and said, "I still don't get how you deal with all of this."

"Rubio Charters has been around longer than just about any establishment here in the Keys," he said. "It's as conch as Key lime pie, and I'll be damned if I'll see it go."

"I didn't mean stop the business. What I mean is, why don't you just hire guys to do this for you?"

He nodded. "I've thought about it. But they aren't all bad, bro. Usually, I get people worth their salt."

I patted my old friend on the shoulder. "Let's go and get some lunch over at Pete's. My treat. He told me he caught a haul of grouper last night. Plus, I've got something to show you."

His eyes lit up at that. "The last time you spoke like that, you found a German WWII submarine. What are you up to now?"

The drive over to Pete's took only a few minutes in my black Toyota Tacoma 4x4. His restaurant is on Mangrove Street, just a few blocks away from the ocean. As we drove, I noticed that the streets were much busier than usual, with lines of people filling the sidewalks and scampering across crosswalks. I remembered that the cruise ship *Princess Louisa* was scheduled to be in port for another day due to unexpected engine trouble and knew that it would be replaced soon after it left, a common occurrence in Key West, especially this time of year.

We pulled into a small parking lot in front of a structure that had the words Salty Pete's Bar, Grill and Museum plastered in white paint across a dark blue backdrop. I was happy to see that the lot was nearly full. When I'd first moved to the Keys, the place had been rundown and barely made enough money to pay the electric bill, let alone make a profit. But thanks in part to Pete's help, we'd found the Aztec treasure, and Jack and I had used part of our small finder's fees to fix up the place. Now, it was one of the most popular places to eat in all of the Keys.

The three of us headed up a small set of steps and through a pair of mahogany double doors. As soon as the doors cracked open and the bell rang, the smell of grilled seafood wafted through the air and into my nose, causing my mouth to water. Osmond, a massive Scandinavian guy who went by Oz, was one of the best cooks in all of the Keys and never failed to impress. The restaurant looked almost new, with freshly painted walls, shiny hardwood floors, new booths lining the edges, and custom-made tables and chairs in the middle. But it still had its old-style charm, with pictures hung all over the place, many of them black-and-white, and old wooden helms and a few giant stuffed marlins.

We greeted and moved past Mia, the head waitress, and up a wide set of stairs near the back of the dining area that led up to the museum on the second floor. It had rows of glass cases filled with artifacts from all over the Keys and even had a section devoted to the Aztec treasure, including pictures of the site and a golden statue of Montezuma. We stepped through a sliding glass door and out onto the balcony, which had a large seating area and a 180-degree view of the ocean. Given that it was in the eighties, there were only a few tables taken, and we sat down on one in the corner that was well shaded by a large umbrella.

Mia appeared a few seconds later, smiling as she filled three glasses in front of us with ice-cold water. As usual, she had her dark hair in a ponytail and wore a red Salty Pete's Bar and Grill tee shirt that was tied back behind her.

"Pete's out back tinkering with an old Mercury outboard," she said. "I sent Jess to let him know you're here. You guys know what you want?"

I decided on a blackened grouper sandwich with their specialty sweet potato fries and grilled shrimp kabobs over pineapple slices for an appetizer. I also ordered a glass of Key limeade to wash it all down. The good thing was you couldn't really go wrong with Oz's cooking. I'd tried everything on the menu and liked it all. Ange got the grilled mahi and Jack the jerk chicken with a side of a dozen raw oysters.

Leaning back in his wicker chair, Jack stared at me and said, "How much longer are you planning to keep me in suspense, bro?"

Just as the words left his mouth, the sliding door opened and Pete walked out onto the balcony. Pete Jameson is a well-known figure in the Keys, a man who's lived here all his life and spent most his living hours out on the waters fishing and diving. He moves a lot quicker than you would imagine, given that he's in his early sixties and has a short, chubby physique.

His skin was bronzed from spending hours every day out in the sun and the top of his head, was completely barren of hair. But the most distinct feature about Pete was his right arm, which was missing just a few inches above the elbow, and his metal hook in lieu of a hand.

"Well, if it isn't three of my favorite people in the Keys," he said, smiling as he greeted each of us. Placing a hand on Jack's and my shoulders, he added, "Did you guys see the exhibit for U-3546? I added a few new pieces."

U-3546 was the German U-boat that my dad had discovered and given clues for me to find just before he was murdered. She rested in one hundred and sixty feet of water, about thirteen miles south of Islamorada, and we'd all spent much of our time over the past few months diving, exploring, and photographing the wreck.

"I'll have to check it out after lunch," I said. "Did you see that it was named a historic site?"

His eyebrows grew wide and he nodded. "It's about time. That wreck is one of the most astonishing things I've ever seen beneath the waves, and I've seen more than a handful of most salty aquanauts combined."

Mia appeared, holding a large plastic tray of food in one hand and a glass pitcher of Key limeade in the other. She smiled as she set our plated food in front of us and refilled our glasses. Unable to control myself, I grabbed hold of the sandwich and took a bite of the delicious fresh grouper.

Seeing my reaction, Pete plopped down into the fourth wicker chair and patted me on the back. "And to think," he said, "the first time you came into my place, you weren't even here for the eats."

Ange laughed. "Some things don't change."

Jack, Pete, and Mia all stared at her inquisitively.

I swallowed and cleared my throat. "What Ange means is, today I'm not just here for the food. Though, with Oz on the grill, it sure is one hell of an added bonus."

Mia raised her eyebrows. "What are you saying?" she asked. "Don't tell me you've stumbled upon another Spanish galleon."

The table went quiet and I glanced back at her, unable to keep a boyish grin from manifesting itself across my face.

"Damn, Logan," Jack said. "Don't you ever just kick back and relax?"

I threw my hands in the air. "I didn't go looking for it. It just stumbled into my lap."

After a short pause, Pete glanced at me inquisitively. "It?"

Mia had other tables to check up on but couldn't bring herself to step away. In a moment, the table seemed to rise in anticipation, like when you're at a movie theatre and the title screen is about to play. Instead of using words, I reached to my side and grabbed the dagger, which was still wrapped in the leather cloth I'd received it in and wedged between my holstered Sig and my belt. Unwrapping it slowly, I held it out in front of me, then set it on a small empty space on the table beside the salt and pepper shakers and a bottle of Swamp Sauce.

For a few seconds, they just stared at it. Then Pete reached across the table and snatched it with a calloused hand.

"It looks old," Jack said, leaning over to stare at the dagger as Pete examined it.

"There's a name inscribed here," Pete said. "And

a date. Beatrice Taylor, 1665."

Ange nodded. "And there's a symbol too," she said, pointing beside the name and date.

"What is that?" Pete asked, tilting his head. "A heart?"

I shrugged. "Your guess is as good as ours. But it sure looks like it. So what do you guys think?"

Pete held the dagger out in front of us and said, "Well, it's a knight dagger."

"A knight dagger?" I asked.

"Yeah. It's a variant of a rondel dagger. It was popular in Europe in the late Middle Ages, and this one has a solid gold hilt and steel blade. My guess is that this particular blade was designed for ceremonial purposes." He shook his head and added, "It's incredible that such an old piece lasted so many years under the ocean and still looks like this."

"I was told that it had been encrusted with barnacles and other sea life," I said. "They could have formed a protective layer, keeping the dagger from total corrosion."

Pete nodded. "It probably came from an English merchant vessel of some kind. Or possibly it came off one of the ships in the 1733 Spanish fleet, or any of the hundreds of other wrecks in the Keys."

"But why would a European merchant vessel be sailing in modern-day Florida Bay?" I asked.

Jack's eyes grew wide. "Wait, where did you find this?"

"I didn't find it," I said and explained all about Chris and how his uncle, an old shrimp captain, had found it years ago while hauling in his catch.

"That's some shallow water out there," Jack said. "And there are hundreds of small islands, sandbars, cuts, and reefs." He shook his head and added, "Not

50

the place for a merchant vessel."

"And that rules out the 1733 Spanish fleet theory," Pete said. "Or any galleon for that matter. A Spanish galleon fully loaded down with treasure, cargo, and contraband would draw nearly thirty feet of water. A ship like that couldn't have made it anywhere close to Florida Bay, even if it wanted to."

I took a few more bites from my sandwich, finishing it off, and tossed a few sweet potato fries down the hatch as well. I looked out over the blue ocean beyond and marveled at all the secrets it still kept hidden beneath the surface after all these years.

"So, if it's not from a galleon or merchant vessel, where did it come from?" Ange asked.

As we finished eating, Pete stayed uncharacteristically quiet, seemingly lost in thought. After a few minutes, a faint smile appeared on his face and he said, "It must have been a sloop or a schooner, and there's only one type of captain who would dare set sail into such shallow and treacherous waters in those days." He paused, took a drink of water, grinned and added, "A pirate captain."

FIVE

We sat on the balcony, chugging down a few Paradise Sunset beers and talking about the dagger long after our food was gone. Pete's mention of the word *pirate* had us all both intrigued and skeptical.

"I didn't know there were very many pirates in the Keys," I said.

"There weren't," Pete replied. "In fact, these islands scared the hell out of even some of the most notorious pirates. But there are a few stories."

"Any about sunken pirate ships?" Ange asked.

Both Jack and Pete shook their heads.

"Never heard anything like that before," Pete replied. "Nowhere near Florida Bay, anyway."

"What about the name?" Ange said. "Who is this Beatrice Taylor? We did a few internet searches and couldn't find anything on her."

Pete shrugged. "This dagger was probably stolen. Could be anyone."

After another fifteen minutes of drinks, theories, and a few of Pete's sea stories, we set out to search the entirety of the area that Chris's uncle dragged his net through. Jack, Ange, and I rose to our feet, but Pete stayed put.

"What you guys need to do is mow the lawn," he said, a term used to describe a salvager searching the ocean floor over a large area for lost antiquities. "Get that equipment out that you used to find the *Intrepid*, and start going back and forth. Just be careful. That kind of activity will draw attention around here. And people who frequent those waters will grow suspicious real fast."

Having been sitting for so long, I stretched and patted Pete on the back.

"Thanks for everything," I said. Then I grabbed the dagger off the table, wrapped it back in the leather cloth, and stowed it away beside my holstered Sig.

We headed back through the sliding glass door, past the rows of artifacts and down the stairs towards the main entrance. I handed Mia a folded twenty-dollar bill on the way out and told her that the food was amazing as usual.

Pushing through the double doors, Jack swiveled his head back. "I don't have a charter for a few days. We should head out there in the morning and get started."

I smiled as I followed him alongside Ange, heading down the small set of stairs just outside the doors. As we reached the bottom step and moved along the gravel driveway towards my Tacoma, I spotted a silver Mercedes with its driver's-side window rolled halfway down. It was parked along the other side of the street, roughly a hundred feet away from us. There was a guy looking in our direction, his

53

eyes concealed behind a pair of dark sunglasses and the rest of his body undistinguishable behind the tinted window and shadows of the interior.

When we reached my Tacoma, I saw that we were hidden from the Mercedes by the other vehicles in the lot and a small cluster of cocoplum bushes.

Handing the keys to Ange, I said, "Start her up and wait here a second." She looked at me, confused, as I placed the set of keys into her hand and added, "I'll be right back."

"What's going on?" Jack asked.

I didn't answer and was out of earshot a few seconds later, keeping to cover as I moved down towards an adjacent side street. After eight years in Naval Special Forces and six years working as a mercenary, I'd learned to trust my instincts. I knew all too well that if I ignored them, it could mean a very bad day.

Keeping my distance from the Mercedes, I crossed Mangrove Street and wrapped around the back side of a tackle shop and a scooter rental pavilion. Moving in close, I crouched down and approached the driver's-side door from the back. With my right hand pressed against my Sig, ready to draw it at a moment's notice if necessary, I stood up tall and casually stepped in front of the half-open window.

"Something I can help you with?" I said, causing the guy to snap his head sideways and backward as I caught him off guard.

He looked at me through his dark sunglasses, and his mouth dropped open as if a weight were tied to his bottom lip. Without a word, he slid a jittery right hand towards the ignition, clasped the key already inserted, and started up the engine. Putting it in gear, he hit the gas, screeching the tires over the pavement and sending the Mercedes flying south on Mangrove Street.

I stood unmoving with my hands on my hips, watching as the car took a sharp left, almost hitting a woman on her bicycle before disappearing from view. *Well, that was odd*, I thought, shaking my head. I walked back across Mangrove Street towards the gravel parking lot of Salty Pete's.

Ange and Jack stood where the driveway met the sidewalk, both having confused looks on their faces.

"What the hell was that about?" Ange said, still looking in the direction where the Mercedes headed.

I shrugged. "No idea. But whoever that guy was, he was watching us for some reason."

Ange stood for a moment, working something out in her mind. "Wait," she said. "You don't think it was one of those predators from last night, do you? Or maybe a friend of theirs?"

Jack glanced at her, his expression shifting from confused to intrigued. "Last night?" he said. "What did you guys get into now?"

"It was nothing," I said, waving a hand at Jack. "Just a couple of drunk jerks trying to take advantage of a woman." Then turning to Ange, I added, "And, no. I don't think those guys were professional criminals. Professional assholes, yeah. But that guy in the Mercedes was following us for a different reason."

I walked past Ange and Jack, heading towards my Tacoma.

"What reason is that, bro?" Jack said.

I shook my head. "I don't know. We should keep our eyes peeled for him or others wherever we go." I hopped into the driver's seat, reached for my waistband and pulled out the dagger. "But for now," I said, "I'm much more interested in figuring out who this is and how their dagger managed to wind up in Florida Bay."

Ange took a quick look around, then they both climbed in. On the drive back over to the marina, I decided to call Professor Murchison's office over at the college. I'd sent him a text the previous day and was surprised that I had yet to receive a reply. He was usually quick to respond and eager to enlighten with any knowledge he possessed on a subject.

After the third ring, a woman's voice came over the speaker. It was his assistant, and when I inquired about the professor, she told me that he was in Switzerland and that the service was poor in the remote region he was visiting. When I asked how long he was supposed to be there, she said he should be back in civilization in the next few days, providing he didn't decide to extend his stay. I thanked her, hung up the phone and pulled my Tacoma into the Conch Harbor Marina parking lot, easing the front tires a few inches from a railroad tie in the front row.

We walked down the dock towards the Baia and sat around the outdoor dinette, going to work on our laptops and brainstorming our plan for the following day. The excitement of setting out on another treasure hunt overtook me, and I felt like I was chasing a child's dream going after a second potential wreck.

When we finally hit the sack, I lay in the main cabin's king-sized bed beside Ange and thought about the guy in the Mercedes. I'd never seen him before and hadn't a clue what he wanted. But after years of doing the kind of work I was good at and dealing with all sorts of scumbags, I knew that one thing was certain: he was following me. And if I ever saw him again, I'd do more than just casually ask if there was something I could help him with.

SIX

The next morning, we awoke early, cruising out of the dark marina and arriving at our destination just in time to watch the sun rise slowly over the Upper Keys. It was a beautiful day to be out on the water, with a slight breeze from the southeast and not a cloud in the sky.

We hadn't seen any other boats out on the water except a few shrimp trawlers cruising out for a day's work, but that didn't stop us from casting intermittent glances all around us with binoculars just to make sure that no one was following us. When we were confident that we had the stretch of ocean to ourselves, we went straight to work.

The first order of business was to create a survey of the ocean floor using active sonar equipment. Active sonar works by sending out a loud, high-pitched sound referred to as a ping. When the ping comes into contact with a solid object, the sound wave is reflected back to the sonar device. The sonar then uses the amount of time it took for the ping to return, combined with many other sound pulses, to generate a replication of the seafloor. Back when I'd purchased the Baia a year earlier from a retired surgeon named George Shepherd, he'd informed me that the boat was equipped with built-in side-scan sonar, which allowed me to navigate safely through the many narrow cuts and channels in the Keys. It also came in handy at times like this, when I desired a digital replication of the seafloor.

Firing up the equipment and linking it via USB to my laptop, we began our search. Jack and Ange sat around the outdoor dinette, watching the laptop screen as the world below came to form. Most of our search area was less than twenty feet deep, allowing us to see the bottom clearly from the deck. But there were a few locations where the water was deeper, so we focused primarily on those spots with the sonar.

I kept the Baia at a steady ten knots, which was slow enough to give the sonar adequate time to do its job. It was a slow and arduous process, fueled by a constant supply of Colombian medium roast coffee, coconut water, freshly sliced mango, and leftover lobster. We kept at it long into the night, and by noon the following day, we had ourselves a complete map of our search area.

"What do you think, Jack?" I asked as the three of us peered at the laptop screen, looking over the fruits of our labor.

He shrugged. "It's hard to tell, bro." Then, pointing to a few unique underwater formations, he added, "These spots here seem promising. The problem is that dagger was probably underwater for nearly three hundred and fifty years. If there was anything else with it, it could be scattered for miles."

I nodded. Aside from the search and discovery of the *Intrepid*, I didn't have a lot of experience in the treasure hunting department. But I did know about salvage and the incredible effects the ocean can have on objects and shipwrecks over long periods of time. During my time in the Navy, I'd spent a few years as an instructor at EOD school at Eglin Air Force Base in Fort Walton Beach, Florida. There, I was able to fine-tune my knowledge of salvage among some of the best in the world.

After eating a quick lunch of BLT sandwiches and potato chips, I headed into the guest cabin and came back out holding a large plastic hard case. Jack and Ange both smiled as I appeared, and I set the case on the aft deck beside the transom and unclasped the plastic hinges. Lifting open the lid, I revealed a yellow cigar-shaped device that was a foot wide, five feet long and looked like a torpedo.

"In the words of Salty Pete," I said, glancing down at the device, "let's mow the lawn."

Ange leaned over. "Finally, a little excitement." She was wearing a pair of denim shorts that complemented her long, tanned legs nicely and had just a white bikini top covering her upper body. She stood tall and turned her gaze aft, looking out over the water through a pair of aviator sunglasses. In an excited voice, she added, "I call the first hit."

I smiled as I lifted the device from its case, hooked it up and set it into the water off the back of the swim platform. Much like the guy walking around on the beach with a metal detector, the magnetometer picks up anything metal resting beneath the waves. And I'd pulled out all of the stops when I'd purchased this one. It was top-of-the-line and powerful enough to detect even the smallest metal objects through over a hundred feet of water.

Once the magnetometer was on and working properly, I let out enough slack in the tether so that we'd drag it twenty feet behind the Baia. Jack had the laptop up and running with a combined survey of the entire seafloor, which we could use to mark locations where the magnetometer found something, or hot spots as we called them.

I maneuvered the Baia to the northwest corner of the grid, turned us around and cruised steadily south, the yellow torpedo shooting through the water behind us just a few inches under the surface. After less than five minutes of towing the magnetometer, we heard its digital control station beep to life. Ange, who was standing on the swim platform, turned to face Jack and me with a big grin on her face.

Reading her mind, I idled the Baia, grabbed Ange's mask from the storage compartment beside me, then walked over and handed it to her.

"Just seventeen feet to the bottom," I said, stepping onto the swim platform beside her and leaning over the stern. I glanced at the magnetometer's control screen, then pointed below and added, "Looks like it's coming from right there."

By the time I looked back up at Ange, she'd already slipped out of her shorts, revealing a sexy white bikini bottom.

Still grinning, she slid her mask over her face. "If I find this thing on the first bite, you owe me the finest bottle of champagne, Dodge."

I laughed and replied, "If you find a wreck on the first hit, I'll buy you a case of it."

She smiled, stepped towards the edge of the swim platform, and dove headfirst into the water. She hit the water perfectly, barely making a splash, and I watched as she glided through the clear water towards the bottom.

I knew that if we dove down every time the magnetometer went off, we'd probably be at this for weeks, but I humored Ange. It was the first hit, after all. From here on out, though, we all agreed that the best course of action would be to finish mowing the lawn, gather up all of our data, then search the areas with the highest activity first and work our way down the list.

Less than a minute later, Ange broke the surface holding an object in her hands that was covered in rust, barnacles, and seaweed. Ange slid her mask down to hang around her neck, then handed me the object, which I realized was an old abandoned crab pot. The metal links were mostly broken, and it was covered in so much muck that you could barely see inside it.

"At least we know the meg is working, bro," Jack said, laughing as he leaned over the sunbed to see what Ange had found.

I threw the pot back into the water with a splash, then held my hand out to help Ange up the ladder.

"I guess you're off the hook," she said as I pulled her up and handed her a towel.

I grinned. "I guess so. Lucky for you, I was going to buy you a bottle of champagne tonight at dinner anyway."

As she dried off, I stepped into the cockpit and brought the engines back up to ten knots.

"One down," Jack said, nestling back into the cushioned half-moon seat around the dinette, "a thousand more to go."

SEVEN

Silberhorn
Bernese Alps, Switzerland

Professor Frank Murchison lay flat on his chest, his body barely fitting through a narrow crevice deep within the dark cave. He extended his wiry frame as far as he could, then stretched out his hands, which tightly gripped a Nikon D3 camera housed in a rugged waterproof case. Holding the camera steady, he snapped a few pictures, the bright flash illuminating the darkness for an instant each time.

Once satisfied, he eased the expensive camera back onto his chest, then reached with his right hand for the flashlight strapped to the side of his belt. Switching it on, he scanned the beam in front of him, admiring the ancient cave paintings that artistically adorned the flat wall of rock.

Incredible, he thought as he brought his left hand

up to his face and wiped a fine layer of sweat from his brow. There was barely enough space for him to complete the action, with the never-ending slabs of rock sandwiching him together from both sides.

He continued to admire the cave paintings that had been seen by just a small handful of eyes over the past thousands of years. It was hard for him to tell for sure at first glance, but judging by their design, location, and medium, he imagined that they dated back roughly five thousand years.

Once he'd taken enough pictures, he inched his way backward, traveling for over five minutes before reaching a space large enough for him to dust off his pants and jacket and rise to his feet.

Frank Murchison was just under six feet tall, weighed one hundred and eighty pounds and had thinning dark hair and tanned skin. Though he was in his early fifties, he moved and had the energy of a man much younger. Having spent twenty years as a professor of history and archeology at Harvard, he'd finally had enough of the cold and headed south to work at the closest college to the equator in the United States: Key West Community College. It might not have been the best career move, but Frank had never regretted the decision for a second. To Frank, no longer teaching at one of the most prestigious universities in the world simply meant that he had more time to go on funded academic expeditions around the world—an aspect which had always been his favorite part of the job.

He grabbed his backpack from the ground, stowed his camera, then headed back towards the opening of the cave alongside the two mountain guides who'd found the paintings. The three of them had traveled deep within the bowels of the intricate cave system, to portions few men had ever reached before. It had taken two hours, and they'd used both Frank's high-end electronics and the incredible memory of the two men to navigate without becoming lost in the thousands of branches and sharp turns.

The cave had only been discovered a few months earlier, when climbers had fallen through a thin sheet of ice on the southern slope of Silberhorn, a twelve-thousand-foot mountain between Bern and Valais. Though it had yet to be extensively explored, it was believed to be one of the longest caves on earth, following many of the same geological patterns as nearby caves such as Hölloch and the Grotte aux Fées.

Few people had explored it since its discovery. This was due primarily to its isolated location and the fact that navigating the cave was treacherous, resulting in three deaths in only a few short months.

As the trio trekked their way towards the opening of the cave, the dark rock faces surrounding them on all sides slowly transitioned, giving way to thick sheets of ice and hard-packed snow.

A swift, bone-chilling breeze swept into them as they spotted the faint glow from the outside world radiating from less than a quarter of a mile ahead. Frank wore a thick blue North Face jacket and pants, along with waterproof hiking boots. The light from the distant sun bled through portions of the ice, revealing his tanned skin and part of his thinning dark hair that snuck out from under his thick Ushanka hat.

Near the entrance of the cave, the three grabbed the rest of their gear. Large hiking backpacks that contained everything they'd needed for their two-day journey to and from the train station at Jungfraujoch, the highest railway station in Europe.

Stepping out of the narrow entrance, which was almost completely covered in snow and ice, Frank took a deep breath of fresh air and stared off in the distance at the beautiful mountain range surrounding him. Massive snowcapped peaks and, far off in the distance, beyond the cloudless horizon, a lush green landscape littered with crystal-clear lakes and rivers.

After pausing for a moment to take it all in, Frank joined his companions as they began their two-day journey, passing through some of the most awe-inspiring scenery in the world. When his tired and hungry body finally reached the train station in Jungfraujoch, he paid his companions a generous fee, then decided to spend one night at the Hotel Alpina. Once showered and changed, he sat out on the hotel balcony, which had a great view of the small village and the mountains surrounding him.

After ordering a plate of rösti, a popular Swiss dish similar to hash browns, and a Swiss lemonade soda called Elmer Citro, his first order of business was to check his messages. Leaning back into his solid oak chair and reaching into his pocket, he pulled out his smartphone, which displayed only a dark, blank screen. His phone hadn't had a single bar of signal throughout the entire duration of the trek. So though he was eager to upload the hundreds of photos he'd taken to his laptop, his first order of business was to turn on his phone and check his messages.

After scrolling and reading through droves of work emails from colleagues and contacts all over the world, he paused as he saw a message from Logan Dodge that had multiple attachments.

What are you up to now? he thought, a smile appearing across his face.

He opened the message, glanced at the pictures on the screen, and for the second time in just a few days looked at a piece of history that was both remarkable and unexpected.

EIGHT

Even as the rubber tires of the Boeing 747 screeched down on the tarmac, Frank kept his eyes glued to the screen of his phone, admiring the picture of the old dagger and wondering what its story was. From the moment he'd first laid eyes on it back in Switzerland, he had been filled with a strong desire to find answers, and that desire had led him to take a detour on his trip back to the States, stopping over for a day in London.

He caught a ride on a classic black hackney carriage, telling the driver to take him to the Maritime Museum. It was a dark overcast afternoon with a slight drizzle of rain slapping against the window as Frank looked out at the city. He watched as the taxi drove down Woolrich Road, over the Lower Lea Crossing and eventually into the old Blackwall Tunnel, cruising under the Thames and popping out in North Greenwich.

The National Maritime Museum in Greenwich is the oldest and largest maritime museum in the world. Its massive grounds are situated between Greenwich Park to the south and the University of Greenwich to the north.

The driver pulled up alongside the curb directly in front of the main building, then put the engine in neutral, opened his door and slid out. Frank stepped out of the cab under the cover of the driver's black umbrella, then unraveled his own and headed toward the side entrance of the main building of the Museum. It was a massive structure with a tall whitewashed exterior complete with pillars, palisades, and a Union Jack waving lazily high above its tallest point.

Pushing through a large glass door, Frank headed towards a counter where two women sat beside a cluster of security personnel and a walkthrough metal detector.

"How can we help you, sir?" a dark-haired woman in her forties and wearing a museum staff uniform said. "Are you here for research?"

Frank smiled and stepped towards the counter.

"Yes," he said, reaching for his leather wallet lodged into the back pocket of his tan slacks. He pulled out his Harvard staff identification card and handed it to the woman. "I'd just like to check out a few sources. Should take only a few hours."

The woman nodded and handed the card back to him.

"Do you know how to get there?"

"Blindfolded," he replied with a grin, then slid the card back into his wallet. He hadn't worked at Harvard for years, but he still utilized a few of the perks.

After passing through security, Frank moved

along the side of a massive room, filled with various maritime artifacts and people admiring them near the center. The museum housed some of the most extraordinary maritime pieces in all of history, but Frank had been there many times before, so he barely glanced at some of the ship models in the distance before heading towards an elevator at the side of the room.

When he reached the elevator, he stepped inside, the doors closing behind him as he pressed a button. When they opened again, he found himself two levels down and was greeted by a woman sitting behind a large wooden desk.

"Welcome, Dr. Murchison," the woman said before he'd even fully exited the elevator.

Frank greeted the woman, who'd been working down there for the past twenty years, then headed past her desk. The bowels of the museum were a massive underground labyrinth that connected the main building to the other buildings surrounding it. It was tens of thousands of square feet of archives, rows and rows of storage facilities containing original maritime texts dating back to the fourth century AD. In other words, it was a history nerd's dream come true.

Frank sat down at a computer, typed in a few keywords and a date range, then began his investigation. As he usually did when searching for information in the massive database, he began the search by being specific, searching the keywords Beatrice Taylor and the date of 1665. When no results popped up, he tried another search. He repeated the action a few times, scanning over page after page of search results, hoping for something to catch his eye.

After three hours and two cups of coffee, his dreary eyes skimmed over a few lines of text, then he had to stop himself from instinctively clicking to the next page.

Very interesting, he thought as he spotted what he thought might be a lead, then dug deeper into the research. A few hours later, he headed away from the computer and into the actual archives in order to look over a few of the documents firsthand. After a few minutes of walking, he pulled out a drawer, skimmed over an organized group of folders, and pulled one out near the middle. After seeing that what he'd found wouldn't be useful, he carefully set it back and pushed the drawer back in.

A few rows down, he pulled out another drawer of documents. Grabbing a folder, he pulled it out carefully and found the page he was looking for. There, in the old ink and coarse paper it had been handwritten on hundreds of years earlier, he read the following lines of text written by the governor of Jamaica, Sir Thomas Modyford, to the crown of England.

On the fourteenth of February, 1667, I received a report that the sailing master aboard the Crescent, John Taylor, overtook command of the ship through an act of mutiny along with much of the crew. The status of Captain Adley and his fellow officers remains a mystery. As for the mutineers' intention, I have good reason to believe that they have turned to piracy and will be a threat to British transport in the Americas if not dealt with properly.

Frank knew as well as many who studied piracy in the Caribbean that much of it was founded on corruption and hypocritical actions. Though the English crown's official stance on piracy was that it threatened global trade, they financed and supported many pirates, including Henry Morgan, in exchange for the buccaneers only attacking Spanish ships. But since this Taylor had stolen an English ship, he'd thrown any possibility of working with the English crown aside.

Moving along onto other documents pertaining to John Taylor and the *Crescent*, he was surprised to learn that the man had changed his name and had become one of the most notorious pirates of his time. What amazed Frank the most was that he'd never heard about the story before. As he continued reading, his eyes grew wide as he read the text over and over. The chilling realization settled upon him that in all likelihood, the dagger had come from a lost pirate ship.

Moving along to his final stack of documents, he read about a young woman whom John Taylor had known back in London. His dreary eyes lit up with excitement as he scanned over her name, read a few more pages, and then smiled. He removed his glasses, set them on the stack of old texts in front of him, and let out a long sigh.

"This is her," he said to himself, his voice the only sound to be heard in the bowels of the archives. He held up one of the images Logan had sent him of the dagger. It was zoomed in to allow Frank to read the name and date inscribed into the hilt. "This has to be her."

NINE

We continued to drag the magnetometer through the crystal-clear water, marking locations on the survey we'd created of the seafloor as we went along. Most of the hits were relatively small, similar in size to the first one, which had ended up being an old crab pot. But occasionally we'd stumble upon a substantial amount of metal and hop into the water to take a look.

Fortunately, since most of our search area was in shallow water, we didn't have to don scuba gear to investigate. At one uncommonly large hit, I idled the engine and decided to take a peek. Though the peak heat of the day had passed and the sun was beginning its descent towards the horizon, I was hot and wanted to cool off.

Usually when we're out on the water, we cruise much faster than ten knots, creating gusts of much-appreciated wind. Cruising so slowly had caused a few patches of sweat to bleed through my tee shirt, and nothing sounded better than a dip in the water.

I grabbed my Cressi frameless dive mask along with my freediving fins, then slid out of my tee shirt, stepped down onto the swim platform, and dove into the ocean. The water felt amazingly refreshing as I cut through it, kicking smoothly towards the seafloor, which my depth gauge on the Baia had told me would be just over thirty feet down.

As I swam down, I spotted a large patch of rock covered in coral, anemones, and seagrass. It was teeming with colorful life, from a large red snapper and a spotted drum to a few beautiful parrotfish. It had always intrigued and amazed me that the parrotfish was able to change its sex and color multiple times throughout its life. These particular ones were both light shades of silvery-tinted turquoise.

Positioning my body right over the rock face, I took a look around, searching the area where the magnetometer had detected the large amount of metal. As I finned over the back side of the rock, I saw something strange about part of its shape. It had a nearly flat edge covered in barnacles and other sea growth but still managed to look foreign to its marine environment.

My mind instantly played back to my first time searching for the lost U-boat south of Islamorada that my dad had found. After years of being submerged beneath the ocean, I had to practically swim into its hull before realizing what it was, and that was an entire German submarine. What we were searching for now wasn't made of solid metal, and it had been lost beneath the waves hundreds of years longer than the U-boat, making finding anything pertaining to the wreck extremely difficult.

I wrapped my hands around the edge of the unusual surface, then cleared my mask and blinked a few times as I examined it closely. My eyes grew wide and I shook my head. It was a large sheet of metal that looked like either the hood of someone's car or maybe the side panel of an old trawler that had been washed overboard during a storm. Either way, it sure as hell wasn't part of an old wreck.

Before heading back up towards the surface, I took a look around and spotted a good-sized hogfish hanging out close to the rock formation and sheet of metal. Finning back to the surface, I broke up into the open air and called Ange, asking her to grab my speargun from the salon. She came back a few seconds later, holding the top-of-the-line speargun in her hands and extending it to me as I treaded water.

She grinned and said, "I'm guessing you didn't find an old wreck either?"

I laughed and replied, "Strike two. But I won't let the disappointment keep me from getting my woman the meal she deserves."

I relaxed for a few seconds on the surface to catch my breath and to load up a two-pronged spear. Placing the metal spear into the grooved wooden track, I pulled back on the rubber tubing, then locked it into place. This particular speargun had a draw strength of eighty pounds, enough to send just about any regulation fish to a swift end.

With the speargun in my hands, I smiled and nodded to Ange before taking in a breath, bending my upper body downward and dropping beneath the waves. Spearfishing had been one of my favorite activities ever since I was young. It combines so many things that I love into one activity; the feeling of weightlessness as you glide underwater, the beautiful scenery of marine life, and the thrill of the hunt as you strategically locate and take down your prey. It also usually results in a feast of the freshest seafood you can eat, from the ocean to the grill in just a few minutes.

I finned almost effortlessly to the bottom, pressed my chest against a small clearing of fine sand surrounded by seagrass, and waited. I waited patiently as the world beneath the waves came alive, with various fish swimming just inches away from me. After being down for a minute, I spotted the large hogfish I'd seen moments earlier, its pig-like snout rummaging for crustaceans buried in the sand on the other side of the rock formation.

Pressing my hands softly against the sand, I gave a few slow kicks, closing in on the unsuspecting fish. When I was within ten feet, I aimed the tip of the speargun below the front half of the hogfish and pulled the trigger. The spear rocketed through the water and struck the large fish right through its vital organs. The spear was large enough, and hit the hogfish with enough force, that it was dead almost instantly.

I moved towards my dinner, pulling it in until I could grab it, and finned back up towards the surface. When I broke free, I held the hogfish up as best as I could, showing it off to Ange and Jack, who were both looking over the transom.

"Damn," Jack said. "That looks like it's at least twenty pounds."

"And it feels even heavier," I said, lowering the fish so it was more neutrally buoyant in the water.

I handed it to them, then removed my fins, climbed out, and toweled off. Within ten minutes, Jack and I had the entire fish gutted, cleaned, and sliced into delicious slabs of meat. We chose the best filets to grill up for dinner, then I put some in the fridge and stowed most of it away in vacuum-sealed bags in my freezer. I'd have hogfish for a week, one of the many perks of living in the Florida Keys.

We doused them in Swamp Sauce, a local sauce from up north in the Everglades, then fired up the grill, cooking the fresh fish right on the deck along with a pile of golden potatoes and some of the leftover lobster. Once cooked, we sat around the dinette, enjoying the tantalizing fish that seemed to melt in our mouths and turning the Baia around so we could watch the beautiful sunset over the horizon. Ange had whipped up a few mojitos, and I leaned back into the cushioned seat, joking around with them and enjoying the meal as we watched the sky come to life with bright streaks of color.

Just as we finished eating, our stomachs full from the all-you-can-eat fresh seafood, I received a phone call from Professor Murchison. It caught me off guard, as I hadn't heard a word from him since I'd sent him my questions regarding the old dagger a few days earlier.

Sliding my iPhone out of my cargo shorts pocket, I pressed the answer button and held it up to the side of my face.

"Boy, am I glad to hear from you," I said. "How are the Alps?"

"Cold and fascinating, as usual," he replied. "And if you're glad now, wait until I tell you what I found out about that piece of yours."

I could hear the excitement in his voice. From the first moment I'd met Professor Murchison, I could feel his passion for history, and it was so contagious that it spread like wildfire among whoever he was in contact with.

I smiled and said, "Well, any information would be better than what we've learned so far."

"Are you sitting down?" he asked. "It's kind of a lot."

I switched to speakerphone and leaned back.

"Yeah, and I've got you on speaker with Ange and Jack."

The two of them each said a quick hello, and then Frank got straight to it.

"Sorry I haven't gotten back to you sooner," he said through the speaker, which was booming loud enough for all three of us to hear him easily. "When I first saw your message and the pictures of the dagger, I knew instantly that it was an old knight dagger. But offhand, the name inscribed on the hilt didn't ring any bells, so I decided to do some investigative work." He cleared his throat and continued, "I stopped by the Maritime Museum in London, which contains massive rooms filled with everything from ship journals to crew pay records, and tens of thousands of letters. It was deep within the archives, after an entire evening of searching, that I found something."

He paused for a moment and I knew what he was doing. Frank seemed to have a flair for the dramatic and liked to keep people, especially his students, on edge.

Ange couldn't take it anymore and said, "Well? What did you find?"

His smooth and energetic voice came over the speaker. "I figured out who she is. It took quite a bit of digging and piecing together. It was especially difficult, since her name was never legally changed to Taylor." The three of us looked at each other, filled with both confusion and curiosity. A few seconds later, Frank added, "The story begins back in 1649, when a twelve-year-old English orphan named John Taylor became a cabin boy on a ship called the *Lady Margaret*. For fifteen years, Taylor sailed all over the Atlantic, from the Bahamas to Halifax, and all over Europe, working aboard various ships. He worked hard, learned everything he could about sailing, and rose fast, developing a good reputation amongst his peers. I don't have an exact time frame here, but it was somewhere around 1664 that he met the beautiful daughter of one of his ship's financiers. Her name was Beatrice Littleton, and the two fell madly in love with each other. They wanted to get married, but of course, her father disapproved of it.

"You see, Taylor had sailed all over the world. He'd proved his salt and his courageousness countless times through heavy storms, damaged hulls, and months of working from sunup till sundown on shipwide half rations. But no matter what he did, Taylor couldn't escape his past. It held him back like a metal noose around his neck, keeping him from many well-deserved promotions, as they were instead handed to sailors of greater hereditary importance in English society. Beatrice's father refused to let the marriage take place, and as far as I can tell, the two decided to elope but weren't able to."

As Frank paused for a moment, I realized that all three of us were sitting on the very edge of the cushioned seats, our bodies hunched over my smartphone.

"What do you mean they weren't able to?" I asked. "What happened?"

Frank cleared his throat and said, "Seeing the romance building between them, Beatrice's father talked to the captain of Taylor's ship. Taylor was then forced to go on an unexpected voyage to Jamaica and back. It was scheduled to last nine months but ended up taking even longer. It was when he returned to London in April of 1665 that he learned the horrible news. Beatrice had gotten sick during the Great Plague of London and had died two months earlier."

Frank said the last words slowly and paused for a few seconds. I glanced over at Jack, then at Ange, whose mouth was wide open and her eyes unblinking.

"How terrible," Ange said. "What did Taylor do?"

Frank sighed. "Well, I don't know what he did at first. But a few months later, he set sail again for the Americas, this time on a newly constructed English schooner called the *Crescent.*"

Frank then continued, reading a portion of a letter sent from the governor of Jamaica, informing the crown that Taylor had taken control of the *Crescent* and turned to piracy.

"It was around this time that Taylor changed his name to one more well known in modern times. John Shadow."

The three of us glanced up at each other, a combination of excitement and disbelief overtaking our facial expressions. John "Blood" Shadow was right up there with Blackbeard and Henry Morgan as one of the most ruthless and notorious pirates ever to set sail. I'd read about him growing up and was amazed to hear Frank mention his name.

Frank continued. "During the Golden Age of Piracy, it was said that Shadow had raided over thirty Spanish and English ships, accumulating a massive fortune. But the history books conflict when it comes to what exactly happened to Shadow and his treasure. Some scholars believe he ran away with his crew to a secret port in South America. Others that he was murdered by his own crew, and his treasure was taken and split amongst them. But no one knows for sure."

"What do you think happened?" Jack asked.

Frank's voice grew more excited as he said, "Well, here's where the story gets really interesting. In 1672, after years of his raiding Spanish galleons and English merchant ships, the English crown finally grew sick of Shadow and decided to take swift action. They sent the *Valiant*, a massive forty-gun frigate, and put it under the command of Captain William Gray, an English officer who rose to become the crown's most successful pirate hunter. Later that year, the *Valiant* and Captain Gray confronted the *Crescent*, and the two ships engaged in a battle that eventually resulted in the sinking of the *Crescent* and the death of John Shadow."

"Wait," Ange said. "So if this Captain Gray sank the *Crescent*, didn't he recover Shadow's treasure as well?"

I could hear Frank's breathing through the phone, and after a few seconds, he said, "That's the thing. Gray supposedly searched the wreck but never found any treasure aboard. Which means that Shadow must have hidden it away somewhere."

The story was fascinating, and I hung eagerly on each word that came out of Frank's mouth. But there was something that didn't make sense, a key part of the story that didn't fit.

"So if Gray killed Shadow and sank the *Crescent*, why is there a historical debate about what happened to the pirate?" I asked. "I mean, that sounds pretty official to me."

"It's because of Gray's character," Frank replied. "It came into question once it was discovered that he'd lied about the location of the *Crescent*'s wreck site in order to keep the treasure all to himself. Historians believe that if he lied about the location, he and his crew could have easily lied about a lot more. There are simply too many flaws in Gray's character to use him as an entirely reliable source. But the dagger you've got was found in Florida Bay, and I have no doubt that it belonged to Shadow. The fact remains that you guys could be close to discovering a notorious lost pirate ship, and solving one of the Caribbean's greatest mysteries."

TEN

After talking with us on the phone for well over an hour, Frank ended the call by informing us that he was catching a morning flight back to Florida and that he should be back in the Keys the following evening. Once the line went dead, we sat in silence for a moment, taking in everything he'd said. After half a minute, I broke the silence when I leaned back into the cushioned seat and laughed.

Grabbing the dagger from the table in front of me, I held it up to the cockpit lighting. "This dagger belonged to Captain John 'Blood' Shadow."

"That's crazy to think, bro," Jack said. "Maybe if we find the wreck, we can figure out where his treasure is as well."

We all thought it over for a few minutes, still amazed how we'd managed to find ourselves in the current situation.

Suddenly, Jack smiled, stood up and said, "You

know what? You both have had your turns picking a hit to explore." He slid the laptop monitor to face him, then looked over the map we'd created and added, "I'm feeling sufficiently excited about this venture after that talk. I think it's my turn."

Ange laughed. "Little late, isn't it?"

By way of an answer, Jack grabbed his dive flashlight.

I glanced over at his empty glass, then laughed. "I think I saw a 'don't drink and swim' sign while we cruised past Fleming Key."

"That's only for landlubbers," Jack said with a grin. "I swim better with a little buzz. Besides, that's my lucky tequila I was drinking."

I raised my hands in the air. "Fine," I said. "Where are we headed?"

"This one," Jack said, pointing at a hit on the screen.

It wasn't the biggest one, but it was surrounded by a bunch of other similar-sized hits. Jack stepped over to the helm and started up the engines, and within a few minutes he had us floating right over his selected spot. After taking one more look at the map, he slid on his mask, switched on his dive flashlight, and dove over the starboard gunwale.

"We didn't make a bet," I said as I stepped over and looked down into the dark water, watching as his flashlight scanned along the seafloor below.

Ange laughed, and before she could reply, Jack had already returned to the surface. He was empty-handed, but a big smile materialized on his face after he let out his breath.

"What is it?" I asked, eyeing him skeptically.

"Grab me your crowbar, would ya?"

I looked at my old friend, confused, but just

shrugged and moved into the salon, where I kept my crowbar in a storage closet. Returning a moment later, I handed it to Jack, who gripped it tightly, took in a breath, and dropped back down beneath the waves without another word.

"Well, I'll give him this," Ange said, no longer able to contain her curiosity as she stood up and moved beside me, "he sure has a flair for the dramatic sometimes."

A little over a minute after he reached the bottom, I saw him grab an object and kick towards the surface. Whatever it was, I knew that it was heavy. He was barely able to bring it all the way up as I leaned over the gunwale and wrapped my arms around its hard, barnacle-covered exterior. It only took a few seconds for Ange and me to realize what it was.

"You have got to be kidding me," Ange said, staring at it with awe.

Jack popped up out of the water, a big smile still on his face as I hauled it up and set it on the swim platform.

"What did I tell you, bro?" Jack said as he pushed down his mask, swam around to the stern, then pulled himself up and sat next to the cannonball he'd just brought up from the seafloor. "I think it's a six-pounder. But it's heavier with all this crap caked all over it."

After scraping and scrubbing almost all of the barnacles and grime from its surface, we were able to see that it had a distinct symbol carved into it that looked like an arrow. Jack told me that he thought it was the mark of the Royal Navy but didn't know for sure. I moved over to the laptop and marked our location as a potential wreck site.

Glancing over at the bottle of liquor resting beside me, I said, "Man, that's some lucky tequila."

Ange laughed, and Jack grinned from ear to hear, looking back and forth between the cannonball and his bottle.

We snacked on leftover fish and lobster as we planned out the following day's search. We'd managed to meg over half of our search area already and had accumulated over fifty hits, ranging in size from as small as a bottle cap to large enough to be a cannon or ballast stone. With Jack finding the cannonball, none of us had ever been more excited for daybreak to come so we could jump back into the water and see what else there was to find.

It was well after ten o'clock by the time we finished, and the sky was dark, the sun having disappeared long before. Since it was a calm evening with very little wind, we cruised just a few miles away into a small bay near the Dolphin Research Center on Vaca Key and dropped anchor for the night.

I switched off the outside lights and turned on my security system before following Ange and Jack down into the lounge, locking the door behind me. Jack crashed in the guest cabin, and Ange and I headed for the main cabin. We pulled off our clothes and collapsed onto the king-sized bed, tired after the long day of searching. I lay on my back with Ange draped over me, her blond hair smelling of wildflowers and the ocean as it rested on my right pec.

"It's such a sad story, Logan," she said, not moving her head in the slightest. "I wish Taylor had sailed away with her. Just sneak off in the middle of the night, elope, and live on their own."

I smiled. "It's crazy to think that he would do something so radical as turn pirate. And that he'd be able to convince most of the crew to do the same."

"People do crazy things sometimes when they hit rock bottom," Ange said. "Plus, did you hear what Frank said? How Taylor had worked his ass off for years but never got the promotions he deserved because of his family? Then the love of his life dies. That would push anyone off the edge. Hell, I'd have probably turned pirate too."

I grimaced. "You would've made one hell of a pirate, Ange."

She laughed, and within a few minutes we were both passed out, lulled to sleep by the gentle rocking of the Baia.

What felt like only a few seconds later, my eyes sprang open and I listened intently, my instincts taking over. I sat still for a moment, not knowing for sure why I'd woken up. I must have heard something, I thought as I slowly lifted my head up off the feather pillow. Keeping my body still and my breathing quiet, I felt a subtle but unnatural sway of the boat and realized that somebody was moving aboard the Baia.

I sat up on the bed, then listened for any sound, expecting to hear Jack shuffling quietly about in the salon. Instead, my eyes grew wide as I heard the sound of the door leading out to the cockpit rattle softly, then hinge open.

I pulled off the white comforter, slid out of bed, and reached for my Sig resting on the nightstand. I was wearing only a pair of gray workout shorts as I moved barefoot towards the main cabin door. Ange woke up suddenly, her blue eyes bursting open and her upper body pulling herself up instinctively.

"What's going on?" she asked quietly. She was

fully alert, her body and mind managing to shake off her deep sleep instantly.

By way of an answer, I placed a finger against my lips, then pointed aft where faint footsteps could be heard stepping down into the salon. Before I could blink, she climbed out of bed, pulled one of my tee shirts over her naked body and grabbed hold of her Glock 26 9mm handgun, grasping it with both hands.

Turning away from Ange, I took a step aft and brought my head just a few inches away from the cabin door. The sounds were closer now. It sounded like two people, moving quietly towards our location. I didn't have time to wonder why my security system hadn't gone off or how whoever it was had managed to break the lock.

Gripping my Sig tightly in my right hand, I nodded to Ange, who stood just a few paces behind me, and jerked open the door. Before whoever it was even knew that I was there, I was through the door, my Sig raised chest height as I stepped towards their two shadowy figures.

The guy closest to me held something in his hands, and by the faint light of the moon trickling through the still-open salon door behind them, I saw it glisten and realized that it was a pistol.

"Drop it!" I yelled, but before the words had escaped my lips, he raised the firearm towards me.

Without hesitating, I pulled the trigger, putting a bullet in his left shoulder. The sound rattled the air like thunder in the tight confines of my boat. His body twisted and he let go of his handgun, sending it rattling to the deck.

The second guy, seeing his buddy wailing in pain, didn't try anything. Instead, he turned on his heels and almost tripped as he climbed up the stairs, heading back out into the cockpit. The first guy, having learned his lesson, stumbled as he turned around. Just as he took the first step, Ange switched on the salon lights, allowing me to see him clearly for the first time. He had dark skin and was wearing basketball shorts, a white cutoff tee shirt, and a backward ballcap.

I lunged after him as he took the steps as fast as he could, his blood dripping onto the white fiberglass below. I reached him just as he took the final step, swiping his right ankle and causing him to tumble over, his face slamming hard between the console and the dinette.

It took me all of half a second to race up the stairs, and as the guy tried to get to his feet, I hit him with a hard front kick to his face. His nose crunched and his head jerked back, hitting the deck with a loud thud that knocked him unconscious.

Moving past the bloodied guy on the deck, I watched the second guy, who was dressed in a pair of dark jeans and a black tee shirt, just as he climbed into a small inflatable dinghy. I sprinted towards him. He frantically untied the nylon rope attaching his small inflatable to the Baia, but he must have been stupid to think he could escape me without an outboard.

Sprinting for the stern, I jumped down past the transom onto the swim platform and hurled my body through the air, crashing into the thug. I slammed him across the face with my elbow, causing him to jerk his head sideways and send a spray of spit and blood through the air as we tumbled against the starboard pontoon of the inflatable. As I fought to hold him down, he hit me with a strong kick to the chest that sent my body falling backward, and I almost tumbled into the water at the forward part of the dinghy.

I regained my balance, and as the thug came at me, I snatched an oar from the deck, reared it back, and slammed it against the side of his face. The oar broke in half and the thug grunted in pain as his body flipped over the side of the dinghy and into the water with a splash.

I dropped the broken half of the oar still clutched in my right hand, then moved towards the guy as he gagged and struggled in the water. Just as I was about to rip him out of the water and put him to sleep, I heard the sound of two powerful outboard engines come to life in the distant darkness.

"Logan!" Ange yelled, her voice booming from the deck of the Baia.

I turned to glance in her direction and saw her standing alongside Jack up against the transom. They were both armed, Ange with her Glock and Jack with his compact Desert Eagle. As I looked at Ange, I saw that she was pointing in the direction where the engine sounds were coming from. Glancing over my shoulder, I saw the faint blurry white hull of a boat as it rocketed straight towards us, leaving a silvery streak of rippling moonlight in its wake.

I looked back at the guy who was still thrashing wildly in the water. Bending over the pontoon, I grabbed hold of his soaked black tee shirt with one hand and tightly gripped his left arm with the other. In a quick motion, I pulled him out of the water, grabbed my holstered Sig, and slammed the handgrip against his temple, knocking him unconscious.

With the guy out of commission, I drew my attention back to the approaching boat, which was now within a quarter of a mile from the Baia.

"There's at least three of them, and they're armed

with AK-47s!" Ange said in a powerful and serious tone as she stared at the approaching boat through the optics of my night vision monocular.

I could see them too, standing aboard what looked like a twenty-four-foot Proline center-console, their weapons glistening faintly as the engines shot them through the water. It was clear that these guys weren't looking to have a friendly chat and though I had no idea who they were or what they wanted from us, I knew our only choice was to fight them off somehow. The only problem was that we were outgunned.

My mind drifted momentarily to the stockpile of weaponry I had locked away in the main cabin safe, wishing I had enough time to run in there and saddle up with something a little more effective than my Sig. But I knew that the boat would be on us in just a few seconds.

I faced the approaching boat, gripped my Sig with two hands, and took aim towards the windscreen. In my peripheral vision, I saw Ange and Jack do the same. As the boat turned slightly, giving me a good view of one of the thugs beside the pilot, I pulled the trigger in a smooth, repetitive motion, sending a succession of 9mm rounds straight towards the thugs.

Ange and Jack fired as well, and our combined efforts sent a barrage of bullets towards our unknown assailants. One of the shadowy figures flew back and dropped out of sight right away, and the rest quickly took cover behind the gunwale and bow, escaping the storm of gunfire before they too met a painful, bloody end.

We stopped firing as they disappeared from view, knowing that our bullets would have little success at stopping or even slowing the boat if we fired at the hull. Within seconds, the boat cruised within a few hundred feet of the Baia. I kept my Sig raised, my vision narrowed, and my finger ready on the trigger. In an instant, and just as the boat was right on top of us, two of the thugs came back into view, springing up from their hiding places and aiming their shouldered AK-47s straight towards us.

"Take cover!" I yelled.

I fired a few rounds, but seeing that the two of them were already firing automatic streaks of bullets my direction, I had no choice but to dive headfirst into the water. Kicking my feet as hard as I could and dragging myself down with my arms, I narrowly avoided a few bullets as they torpedoed through the water and broke apart around me.

Glancing up through the inky blackness, I watched as the boat cruised by and heard the loud propellers as they crashed through the water in a powerful white vortex just overhead. As the boat passed, and when the bullets stopped exploding into the water around me, I quickly kicked for the surface.

Breaking out of the dark water into the open air above, I heard the hissing of air coming from the inflatable beside me and the shuffling of feet aboard the Baia. I instantly drew my gaze to the thugs on the boat, who'd stopped firing and were hauling ass away from us.

With my Sig still clutched in my right hand, I brought it out of the water, took aim, and fired off round after round towards the thugs. Though they'd already cruised over a few hundred feet away and were increasing that gap with every second, I managed to hit one of them in the back, causing his body to lurch forward and collapse to the deck beside the pilot.

The mysterious center-console continued its frenzied escape into the darkness of the night, its engines growing quieter and quieter as it headed north into the Gulf. I turned my attention back towards the Baia.

"Are you guys okay?" I asked as I kicked my way behind the now-mostly-deflated dinghy towards the swim platform.

A second later, Ange said, "Never better." She stepped down, then, holding out a hand to help me up the ladder, she looked me over and added, "Please don't tell me you got shot."

I shook my head as we locked hands, then climbed up onto the swim platform beside her.

"A few of those rounds came close," I said. "But you know how much I hate to disappoint you."

Jack moved over to the transom and handed me a folded towel. He was still gripping his Desert Eagle in his left hand, and his eyes were wider than the horizon on a cloudless afternoon out on open water.

"Who the hell was that, bro?" Jack asked, turning to stare off in the direction where the boat had disappeared.

I shook my head. "I don't know." Then, toweling off my dark brown hair, I added, "But we should radio the Coast Guard and inform them where they were heading. Tell them to keep an eye out for them."

Jack nodded, then turned on his heels and strode for the radio attached to a fiberglass panel beside the helm. While he called in a report, I finished drying off and looked over at the thug lying motionless in the barely floating dinghy, his chest riddled with bullet holes.

"Damn," I said, staring down at him. "These

guys don't like to leave loose ends."

"Yeah, well, they failed, then," Ange said, motioning towards the other thug I'd taken out, who was still sleeping like a baby on the deck beside the dinette.

After toweling off, I stepped up into the cockpit and we zip-tied the thug's wrists and ankles together. Jack finished his call and informed us that the Coast Guard was sending out a few patrol boats from the station in Marathon to look for the attackers.

After a brief moment of silence, Ange said, "You think those guys were after the pirate ship?"

I shrugged. "I don't think so. I mean, we just learned about it ourselves. And aside from Frank and Pete, there's nobody that knows we're even looking for something."

Ange gasped, rose to her feet and took a step back.

"Logan," she said, pointing at the unconscious thug on the deck.

"What is it?" I asked, wondering what could possibly cause her to act like she was.

"Look," she added and I realized that she wasn't just pointing at the thug. She was pointing at his right hand.

I stepped towards the snoozing thug, bent down and looked at his right hand. Just as I was about to ask Ange what the hell she was talking about, I saw something that made my mouth drop open. The guy had a tattoo of two black snakes slithering around his wrist.

Ange moved beside me and said, "Black Venom."

ELEVEN

It was just past two in the morning when Black Venom's boat disappeared in the night and the three of us were left with two thugs, one dead and one unconscious, and a whole lot of questions. It had been nearly a year since I'd helped take Black Venom down and kept them from getting their hands on the Aztec treasure. Why had the powerful Mexican drug cartel finally decided to come back to the Keys? And, more importantly, how many more had they sent?

Those questions alone caused us to station a watch for the rest of the night, starting with me from 0230 until 0330. I sat on the cushioned half-moon seat around the dinette and took intermittent trips up onto the bow to have a look around the horizon with my night vision monocular.

Slung over my chest, I had my MP5N submachine gun, to go along with my Sig holstered to my side. Part of me wanted them to come back as I peered through the scope at the miles of dark ocean and distant islands surrounding us. I would be more prepared this time around.

Leaning back into the seat, I grabbed my white Rubio Charters mug, which I'd recently filled with a fresh brew of Colombian medium roast and took a few sips. The hot liquid felt good, and the caffeine boost felt even better. It had been a long day out on the water, and I'd been looking forward to a long and peaceful night's sleep before those bozos had decided to show up.

Setting the mug back on the dinette, I glanced down at the guy I'd shot, who was still unconscious, his limbs zip-tied, and lying on his side on the deck beside the sunbed. We'd used my big first aid kit to stop the bleeding, which I'll admit was more for the sake of my fiberglass deck, which I didn't want to get blood all over. But at least the guy wouldn't die. Who knew? Maybe the authorities would be able to get some information out of him. I highly doubted it, though. The other thug, who'd been less lucky during the encounter, lay beside him, his bullet riddled corpse covered with an old bedsheet.

At 0326, the salon door opened and Ange stepped out. She was barefoot and wearing a pair of black workout shorts and a gray tee shirt.

She smiled at me, then took a quick look around the horizon.

"Any more sign of Black Venom?" she asked.

"Unfortunately, no," I replied. "These guys pissed me off, and I wouldn't mind a little more ass-kicking tonight."

She laughed and plopped down beside me. "Well, if they do come back, I'll be sure to save a few for you."

I smiled. "You're the best." Then I kissed her on the cheek and slid my mug across the table, stopping it right in front of her.

As I rose to my feet, she said, "I only drink black, you know that."

"It is black," I replied. "I just filled it." Then I winked at her and added, "You look sexy in that shirt, by the way."

She gave a dramatic blush, then whipped her hair to the back of her head. I grinned as I stepped down into the salon, closing the door behind me.

At 0530, I awoke to the sound of my phone playing Jimmy Buffet's "Margaritaville." Opening my eyes, I saw Ange curled up beside me. Somehow she'd managed to crawl into bed without me even noticing, which made me wonder if living in the Keys for so long had made me soft. Or maybe Ange was just that quiet. Thinking about the events of the previous night, how I'd awoken and taken down the two thugs sneaking onto my boat, I knew that the latter was most likely the case.

Ange and I both crawled out of bed together and, after seeing that Jack had nothing new to share, we took a nice hot shower and prepared a small breakfast. I scrambled up a few eggs to go along with toast, slices of mango, and orange juice. As we ate out around the dinette, I watched our captive as he sat propped against the starboard gunwale, staring at the deck. His face was bandaged and still a little bloody from when I'd kicked him in the face, and his shoulder had a few layers of white bandages wrapped around it tightly.

"Hasn't said a word," Jack said. "He woke up around four, looked confused as hell, then just sat against the side of the boat. Been sitting like that ever since."

"Charles said he'd meet us at Boca Chica Marina this morning to take him off our hands," I said, referring to the conversation I'd had with Key West's sheriff earlier that morning.

Ange glanced over at the radio beside the helm and added, "And that thing hasn't made a sound for hours. Which means that they probably got away."

When we finished eating, I pulled up the anchor from the cockpit using the windlass, then started up the engines. The sun was just rising over the eastern tip of Vaca Key and the Upper Keys beyond as I eased the throttles forward, cruising us out of the shallow bay.

I put us on a course due southwest, and we flew across the calm morning waters of Florida Bay. Looking off the starboard bow, I could see our search area in the distance and wished this little hiccup hadn't taken place. What with Jack finding the cannonball, I felt like we were close. Just a few more days of searching, and I was confident that the *Crescent*, and perhaps even its treasure as well, could be ours.

I glanced back at our captive, who was still sitting motionless, his body tied off to a pair of starboard cleats. *Someone always has to throw a wrench in the plans*, I thought, shaking my head as I turned back to look through the windscreen.

I kept the throttles at the Baia's cruising speed of thirty knots as I piloted her under the Seven Mile Bridge, passing right between the small Pigeon Key to the west and Boot Key to the east. Once past the bridge, I turned to starboard, heading west and cruising within a few hundred feet of the tiny Molasses Keys.

My mind instantly shot back to that day three months earlier when I'd crashed into it while taking down Pedro Campos and his small drug-smuggling operation. He and his twin brother, Hector, were both massive guys who'd been former MMA fighters before deciding to break bad. My dad had been working undercover during one of their operations to try and take them down when they'd grown suspicious and murdered him. That had been a big mistake on their part, and once I'd learned about it, I had gone on a mission to avenge his death and brought both of them, and their operation, to ruin.

I cruised through the Middle Keys and into the Lower Keys, eventually reaching Naval Air Station Key West, where I soon eased back on the throttles and turned into Boca Chica Channel. I pulled the Baia slowly right up to the day-mooring section of Boca Chica Marina and spotted two police cars and an ambulance parked along the waterfront on Midway Avenue. As I killed the engines, I heard a massive Boeing C-17 as it took off from the air base, its jet engines roaring as it flew just overhead.

Glancing over towards the marina office, I saw Sheriff Wilkes approaching from the direction of the police vehicles alongside three other officers.

"Finally we can get rid of this guy," Ange said as the three of us forced the thug to his feet. "I'm getting sick of looking at him."

Even as we moved him over to the port gunwale, he didn't say a word or even move his eyes in the slightest. He looked like a lethargic zombie, and I was happy to get rid of him as well.

Sheriff Charles Wilkes was an imposing black man who was just slightly shorter than my six foot two inches. He had a lean muscular frame and looked and moved much younger than his forty-nine years. He walked right up to the port side of the Baia, eyeing both us and the guy we were holding through a pair of dark Oakley sunglasses for a few seconds.

"He said anything yet?" Charles asked in his low and powerful voice.

"Not a peep ," I said.

The three of us lifted him up over the gunwale, then Charles and the other officers grabbed hold of him. Officer Kincaid cuffed the thug, then cut the zip tie holding his ankles together.

"Jeez, Logan," Charles said, looking the thug over from head to toe. "He looks beat to hell. It's no wonder he hasn't said a word. Maybe he can't."

"Hey, he got off easy," I said sternly, motioning towards the corpse on the deck hidden beneath the sheet. After lifting the dead body up and handing it to two other officers, I added, "If any of his buddies board my boat again, I won't be aiming for their shoulders."

Charles thought it over for a moment, then nodded. "Fair enough. We'll have the body sent over to the Monroe County Medical Examiner. We're taking the other guy to the station in Key West, then he'll be taken up north. I'm guessing you're aware that the Coast Guard didn't find any sign of the boat anywhere this morning."

"Yeah," I said. "I figured as much when we didn't hear anything."

Charles stood beside the Baia for a moment while the other officers ushered the thug over to one of the police cars and carried the body into an ambulance.

Charles turned to me and sighed. "Look, I don't have to tell you what kind of shit could come out of all this. The last thing I want is for my home to turn into a Mexican cartel war zone."

"Me too," I said. "But I'm guessing these guys want their revenge for what happened last year. And like I said, if they come near me, I'm going to defend myself with whatever means necessary."

Charles nodded, then looked over at the officers as they put the thug into the backseat of one of the cars.

"We'll be in touch, alright?" he said before nodding to each of us. "You guys just be careful."

"You too, Charles," I said, and he turned and headed towards the two police cars.

We watched as he climbed into the lead car, and they pulled out onto the road, heading towards US-1.

We filled up the Baia's tank, and as I was about to start up the engines, Jack told me to hold up.

"You guys hungry?" he said, motioning his head towards Navigator's Bar and Grill, which sat just a short walk down the beach.

"I thought they didn't open for a few more hours," I said, hoping to be wrong, since Navigator's served some of the best breakfast bowls I'd ever had.

Jack smiled. "I know the owners, bro. I eat here all the time, and I'm sure they won't mind the company."

I glanced over at Ange as she said, "I'm starving. I guess that breakfast we had just didn't cut it."

I slid my keys out of the ignition, locked up the Baia, then turned on the security system before hopping onto the dock beside Ange and Jack. Jack hadn't been kidding about being friends with the owners. Not only were they happy to serve us an hour before they opened, but they called out Jack's name gave him a big hug just seconds after he walked in the door.

We sat around an outside table under the shade of a green umbrella and a few palm trees, our bare feet in the sand. We had a beautiful view of the mooring sailboats, along with the busy channel beyond. We ate a variety of delicious food, including one of their specialty breakfast bowls, a pulled pork sandwich, and fresh fish tacos with mango sauce.

While eating, we talked about everything from the cannonball Jack had lifted from beneath the waves to what we were going to do about Black Venom.

"If I know anything about Black Venom," I said, sipping on a glass of fresh cantaloupe juice, "we sure as hell haven't seen the last of them."

TWELVE

The two men stood across from one another beside the large dining room table of the yacht.

"What the fuck happened?" Felix Callejo said, his voice consumed with rage.

"He… he killed one of our men," the younger cartel said to his superior. He tried to speak confidently, but the degree to which they'd just messed up weighed heavily on him. He was big and muscular but stood hunched over slightly. "And they took Luis."

"How did you let that happen?" Felix fired back, his eyes fuming and his jaw clenched. He wasn't physically imposing. At roughly five and a half feet tall and one hundred and sixty pounds, he was much smaller than the man he was berating. But after decades of criminal activity and dealing with the most hardened criminals in the world, Felix Callejo had an aura about him that could make even the toughest thugs feel a foot tall.

Antonio stood still for a moment. He wanted to choose his words carefully. Too many times, he'd witnessed fellow cartel members unable to hold their tongues or control their wits when faced with an angry higher-up. And that never ended well.

"He's highly trained," Antonio said, his words stumbling awkwardly out of his mouth.

"I know that he's trained," Felix fired back. He was all rage. His eyebrows pulled down and together, his lips narrowed and he'd stepped close to Luis, allowing the younger man to see the anger deep within his green eyes. "We told everyone involved in this operation that from the beginning. Are you telling me that you weren't listening, or are you trying to tell me something that I already know?" He looked at the younger man expectantly. "Well? Which is it?"

By way of an answer, all Antonio could do was look at his hands and try to quell his imagination as it ran wild, thinking about what Felix was likely to do to him. In his mind, he could see the faces of men who he himself had thrown overboard with chains tied around their ankles at the order of Black Venom higher-ups. He would be joining them soon, he convinced himself, and it caused a layer of sweat to form on his brow.

Felix shook his head and barked, "Pathetic. You know very well the consequences of failing so miserably under my command. Your actions today have put our target on alert. And now one of my men is in their hands. Do you even fucking realize how much harder you've made this?"

Just as it seemed that Felix's booming voice couldn't get any more pissed off, a sound broke the uncomfortable silence.

Felix grunted, reached into his pocket, then pulled out his cell phone. He gazed at the screen momentarily, his face shifting from pissed off to irritated.

Glancing up at Antonio, he said, "We're not finished here."

Felix then moved across the room, motioning for the two big guys standing stoically at the back of the lounge to follow him. Moving through a set of metal doors, he entered the most secure room on the entire yacht and told his henchmen to bring the call up on the seventy-inch plasma screen that was mounted to the aft-facing wall. The rest of the room was lined with floor-to-ceiling tinted windows that offered an incredible bird's-eye view of the ocean below and the deep blue horizon beyond.

The two guys did as Felix asked, and a few seconds later, the call connected and the image of an old, dark-skinned man with gray hair appeared on the screen. He had a stone-cold expression plastered across his face. He was wearing a white button-up shirt and sitting on a black leather couch, with a large window revealing a thick green jungle behind him.

"What is the status of Logan Dodge?" the old man asked in Spanish, getting straight to the point. He had a silky-smooth voice and stared unblinking into the screen, right at Felix.

Felix stared back at his boss, remaining as calm and confident as he could. He knew the leader of Black Venom well and knew that if he backed down even the slightest, the old man would tear him apart.

"We've been tracking his movements, Jefe," Felix replied. "We have a plan to take him."

The old man sighed and narrowed his gaze.

"A plan?" he grunted, then cleared his throat and

leaned in closer to the camera. "You left Cartagena ten days ago. You should have him on my doorstep in chains by now."

"It's not that simple with him. He's highly trained, and so are many of his friends. If you sweep in and try to grab him, we'll lose a handful of men in the process."

Felix left out the fact that he'd just lost two of his men, not wanting to anger the cartel leader any further.

Jefe waved a hand in the air. "He's already killed more than a handful. I don't want excuses, and I don't want any more planning. I want Logan Dodge, Felix. And if you can't bring him to me … well, then I might have to start looking for a new second-in-command."

The message was received loud and clear. Before Felix had even replied, the leader of Black Venom disappeared, his image replaced by a solid black screen. A new anger surged within Felix as he thought over the words Jefe had said.

"Who in the hell does he think he is?" he said to himself.

He thought about all of the years he'd spent killing, struggling, hustling, and putting his neck on the line for Jefe and all of Black Venom. For the leader to go and say that he'd replace him if he couldn't come through struck a chord deep within Felix's psyche.

"Cesar!" Felix yelled towards the door.

A second later, the door slid open and a tall, muscular man stepped inside. He walked with strong, confident strides and had dark hair cut close to his tanned scalp and a black tattoo around his left eye.

"Yes, Felix," Cesar said, walking right up to him.

106

"How is the plan coming along?"

"As we'd hoped," Cesar replied. "We have a taker, and he's willing to do the job for half what we'd budgeted."

Felix nodded. "Good. And the chloroform?"

Cesar paused a moment, then said, "We decided on something a little... stronger."

As Felix opened his mouth to ask what he meant, Cesar stepped out into the hall and came back holding a large plastic hard case. Setting the case on the table in front of them, he unclasped the hinges and pulled out a strange-looking long-barreled rifle. Then he grabbed a dart from a clear case and held it out in front of Felix.

"It's the ones they use to take down elephants in Africa," Cesar said with a grin. "He won't know what the hell hit him."

THIRTEEN

After an early lunch at Navigator's, we hopped back aboard the Baia and cruised around the island into Conch Harbor Marina. We spent the rest of the afternoon narrowing our search grid to an area surrounding the location where Jack had found the cannonball. Our digital replication of the seafloor had many hits from the mag nearby, some small and some large enough to be significant remnants of a pirate ship.

We all knew, however, that just because we'd potentially found a remnant of the wreck, it didn't mean that our search was close to being over.

"It could take years to find the entire haul in open water like that, bro," Jack said. "Remember the *Atocha*? The Spanish galleon that was sunk by a massive cane back in the 1600s over by the Marquesas Keys? Well, she was discovered in 1985, and it took years to find everything. Hell, the salvage crew believes there are still artifacts down there to this day."

I nodded. "The important thing is that we get closer every day. Today it's a cannonball. Tomorrow? Maybe a cannon, or a block of gold doubloons."

We also talked about the massive elephant in the room and how exactly we planned to deal with them. The last thing I wanted was to put anyone in danger, especially considering that Jack had a young nephew at home. Sliding my cell phone out of my pocket, I sat on the transom, slid my legs over so that I was facing over the stern, and dialed one of the few numbers I knew by heart.

Scott Cooper, my division officer back when I'd first arrived at my SEAL team in the Navy, answered on the second ring. Scott is one of the greatest warriors and one of the smartest guys I know. Before joining the Navy, he'd been a Rhodes Scholar, and after his service, he'd pursued a career in politics. Currently, he's a senator representing the state of Florida, and though he's a busy man and spends most of his time in Washington, D.C., we always have each other's backs when trouble comes.

I told him everything. About the dagger, the pirate ship, and about Black Venom. We talked for almost thirty minutes, and he told me that he would do everything that he could to help, starting with a call to CIA Deputy Director Wilson to see if there had been any recent tracking of the cartel's movements in the States.

When I ended the call, I joined the others, who were huddled around the laptop, and we worked and relaxed on the deck until the sun went down. After Jack headed home just after eight o'clock, Ange and I sprawled out on the sunbed and drank a few Paradise

Sunset beers while watching the goings-on in the marina.

The marina was pretty busy, and almost every slip was occupied. What I loved about sitting out on the boat and people watching in the marina was the diversity; we saw everyone from local fishermen and charter captains to weekend warriors to adventurers making a pit stop in their sailboat on their trip around the world.

Ange snapped me from my thoughts as she said, "You know, you were right when you said Black Venom isn't going to back down."

I nodded. "Which is why we need to be cautious and alert at all times until we take them out."

Ange paused for a moment, looking off into the distance.

"What?" I said, sensing that she had something on her mind.

She sighed. "Look, I'm as hard-headed as anyone, and the last girl in the world to back down from a fight. But maybe it isn't the best idea to be here right now."

I chuckled. "What? You think I should fly around the world and lay low someplace in Asia until everything cools off?"

She shrugged. "I'm just saying it might be a good idea. I don't know why they waited so long to come after you, but right now, you're a sitting duck here in the Keys."

"We'll be careful, okay?" I said.

"I've heard that before. What did Scott say?"

I told her the gist of our conversation, and though Scott helping us out made her feel a little better, I could tell that she was still concerned. It was strange; I'd known Ange for a while and hadn't ever known her to be the worried type. I wondered if it had to do with our relationship. We'd been sort of dating, on-again, off-again, for a few years, but the past five months, we'd been almost inseparable, spending practically every minute of every day together. I could feel our relationship heading toward the next level, and my instincts told me that she could feel it too.

The truth was she made a lot of sense. Though I wanted to find the pirate ship and treasure, staying in the Keys was a major risk. But I've never been one to back down from a challenge. I'd taken care of Black Venom before, and I could do it again.

When the clock neared midnight, Ange slid off the sunbed and seductively stepped down into the salon, sliding out of her tank top and shorts and smiling back at me wearing nothing but her bikini bottom. I followed close behind her, killing the outside lights, locking the door, and turning on the security system before joining her in the bed. For one night at least, we forgot about the dangers threatening us and enjoyed each other's company as if nothing had happened.

FOURTEEN

The following morning, I woke up naturally to the morning sunlight bleeding in through the partly open hatch overhead. After a quick breakfast and shower, we were met by Jack, Salty Pete, and Professor Frank Murchison, who'd just arrived in the Keys the previous evening.

"I think it's high time I see this piece in person," Frank said, grinning at me under the shade of a beige sun hat. He wore a pair of olive-green shorts, flip-flops, a white long-sleeved shirt, and a pair of sunglasses with a thick blue strap to keep them from falling. He generally looked more like a beach bum than a respected college professor to a passerby on the street.

I reached to my right hip, where the dagger was stashed, then handed it to Frank. Grabbing it eagerly but carefully, he unrolled the leather, his eyes lighting up as he gazed upon it in real life for the first time.

After admiring the design for a few seconds, he trained his eyes on the inscription, lifting up his sunglasses to get a better look.

Frank smiled. "I've traveled all over the world to find artifacts, and here you are, finding them just a few miles from where I teach."

"If you think that's cool," Jack said, stepping onto the swim platform and over the transom, "what until you see what we found a few nights ago."

He disappeared into the salon and came out a few seconds later, holding the cannonball in his hands. It caused both Frank's and Pete's eyes to grow wide and their mouths to noticeably drop.

"You boys have got to be kidding me," Pete said. "Where did you find that?"

Jack walked over to the transom and hauled the six-pound ball of iron into Pete's hands.

As Pete examined it, Jack said, "Florida Bay, about a half mile south from where the dagger was found. Pulled it out of the water just the other night."

"Was that before or after you were attacked by Black Venom?" Pete asked.

I glanced over at Jack, who was looking at me, and he gave a slight nod of his head.

"I told them, bro," he said. "I figured it was best that they know as soon as possible."

"You're right about that," I said, then added, "I'm surprised you guys still want to go out on the water with us."

"What? And miss an opportunity like this?" Pete said. "I've been diving and salvaging and searching for anything and everything in the Keys since before you three were born. I've never come close to finding anything like this. You kids realize how rare it is to find a genuine Golden Age pirate ship?"

"Pete's right," Frank said, still admiring the dagger and cannonball. "And besides, I think if this Black Venom is still hanging around in the Keys, what safer place could there be than with a former SEAL and the most deadly sniper on earth?"

Ange grinned. "I'm far from the most deadly," she said, making her best attempt at modesty.

"You're not a very good liar, Miss Fox," Pete said, then turned his attention back to the cannonball. "Well, I can tell you that this is an English cannonball. You can tell from this marking here." He pointed to the arrow we'd noticed earlier. It was faded, worn down, and difficult to see, but still somewhat distinct. "And it feels like a six-pounder, which most cannons aboard a seventeenth-century English schooner would have fired."

I nodded, hanging on every word that he said. Between Pete and Frank, they probably had more experience and knowledge of history and the Keys than any other two men combined.

"What do you make of the symbol beside the name and date?" Ange said, motioning toward the dagger in Frank's hands.

Frank glanced back down at it, then looked closer.

"Huh," he said, looking at the small carved symbol. "I'd never even noticed that before."

"We think it might be a heart," Jack said. "And it would make sense, given the story."

"Could be," Frank said. "I'll have to examine it more thoroughly."

"Well, let's get a move on," I said. "We're burning daylight, and there's a pirate shipwreck out there calling my name."

We decided to take the *Calypso*, since it had a

114

significant amount more space and we hoped it would also be less attractive to potential thugs who might be keeping an eye out for my Baia. Using one of the marina's metal carts, I transported the magnetometer along with Ange and my BCDs, wetsuits, fins, and masks over to Jack's boat.

Down in the salon, I grabbed my black CamelBak, then moved into the main cabin and loaded up an extra Sig and a few more magazines from my safe before locking it back up. Ange and I stowed a few changes of clothes in a Mexican-style sack before locking up and heading over to the *Calypso*.

The *Calypso*, Jack's forty-five-foot Sea Ray, was a great boat, with plenty of deck space for him to accommodate a large group out on the water. After stowing our gear and untying the lines, the five of us sat up on the bridge as Jack brought her out of the marina. On the trip over to our search area in Florida Bay, we gave Frank and Pete a rundown of what we'd done so far, showing them all of our mag hits on the computer. I was glad to have them with us. Not only were they both incredibly experienced and knowledgeable, but they'd bring a few fresh pairs of eyes to our search.

As Jack sat at the helm, Ange and I routinely found ourselves glancing at the horizon in all directions, making sure no one was following us. Though we'd enjoyed relaxing the previous evening, the atmosphere was different out on the water. Our guards were up, and we were no longer able to fully engross ourselves in the excitement of searching for the wreck.

At 1000, Jack slowed the *Calypso* to a stop and dropped anchor at the location where he'd found the cannonball the previous evening. Since the water was roughly twenty feet deep and we wanted to take our time searching the nearby seafloor, we decided to don full scuba gear.

Ange and I stayed topside for the first dive, helping everyone with their gear, though no one needed it. Everyone on board was an experienced diver and had themselves ready to go in just a few minutes, but we did a buddy check anyway. Carrying various equipment with them, including a few handheld metal detectors, they jumped one at a time into the crystal-clear water. Jack was the last one to drop beneath the waves, reminding me that they'd be down for approximately one hour—that was, if they didn't find anything significant enough to cause them to surface.

The water was relatively calm as their bodies became blurry through the water, leaving behind a trail of bubbles. Needless to say, they weren't down for an hour. Ange and I cracked open a few cans of iced tea and were just about to get comfortable up on the bridge when we heard a faint splash, followed by the sound of Pete's voice echoing across the late-morning air.

"Hey, take a look at this!" he said, his voice booming and filled with excitement.

Ange and I stood up, looked down from up in the bridge, and saw Pete floating just aft of the swim platform. He had a big smile on his face and held up what looked like an ordinary rock in his hands.

"A rock?" Ange said, chuckling a little.

"You kids." Pete shook his head. "You mean to tell me you don't know what this is?"

"A ballast stone," I said, trying to defend my generation.

Pete's smile returned. "Yep, and there's hundreds more. It's safe to say you guys have found yourselves a wreck."

Ange elbowed me playfully and called me a kiss-up, causing me to laugh as I focused my gaze on the stone in Pete's hands. The truth was, it had been a lucky guess. I knew old ships carried stones in their hulls to keep them from swaying back and forth too much but had never seen one in person.

If Pete was right, and I had no doubt that he was, we'd found a wreck. But the question as to what wreck we'd found still remained.

We spent the rest of the day diving and exploring every inch of seafloor surrounding the spot where Jack had found the cannonball. Over the course of our search, we found more ballast stones, corroded silverware, a few more cannonballs, and hundreds of musket balls. There are few things I find more exciting in life than the feeling of diving along the seafloor, discovering a hit with a handheld metal detector, and digging into the sand, only to find an artifact that's been lost beneath the waves for hundreds of years. It gave me the chills and overcame me with a feeling I hadn't felt since laying eyes upon the lost German U-boat for the first time, and the subsequent weeks I'd spent exploring it.

As the sun dropped down beneath the waves, we decided to call it a day. We disassembled our scuba gear, washed it all down, and met up on the bridge for a humble dinner of leftover fish, cheese, and crackers. Of course, being the renaissance man that he was, Pete had come prepared, grabbing an aged bottle of Captain Morgan from a case in his gear bag.

"To one of the most interesting days I've ever spent in the Keys," he said after filling us each a glass and raising his high into the air. "I only wish we could have found a sealed bottle of Golden Age pirate rum. That would be the day."

As we ate, I couldn't help but admire the haul we'd brought up in just a single day of diving. Many of the artifacts lay sprawled out on a beach towel on the deck just beside our feet.

"I think we might be getting closer to the heart of this ship," Jack said. "We were finding more and more artifacts as the day progressed."

"I think," Frank said, clearing his throat, "that we've probably already found it. Though it will be hard to tell for sure, since hundreds of years of tides, storms, and currents could spread a wreck like that over miles."

Jack looked at the professor, confused. "What do you mean, we've probably already found it? I know it's been years, but we should see at least some remains of the hull, right?"

Pete laughed and answered for Frank. "What he means is that this wreck is buried. We'll need to get ourselves a mailbox to blow all of the sand and sediment away. Should work nicely on this boat."

A mailbox is a large metal shroud that bends to form a ninety-degree angle and can be used to direct a boat's prop wash downward, where it can blow sediment away and reveal heavier objects underneath. Using it would save countless hours that would otherwise have to be spent manually sifting through mountains of sand.

"You really think this could be the *Crescent*?" Ange asked, looking primarily at Frank.

The enthusiastic professor grinned. "I'm almost certain of it," he said. "Now all we've got to do is identify it. And hopefully soon we'll start hauling up doubloons instead of rusted old forks."

With our spirits high and our excitement rivaling that of a child's the night before Christmas, we rattled up the anchor chain and set off for Key West. Neither Jack or Pete would be working the following day, and Frank had already called the college in order to arrange for a substitute for the next few days. None of them would ever pass up the chance to further explore what could potentially be a Golden Age pirate shipwreck.

FIFTEEN

At just after midnight, a white van with tinted windows pulled off North Roosevelt Boulevard and into the parking lot of the Key West Police Department. The lot was empty aside from a row of parked police vehicles, and the van drove around to the back side of the building and pulled up alongside a lone streetlight flickering lazily overhead. Just as the tires came to a stop on the blacktop, the side door slid open and four guys dressed in black and wearing ski masks hopped out.

They moved quickly for the back door, carrying flashlights, various styles of handguns and a large crowbar. The area was quiet and seemingly devoid of people as one of the guys lodged the tip of the crowbar under different sections of the metal door and soon forced it loose.

With the door open and hanging lifelessly against the side of the concrete wall, the four guys swarmed into the station like an onrushing flood. The inside of the station was dimly lit only by occasional overhead lights, so the guys switched on their flashlights without breaking stride. Their boots stomped against the linoleum floor as they moved across the back of the station, heading for a set of stairs.

When they reached the bottom level, the on-duty police officer stepped out from a door across the room. He was wearing only his police-issued pants, a white tee shirt, and a skintight bulletproof vest. Upon seeing the intruders and the weapons they each carried, he raised his standard-issue Glock 17 and fired without hesitation.

Through the darkness, noise, and chaos, it was difficult to tell if he'd hit any of them. But before he could take cover, the four intruders fired back, sending a barrage of bullets his way. One managed to hit him square in the chest, causing the air to blow out from his lungs and his body to fall backward.

Before the officer could retaliate, the four men pounced on him, relieved him of his weapon and used his own handcuffs to restrain him to a nearby metal door handle.

Leaving the officer dazed and sitting on the floor with the bullet lodged into his vest, they moved down a short hallway towards a small jail cell with a bunk bed on one side. Having heard the commotion, the captured member of Black Venom was on his feet with his hands wrapped around the metal bars and his eyes gazing towards the approaching men.

Without so much as a word, the four men stopped just a few feet away from the prisoner. With his right hand clutching a Colt Python revolver, one of the intruders raised it until the barrel was aimed straight into the prisoner's chest and shot an evil smile. The guy had failed in his mission. He needed to be punished, and Black Venom never left loose ends.

"What the hell are you doing, Cesar?" the prisoner said with fear in his eyes.

"By order of Felix," he fired back. "You are no longer needed in this organization. You have become a liability."

Just as Cesar's finger began to flex on the metal trigger, Luis's eyes grew wide and he said, "Wait! There is another treasure."

His voice was frantic, his breathing shallow and erratic. Cesar's finger moved away from the trigger momentarily.

"What do you mean, there is another treasure?" he said, his voice hard but slightly less menacing than before.

Luis's eyes darted back and forth among the four guys. A thin layer of sweat had formed on his brow.

"I heard them talking," he said. "Logan Dodge and the others. They have found a sunken pirate ship. They pulled up artifacts from underwater."

"Gold?" Cesar asked, listening intently to Luis's frantic plea for life.

Luis shrugged. "A legendary pirate ship is bound to have gold. Maybe even more than they found from the Spanish galleon *Intrepid*."

Cesar slowly lowered the revolver to his side and turned to look at the three men beside him. There was no need to speak; he could see their thoughts in their eyes. Maybe Luis was lying to save his own life—maybe there was no wreck. But all of them knew the repercussions of lying, and not a man in Black Venom would choose those repercussions over a bullet to the head.

Cesar glanced down at his wristwatch. They'd already taken too much time. The longer they were inside the police station, the greater the chances that they wouldn't make it out of there.

Looking up at the tall thug beside him, Cesar said, "Go and get the keys, Antonio."

The large man ran out of sight, searched the shackled officer's clothes, and found a set of keys in the front right pocket of his pants.

As the big guy returned into view, Cesar looked back at Luis. "If you are lying, you will wish I'd put an end to you here and now."

"I know," Luis replied. "I'm not lying. The ship is real."

Antonio handed Cesar the keys, and he inserted them one by one until the correct key clicked, turned, and allowed the cell door to slide open. Luis stepped out, and the five of them ran along the narrow hallway, up the stairs, and out into the night air. Within seconds, they climbed into the nearby idling van and slammed the door shut. The driver put the vehicle in gear and hit the gas, cruising back onto Roosevelt, heading east.

SIXTEEN

The next morning, Ange and I awoke with the sun. Having decided we wanted to get in an early workout with a few laps around Archer Key, we took off in the Baia and anchored down on the northern side of the small uninhabited island roughly nine miles west of Key West. The wind was calm, and there were only a few clouds dotting the sky overhead, making for a relatively flat surface all the way around the island.

I changed into a pair of just-over-the-knee swim trunks while Ange slid out of her denim shorts, revealing a dark blue bikini. After locking up the main door, I sat beside Ange on the swim platform, and we stared off at the mangrove-covered island and the bright sky to the east.

"How about a little wager?" Ange said, grinning as she dripped a few globs of shampoo onto her swim goggles, handed the bottle to me, then rinsed it out in the ocean.

I laughed, then set the bottle aside and used my saliva instead, swirling it around the lenses and rinsing it off in the ocean to prevent them from fogging up during our swim.

"What kind of wager?"

Ange thought it over for a moment. She'd been a competitive swimmer when she was young, and wherever she was working around the world, she almost always made time to get her laps in every week. She was fast, a natural in the water. But, being a former Navy SEAL and the son of a Navy diver, I was confident I could take her. We'd raced before, of course, and though I usually came out on top, she oftentimes surprised me.

"One lap," she said. "Winner gets bragging rights. And the loser has to pay for dinner at Latitudes."

I chuckled, not bothering to bring up the fact that I almost always paid when we went to Latitudes anyway. The truth was, she had me at bragging rights.

"You're on," I said, sliding my goggles into position.

We stood toe to toe on the swim platform, facing into a slow current that was flowing east to west. On Ange's mark, I leapt through the air beside her and splashed softly into the water in a swan dive. Slicing through the water deep enough to almost touch the bottom, I kicked and pulled hard, keeping myself under for a few strong strokes before softly breaking through the surface and beginning my freestyle stroke.

Ange, who'd dived in just a few arm lengths away from me, swam ferociously, staying right beside me before passing me as we made the first turn around the western side of the island. I tried my best to stay with her while also conserving my energy. One lap in an Olympic-sized swimming pool would be a sprint, but the route around Archer Key covers a distance of approximately two miles. Archer Key is roughly two-thirds of a mile long at high tide and half a mile wide, but the waters surrounding the island are shallow, forcing us to swim far enough away from the island to be in the deeper channels.

I kept myself to a breath every three strokes and, glancing up at Ange, realized that she'd increased her lead to a full body length. I picked up my pace slightly, but the last thing I wanted was to gas out on the final stretch. I'd swum with Ange many times and knew that she couldn't keep up her current pace the entire race.

I glanced at the occasional flounder and a large school of herring as we swam ferociously around the island. During most of our morning swims, I was able to observe the marine life more closely and enjoy the wonders of the underwater world, but not this morning. This morning, Ange had me chasing her heels, my heart pounding as I took in big gulps of air and made stroke after powerful stroke.

When we made our last turn and swam into the final quarter-mile straightaway on the northern side of the island, I forced myself into a higher gear. Kicking as hard as I could and pulling myself through the water, I was forced to take a breath every two strokes and quickly caught up to Ange. We swam neck and neck for a few hundred feet, and I glanced at her, in awe of how she'd managed to keep up such an exhausting pace for so long.

With the Baia in sight, I gave everything I had and managed to pull a half-body length ahead of her. My body exhausted, my muscles screaming in pain, and my heart pounding, I willed myself to keep swimming. When we were within a few hundred feet of the Baia, I spotted Ange's blurry tan-and-dark-blue figure approaching closer and closer on my right side.

I had nothing left but kept going anyway, pushing past the walls of exhaustion. I forced myself to complete a series of powerful strokes, but still, Ange managed to continue to cut my lead. Soon we were side by side, freestyling as fast as we could towards the finish line. With my lungs screaming and my body giving out, I noticed Ange as she splashed through the water and passed me by a single stroke at the final few feet before the Baia.

I passed the stern of my boat just a fraction of a second behind her. After pressing a button on my watch, I turned sharply to the left and rose up alongside her with my hands against the swim platform. We both breathed heavily for a few seconds, catching our breath and unable to speak. I'd always been competitive since I was young, but Ange was the same, and we had a way of raising each other to a whole other level.

"Holy crap," I said, panting as I reached up and ripped the goggles off my face. I glanced down at my watch with wide eyes. "That's a new record for Archer."

Ange looked tired as hell with her hair tied back, revealing her reddened face. But even exhausted, I noticed a grin materialize on her face as she removed her goggles as well.

"Are you okay?" I asked.

She laughed, shook her head and athletically pulled herself up out of the water.

"I think you should ask yourself that, Dodge," she said. "You look like you're about to have a heart attack."

I smiled and pulled myself up and sat on the transom as Ange grabbed two towels, handing me one of them.

"I'm never gonna hear the end of this, am I?" I asked, though I already knew the answer.

She chuckled and sat down beside me. "Maybe the day the Keys freeze over."

We both toweled off, then rattled up the anchor, started up the engines, and headed back towards Conch Harbor Marina. It was still pretty early, but the workout had given us both a hearty appetite, and my supplies aboard the Baia were getting low, so we decided we'd head over to the Greasy Pelican for breakfast.

"You've got a few missed calls," Ange said as she stepped out of the salon, wearing a faded Florida Marlins baseball cap and one of my thin flannel shirts.

I was just easing the Baia into slip twenty-four when she handed me my iPhone, and after tying her off, I glanced down at the screen. I had two missed calls, both from Sheriff Wilkes, along with a voicemail in which he informed me that he needed to speak with me as soon as possible.

I called him back as Ange and I walked down the dock towards the Pelican, and he picked up on the first ring.

"Logan," he said, his voice booming through the speaker.

"Yeah, what's going on, Charles?" I said, suspecting from his tone that something serious had happened.

He sighed. "I'd like to meet with you this morning. It's important. Where are you?"

"Ange and I are on our way to the Greasy Pelican."

He paused a moment, then said, "Okay. I'll meet you there in ten minutes."

As he was about to hang up, I said, "Wait, what happened?"

I could tell that Charles was walking, able to hear his footsteps and breathing through the microphone.

"It's that thug you guys brought in yesterday," he said. "A group of guys came into the station last night and broke him out."

SEVENTEEN

Not only does the Greasy Pelican have some of the best seafood in town, it's also one of our favorite breakfast spots. I ordered a warm pile of cinnamon French toast covered in sliced strawberries, sprinkled with a layer of powdered sugar, and doused in their specialty maple syrup. Ange ordered the American breakfast, with eggs over easy, bacon, hash browns and toast, though she kept taking bites of mine as I sipped from my mug of coffee.

Charles walked in through the front door just a few minutes after our food arrived. He was wearing his police uniform and moved with his head on a swivel, as if danger could be lurking around every corner of the restaurant.

"Good to see you, Charles," I said, then offered him a seat. He sat reluctantly, and I added in a more serious tone, "Any of your boys hurt last night?"

He nodded gravely, and when the waitress

approached, he told her he'd just have a coffee.

"So what happened?" Ange said.

Looking up at both of us, Charles said, "Around midnight, a van pulled into the station. Four guys popped out wearing ski masks. They broke into the station, shot the night watch in the chest, and grabbed the prisoner."

I sighed. "I'm sorry, Charles. Is he gonna be okay?"

Charles nodded. "He was wearing a vest, and it was a 9mm. Lucky, too, because based on the other bullet casings, one of the guys shooting had a .357. But he'll be fine. I'm having a few squads come down from Homestead to help out. We run a pretty small operation here in Key West, and the last thing I want is to be overpowered again. I've also contacted the Navy and Coast Guard, and they're on full alert."

"Good," I said, listening intently to his words.

"Did your security cameras catch anything useful?" Ange asked. "Any distinguishable markings on the thugs? Or the license plate of the vehicle?"

Charles shook his head. "They managed to disable the security system as they broke in. And we haven't seen any sign of them since. How about you guys out on the water? Any more interactions or sightings?"

"Nothing," I said.

"Okay," Charles said, rising to his feet. "Well, I've got to go. I just wanted to make sure you two were in the loop as to what's been happening. I'll call you if we obtain any new information."

"Likewise," I said.

As Charles turned to head for the door, Ange said, "Who was the officer that was shot?"

Charles glanced down at his phone, then looked

up at Ange. "It was Officer Ben Kincaid. But he's already been released from the hospital. Just a nasty bruise and whiplash, nothing serious."

As Charles left, I drew my attention back to my food, which had been neglected during our conversation. I went quiet for a moment. I wasn't close to Ben, but we'd hung out often over the past few months and I couldn't help but feel a mean swell of anger. As I finished my plate, I thought about Black Venom and how they had a knack for pissing me off.

After breakfast, we met up with Jack, Pete, and Frank at the *Calypso* and headed back out to the wreck site. We spent the entire day in the water, diving along the seabed, scanning with our metal detectors, and sifting through mountains of sand to find various artifacts. On our way to the spot, we stopped at Blackbeard Salvagers in Marathon, the same company I'd worked with during our exploration of the German U-boat and while searching for the Aztec treasure. Pete was good friends with the owner, who gave us a good discount on a pair of mailboxes and helped us attach them to the stern of the *Calypso*. If we hadn't looked like a full-fledged salvage operation before, we sure as hell looked like one now. The two large metal cylinders were a dead giveaway.

We spent an entire week searching, and though we'd found hundreds of artifacts from the wreck and hadn't had any trouble with Black Venom, we also hadn't found any gold or silver. Based on a few items we'd recovered, including a cannon that Frank said was English and dated it back to the seventeenth century, we were confident we'd found the *Crescent*. But the major question lingered in the air: if we'd in fact found the famous pirate's shipwreck, where was his treasure?

As we were sitting up on the bridge eating lunch one afternoon, Frank glanced up from his laptop, his face covered with excitement.

"I think I may have something here," he said.

Frank had spent much of his time over the past week researching anything he could find about John Taylor and the *Crescent*.

Looking up from the screen and seeing all of our expectant faces, he added, "While I was in London, I saved many of the archived files I thought might be useful on a thumb drive. I didn't have time to look all of them over, so I figured I could read them later." He took a sip of coconut water and continued, "Well, I've been reading more about the crew, and I've found something interesting."

Frank rotated the laptop, allowing all of us to see the screen, and pointed to a few lines of highlighted text. "This is Edmond Graham. He was part of the *Crescent*'s crew when it set sail on its voyage that eventually ended in mutiny. He was never seen or heard from again after the incident and was believed to be killed."

"But you think he wasn't?" Pete said, raising his eyebrows.

"Right," Frank said. "I think Taylor used him. You see, this Graham character was a highly educated gentleman who was being sent from England to Jamaica. His trade was civil engineering, and he was sent to help deal with issues Port Royal was having with flooding."

I listened carefully, trying to follow his trail of logic and see where he was going with it.

"So then I read even more," Frank said. "It turns

out, Graham was the leader of an entire team of engineers, and each and every one of those men were never seen again after the mutiny incident."

The table went quiet. The only sound to be heard was the soft flapping of the waves against the hull and a few passing seagulls.

"What are you saying, Frank?" I asked. "What does this have to do with the wreck?"

Frank smiled. "Not the wreck, but the treasure."

"I thought the treasure was supposed to be on the ship," Jack said.

"That's what we thought," Frank said. "But why do you think we haven't found a single doubloon? Surely, if the treasure had been on the *Crescent* when she sank, we would have found something by now. I mean, we've found everything else." Frank shook his head. "No. Captain John Shadow was smarter than that. I'm confident that he hid the treasure."

Ange smiled. "You mean he buried it?"

"That's right," Frank said. "Like a true Golden Age pirate."

I nodded. "And these engineers, you think Shadow used them to help bury the treasure?"

"Eventually, after years of pillaging, yes," Frank said. "And I think they did a hell of a good job with it, and that's why the treasure has yet to be found."

The table went quiet for a moment as we each went over the theory in our mind.

"So, how do we find the treasure, then?" Jack asked. "I'm guessing this Graham guy didn't leave an *X marks the spot* kind of thing."

Frank leaned back against the cushioned seat and looked out over the water surrounding us.

"Well," Frank said, "Shadow was notorious for sailing where most seafaring men feared to go, especially the shallow waters of the Florida Keys. He captained a schooner with a shallow draft and had the tenacity to pull off what few pirates could." He paused a moment as he took another sip, cleared his throat, and added, "If I were to guess, I'd say it's close by. He could have even buried it on one of the main islands of the Keys, and it's been sitting here all these years, waiting to be discovered."

EIGHTEEN

We spent the rest of the evening letting Frank's words and theories as to the whereabouts of the treasure sink in while taking intermittent dives and using the mailbox to wash away more of the ocean floor. The idea that Shadow's treasure wouldn't be with his ship had never crossed my mind, and now that I was thinking about it, I was surprised that it hadn't. In the years he was active, Shadow had raided many ships and accumulated a massive treasure. The idea of him being willing and able to keep it all on board at all times was ludicrous.

We'd spent almost two weeks searching the area in Florida Bay. And while we'd all felt like we were just a few more searches away from the treasure, it now appeared as though we'd been mistaken all along.

The new questions on the table were puzzling all of us: where would Shadow hide his treasure? And how had he utilized the engineers aboard the *Crescent*?

We mulled over those questions in our minds while cruising back to Conch Harbor Marina, long after the sun had been extinguished by the horizon.

The morning after Frank had enlightened us with his extensive research, Ange and I had breakfast on the Baia, then decided to head into town. We wanted to walk around, maybe do a little shopping, and get our mind off Shadow and his treasure. I've found that sometimes the best way to think through a problem is to forget about it entirely. For me, this usually involves doing a completely unrelated activity like playing chess or going to a gun range, but Ange wanted to check out a few of the local stores and restock the Baia.

As we walked down the dock towards the waterfront, I spotted Gus Henderson standing outside the marina office alongside Ben Kincaid. Gus is the owner of the marina, which had been passed down to him from his father and his father's father before that. He was average height, with tanned skin and a few extra pounds along the waistline, and was wearing his usual ballcap and sunglasses. He was watching Ben as he worked on one of the two Sea-Doo jet skis floating beside the dock.

When we reached the shore and walked in front of them, Gus called me over.

"Good to see you guys. Gus, it's weird seeing you out of your hole," I said, referring to his office, where he usually sat sprawled out over a massive blue beanbag chair in front of his television.

"Just doing my rounds," he said with a smile.

"It's good to see you, Ben," Ange said.

"Yeah," I added. "I tried messaging you. Charles

said you had to go up to Miami."

Ben nodded. "They wanted my statement from the jailbreak." He shook his head. "I still can't believe I allowed those scumbags to get past me."

"No one blames you," I said. "They had you outnumbered and caught everyone off guard. I'm just glad to see you going right back to your usual activities."

"Well, those assholes are gonna have to try harder than that if they're gonna keep me down," he said confidently. Then, glancing at Ange, he added, "You guys had any more trouble out on the water?"

"No," Ange said. "We haven't even seen anything suspicious for over a week."

Ben grinned, then motioned to me. "I think you might have scared them off."

"I hope so," I said. "You guys taking these out?" I motioned to the two jet skis.

Ben laughed. "Gus on a jet ski? I don't think anyone will ever see that again."

Ange and I both looked at Gus, who showed signs of slight embarrassment.

"Come on, that was years ago," he said, defending himself. "And that dock came out of nowhere. But the kid's right. I've sworn off jet skis."

Ben turned to Ange and me. "Well, looks like I got a vacant ride if you're both looking for a little adrenaline boost."

I smiled as I looked over his 2008 Sea-Doo RXP jet skis. They were heavily upgraded and I'd gone out on the water with him a few times, sometimes reaching speeds in excess of fifty knots.

Ange nudged my shoulder. "You go ahead," she said.

I tilted my head to look at her. "Are you sure?

138

You love jet skis."

"Yeah, but I'll be fine," she said. "It actually works out, because I was wanting to check out this nearby spa anyway. You guys enjoy your bro date."

I raised my eyebrows. "Since when do you go to spas?"

"You know what, Dodge?" she said with a playful grin. "I think a good old sparring session is long overdue. Maybe that'll put you and your comments back in their place."

I laughed. "Enjoy the spa, beautiful. I'm gonna whoop this guy in a race."

Ange blew me a kiss, then waved as she flip-flopped down the dock, heading towards downtown.

"Hey, you cheated last time," Ben said.

I patted Ben on the back, then knelt down beside him.

"Need any help with this?" I asked, watching as he leaned back into the bowels of one of the jet skis' 215-hp engines.

Ben shook his head, then leaned out of the engine and tightened the seat back on.

"All finished," he said. He rose to his feet, looked out over the water and added, "Let's get out there. The strong ocean breeze is calling my name."

I climbed aboard the other jet ski, then Gus stepped over to untie the lines.

"Don't forget these," Gus said, handing us each a black lifejacket. "Accidents happen."

Ben chuckled as I thanked him. I inserted the key and fired up the engine, my adrenaline rushing as I gripped the handle and throttle. After waving to Gus, we cruised slowly out of the marina, avoiding a few sailboats as they glided by and relishing the calm before the storm.

"Alright," Ben said as we were just about to reach the end of the no-wake zone. "Around Fleming and east. The first one to pass through the Inner Narrows of the Snipes wins."

I nodded. The Inner Narrows was a channel dredged through the seafloor roughly fifteen miles from the marina. When he said go, I leaned forward, held on, and forced my right wrist all the way back, firing up the engine in a powerful roar that accelerated me up over fifty knots in a matter of seconds.

Ben and I stayed side by side as we weaved in and out of the scattered islands of the Lower Keys, passing by them in a blur. There was a slight breeze coming in from the east that created a few small whitecaps, causing our jet skis to occasionally bounce up out of the water.

As we raced past Florida Keys Community College and Raccoon Key, a large yacht cruised out from the waterway between Boca Chica and Stock Island. With the wind blowing ferociously into our faces, we glanced at each other and then smiled, both having the same idea.

Instead of passing around the bow of the yacht, we both shifted our course and hit its large wake full speed. Side by side, we soared high into the air. With my left hand firmly clutching the throttle, I raised my right high over my head and let out a loud yell before splashing back down into the tropical water.

In the final homestretch of the race, Ben and I stayed side by side. I could see the Inner Narrows just beyond the small Duck Key. Seeing Ben begin to veer left, I knew that this was my chance to pull ahead. Duck Key has a narrow channel cutting right through its heart. The only problem is that the water is

140

shallow, and Ben and I both knew that the tide was going out. But I wasn't about to lose a second race in two days.

As we approached closer, I moved alongside Ben, making it look like I too was cruising around the obstacle. But at the last second, I changed course, picked up speed, and flew straight for the middle of the island.

"Are you crazy?" Ben shouted over the roar of both our engines.

For a split second, I reminded myself that this wasn't my jet ski, but I shook it off, confident that I could make it through without damaging it. I forced the engine to give everything it had, pushing it to its limits and topping out at just under sixty knots.

Skirting across the surface, I managed to time the bounces out of the water and fly right over the shallow areas. My heart raced as I glanced down at the water ahead of me, able to see clearly the distinct underwater formations just inches beneath the surface. With one final bounce, I cleared the channel and reached the relatively deeper water beyond.

Ben finally came into view behind me, having circumvented the island. He was cruising as fast as he could, but he was too late. I had far too great of a lead, and I cruised coolly through the Inner Narrows for a relaxed and happy victory.

Ben motored up beside me, shaking his head.

"Alright, you won," he said, clapping sarcastically. "But if you damaged that hull, it's on you."

I laughed. "Not a scratch."

We continued and cruised slowly through the mangrove-infested Five Mile Creek and then headed south under US-1 and into Lower Sugarloaf Sound.

As we were about to enter Sugarloaf Creek and pass by Sammy's Landing into the Atlantic, we spotted a worn-down wharf with a large metal warehouse that looked like it had been abandoned for years. Ben shifted his course slightly, heading towards a few low-floating pilings along the wharf.

"Used to be Adam's oyster company," Ben said. "My dad worked here years ago, before it closed down."

He continued and hit the throttles slightly, cruising his jet ski right up against a portion of the wharf that was broken and angled down into the water. I followed, pulling right up alongside him.

"Why did it close?" I asked, scanning the old establishment, which was covered in vines, rot, and rust.

"Damn oysters just aren't as plentiful as they used to be," he said. "Too much competition and pollution in the water. I guess it was only a matter of time."

Suddenly, Ben killed his jet ski's engine, swung his leg over, and stepped onto the old wood.

"I come here sometimes for target practice," he said, tying his jet ski to a support beam. "You got your Sig, right?"

I grinned and pulled up the right side of my shirt, revealing my piece holstered under my waistband. "Always," I said as I killed the engine and stepped alongside him. "You shoot here?" I shook my head, then looked around. "Nobody gives you any trouble?"

He shrugged. "Well, I usually use a silencer," he said. "But, no. No one's complained yet."

After tying off my jet ski beside his, I followed Ben along the old wharf, the sensible portion of my brain confident that each step would result in the loud cracking of wood followed by me splashing into the water below. But Ben wasn't kidding when he said that he knew the place well. He seemed to know exactly where you could and couldn't step, and I followed him until we reached the shade of the rusted metal structure.

It was low tide, and as we moved away from the open water and its cool breeze, we could smell it. A combination of mud, dead marine life, and rotted wood filled our nostrils as we moved into a wide-open space flanked by shattered windows and littered with assorted machinery left in place by a company that had fallen to shambles.

"Over here," Ben said, motioning to the other side of the room.

He walked along the outer wall, then reached down and grabbed a plastic crate filled with glass bottles. He moved to a nearby windowsill, and one by one, he steadied the bottles on the narrow flat surface.

"You somehow managed to win the race by the skin of your teeth," he said with a grin. "So give me the chance to redeem myself."

I laughed for a few seconds, then realized that he was serious.

"You're not beating me in a shooting match," I stated confidently. Then, before he could reply, I added, "Okay. How about this: you shoot from thirty feet with both hands, and I'll shoot from sixty feet with only my left hand."

"You're really that confident, huh?" he said, jokingly.

"Look, there's not a lot of things that I consider absolutes. But my ability to shoot a gun is one of them."

"Okay, okay," he said, raising his hands in the

air. "Have it your way."

I nodded. "Alright. You're up, Deputy."

He took a few steps forward, facing off at the row of empty glass Coca-Cola, Sprite, and Dr Pepper bottles. Bending his knees, he got into an athletic stance and hovered his right hand over the hand grip of his holstered Glock 17.

"Shooter stand by," I said, then looked down at my watch. "Open fire!"

Just as the words came out of my mouth, he gripped his Glock, slid it out smoothly, and raised it chest height with both hands. He clicked the safety, then fired off round after round, shattering the bottles as he went. He hit four in a row, then wasted a shot on the fifth before finishing them off.

"Six seconds," I said as the loud gunshots dissipated over the quiet air.

The smell of gunpowder took over as he switched on the safety and holstered his weapon. He moved towards the window and placed six more glass bottles on the sill, lined up right where the previous ones had been. As Ben moved to the side, I took position roughly twice as far away as he'd stood, then unholstered my Sig and slid it into my waistband on the left side.

Shooting one-handed is more difficult than with two. Using two hands allows the shooter to stabilize the weapon more easily during a recoil and prepare for successive shots. I'm also right-handed, so I'm less accurate with my left.

Ben told me to stand by, and I took my stance, bending my knees slightly and facing the window with good posture. I narrowed my gaze on the first bottle on the left, a Pepsi bottle with most of its blue label faded away.

144

When Ben announced that he'd started the time, I snatched my Sig, raised it, and fired off the first round in the blink of an eye. The Pepsi bottle shattered, and as I moved on to the next, I felt an unusual tingling pain crawl up the top of my right leg. In the heat of the moment, I spent a few seconds blowing away the remaining bottles. When I came to the final one, I felt a sharp pinch coming from my right leg, and my body spasmed and hunched over.

What the fuck is happening? I thought as my vision began to blur, and I looked down at my leg for answers. The pain had traveled fast, a strange numbing pain that took over my motor functions. With watery eyes, I focused on my right thigh and saw it—a tranquilizer dart sticking through my cargo shorts and deep into my skin, its contents emptied.

I felt a surge of adrenaline take over my weakening body. I reached for the dart with my right hand, ripped it loose and threw it onto the old wood floor. I brought my Sig up and clasped it with both hands as I scanned the room as best as I could through blurry, watery eyes.

"Ben!" I shouted, wondering if he'd been hit as well as I struggled to turn around.

My mind raced as I looked for any movement in the old building, looked for any sign of Ben. But I couldn't see anything. I could barely make out the walls and the floor beneath my feet as I stumbled, my body giving up and forcing me with every passing second to drift closer and closer to unconsciousness.

Suddenly, I felt a surge of pain explode across my face, followed by a powerful blow that knocked my Sig out of my hands. I lurched sideways, almost falling to the floor. Keeping myself balanced as best as I could, I swung a sidekick through the air toward my unknown assailant that I couldn't even see. Feeling only air, I prepared to make another attempt but was struck again. This time the blow came from behind, knocking the air from my lungs as I collapsed forward, my left shoulder slamming into the floor.

Shifting my body around, I saw three dark, blurry figures standing over me. I tried to stand, but the tranquilizer's toxins had traveled through my body and taken over. I knew that it would only be a few more moments before I was gone. I was mad as hell and struggling to stay in control, but it was over.

As my head fell back and my consciousness faded, one of the dark figures stepped closer and crouched down beside me. He tilted his head just a few feet over mine, and his blurry image suddenly came into focus. It was Ben. I could see him clearly, his short hair and his blue eyes staring back into mine, shooting me a stern gaze.

What the hell has he done?

Anger swelled, and I felt a sudden surge of strength take over. I squeezed my right hand into a fist and hurled it through the air as fast as I could. My knuckles made contact with the fragile bones of Ben's nose, causing them to crack audibly and his head to whip back. Blood flowed out, and he wailed as his hands sandwiched the sides of his nose. I tried to sit up and strike another blow, but my body was weak, and I felt a hand grab me from behind and pin me to the floor.

Keeping my blurry gaze drawn on Ben, I watched as he spat a gob of blood onto the floor, then turned and kicked me in the side a few times. I wanted to retaliate, to fight back and beat the shit out of him, but my body was giving out. I could feel the poison moving through my veins, could feel it taking over.

I couldn't think about what was happening, couldn't even try and make sense of it. As my eyes began to close, Ben leaned over and looked down at me. His lips suddenly contorted into a cocky smile. He said something, but I couldn't hear. I saw only his lips move and saw him laugh as he looked down at me, and then everything went black.

NINETEEN

Key West
Later That Afternoon

Angelina walked out of Keys Knees Bakery, holding a plastic bag with a white Styrofoam box inside in one hand and a few shopping bags in the other. Sliding a pair of aviator sunglasses over her eyes, she glanced down at her newly painted white toenails and smiled. Any person passing by would assume she was just another rich tourist, a Southern belle daughter or wife of a wealthy businessman. None would ever suspect that she was actually one of the world's deadliest mercenaries.

Transferring the bag of food into her other hand momentarily, she slid her phone out and glanced at the main screen. It was almost six, and she hadn't received anything from Logan yet.

Maybe he knew I would take longer than

expected, she thought as she walked with light steps along the waterfront back towards Conch Harbor Marina.

Logan knew her better than anyone else. He even knew a little bit about her very secretive past. No one else alive knew that Angelina had actually been born into a wealthy family in Sweden, and that she'd been raised almost into her teens on high-class meals, piano lessons, manicures, and habitual trips to the opera. It wasn't until after her parents had died that she'd turned rogue, run away from her old life and into a world of grunge and violence. But occasionally, her old habits ached for revival, and though she hadn't been to a spa in over two years, she couldn't help but smile and think about how much she'd enjoyed it.

When her sandals hit the mahogany planks of the dock, she picked up her pace a little and tried to spot Logan lounging on the Baia at slip twenty-four. When she was close enough, she stepped onto the swim platform and moved through the cockpit. After disabling the security system with a quick entry on the digital keypad, she opened the door and headed down into the salon.

The inside of the Baia looked exactly as it had when she'd left with Logan earlier. She removed the Styrofoam box from the plastic bag, stowed the food she'd brought for Logan in the small fridge, and moved into the main cabin. Seeing that he wasn't there, she grabbed her phone, called his number and placed the phone against the side of her face. After just one ring, she heard his voicemail message, then hung up.

"His phone's dead?" she said, looking at the screen of her phone in confusion.

She sent a few texts, but didn't get anything back.

That's strange, she thought. She'd known him for years, and she rarely had difficulty getting ahold of him. In the six months they'd spent living together in the Keys, she'd never once seen him shut off his phone.

She wondered if perhaps it had fallen in the water or if he'd forgotten to charge it, unlikely possibilities but still possible. After stowing the clothes she'd bought in town in the main cabin, she locked up the Baia, turned the security system back on and headed down the dock towards the marina office.

She spotted Gus through the window, lounging on a couch with a newspaper in front of him and watching TV. She saw no sign of Logan, Ben, or the jet skis anywhere in the marina or visible open water in the distance. Glancing back at the parking lot, she saw that Ben's Ford F-150 was still parked in one of the visitor spots, and Logan's Tacoma was still parked in the first row against one of the railroad ties.

She turned back towards the office and pushed open the wooden door, causing a small bell to ring overhead.

"Hey, Angelina," Gus said, setting the newspaper aside and sitting up straighter. "Hey, have you seen the guys?"

"I was just about to ask you the same thing. Have you heard anything from them?"

"Nothing," Gus said. "Have you tried calling them?"

"Just Logan, but his phone's off. I don't have Ben's number."

Gus grabbed his phone from a nearby table, searched his contacts, then pressed call and held the phone up to his ear. After a few seconds, his face transitioned to a frown and he lowered his phone.

"Ben's phone is off too."

"That's weird," Ange said, beginning to get noticeably concerned now. "He's not on duty, but he's supposed to be reachable at all times, right?"

"That's right," Gus said, nodding. "I better give the sheriff a call."

Ten minutes later, a police interceptor pulled into the marina parking lot, and Sheriff Wilkes stepped out. Ange met him along the waterfront, and he informed her that he was unable to get ahold of either Logan or Ben.

"Haven't seen Kincaid since yesterday morning," Charles said. "He used up a week of vacation time. Said he was heading up north someplace."

"Well, he was here earlier," Ange said. "They took off on his jet skis."

"What time was this?"

"Noon," Ange said. "Over six hours ago now."

Charles's eyes grew wide, and he thought it over for a moment. He grabbed his phone. "I'm gonna call Jack. See if he knows anything."

Ange stopped him and pointed over the rows of anchored boats to where the *Calypso* was just cruising into the marina. Charles ended the call, and the two of them headed down the dock and met with Jack, who was just returning from a dive charter. Once his patrons had cleared out, they told him what was going on.

"Haven't heard from him all day," Jack said. "That's not like him."

"No," Ange replied. "It's not."

"Have any of you run into anyone or anything suspicious since that guy from Black Venom escaped?" Charles said.

Ange and Jack both shook their heads.

"We hadn't seen them at all," Ange said.

"Yeah. We kinda figured they'd left the Keys," Jack added.

Charles sighed. "Well, until we figure out what happened, we need to assume the worst."

"Let's head out and see if we can find them out on the water," Ange said. "I have at least a general idea of where they were heading."

Within minutes, Ange, Jack, and Charles were aboard the Baia and cruising out of Conch Harbor Marina. Once in open water, Ange gunned the throttles, sending them east along the Lower Keys. All three kept their eyes peeled on the horizon, looking for any sign of Logan or Ben.

TWENTY

Gulf of Mexico
0200

I woke up in a seated position in a dimly lit room. I tried to move my arms but heard rattling and found that they were handcuffed to a metal pipe behind my back. My mouth was dry, my head pounded, and my vision was still blurry as I scanned around the room. I couldn't make out much in the darkness. A long hangar of lifejackets to my right, three mountain bikes, a few inflatable workout balls, and a row of fishing rods secured overhead.

As my senses returned, I felt the ground rock slowly from side to side and heard the distant hum of an engine. *I'm on a yacht*, I thought as I continued to listen and look around.

"How in the hell did this happen?" I whispered to myself as my mind played back as much as I could

153

remember from the moments before I'd blacked out.

A sudden and powerful rage overtook me as I remembered the image of Ben's face hovering over mine, his lips contorted into a cocky smile as I lost consciousness. What had he done? Who had he handed me over to, and where in the hell were they taking me?

I asked the questions in my mind, but I already knew a few of the answers. Even before a big, muscular dark-skinned guy came inside and told me to stand my ass up, I knew exactly who I was dealing with. But the tattoo of two snakes around his left wrist solidified it.

Two more guys entered, then held me down as they removed one of the handcuffs, then clicked it back on, freeing me from the pipe. One of the guys had long jet-black hair that he kept braided. He was overweight and looked at me like I was scum he'd just found stuck under his boot.

The big guy who'd first entered just looked tired. He had a completely shaved head and a tattoo around his left eye. I didn't get a good look at the third guy, but he looked big as well. The first guy's muscles bulged out of his tee shirt as he led the way, holding a pistol in one hand as he told me to move it.

They led me down a well-lit hallway, and as we passed the first door, I heard the faint sound of two women talking on the other side. The fat guy pushed me hard.

"Keep moving!" he barked, and we continued down to the end of the hallway, up a set of stairs, and into a dark room.

They grabbed a second pair of handcuffs, cuffed me to the metal support of a table and sat me down onto a leather office chair. The three men stood beside me, and we waited a few minutes before another group entered and shut the door behind them. They said a few muffled words to each other that I couldn't understand, then turned on a massive flat-screen on the other side of the room.

The sudden burst of brightness caught me off guard, and I had to look down and squint for a few seconds before being able to look at it. Blank at first, the screen soon showed the image of an old man sitting on a couch and staring back at me. He had patches of thinning white hair, olive skin, and dark eyes. He was wearing a black business suit and was sitting on a fancy white leather couch. In the lower right corner of the screen, I could see myself, plopped down in the leather chair, wearing my gray Born to Beach tee shirt and looking like hell.

The man on the screen looked me over for a few seconds, then smiled and leaned back into the couch.

"You see?" a man's voice said in the darkness beside me. It was a low and raspy voice with a strong Spanish accent. "We have captured Logan Dodge, as I told you we would, Jefe."

The old man on the screen gave a slight nod of approval, then said, "I must say, Felix, I certainly had my doubts."

The old man's voice was smooth and articulate, but beyond his posh exterior, I sensed a different man within. He was hardened and evil but did his best to hide his true self beneath a façade of artificial class.

"I will be flying to Tampico tomorrow," the old man added. "You will bring this man to me, and we will deal with him properly."

The evil smile returned as the man's words trailed off. He looked right into my eyes, but I didn't blink or look worried in the slightest. No, I wouldn't give him that satisfaction. Besides, I'd dealt with evil men many times before and wasn't easily intimidated.

"We will be there as soon as we can," Felix replied. "This piece of crap is having engine trouble, so our max speed right now is fifteen knots. We will arrive Thursday evening at the earliest."

The old man was visibly displeased.

"Well, then, fix the issue and be here by Thursday morning," he replied. "I'm eager to avenge Marco's death, and to make an example of this imbecile. The world will see what happens when someone crosses us."

"Yes, Jefe," Felix said. "Is there anything else?"

The old man grabbed a half-filled glass from the table in front of him and took a drink.

"Yes," the old man said. "Remember to watch out for his pissant friends. I have no doubt they will try and save him."

The man standing beside me laughed arrogantly.

"By the time they realize what has happened," he said, "we will be a thousand miles away."

The old man showed no emotion. Instead, he said something I couldn't hear to a few men out of view.

"That's very comforting, Felix," he said sarcastically. "But it's not enough." He paused for a moment, took another swig, then added, "I've sent some of my own men to take care of her. I've heard about her, and the last thing I want is her getting in the way. Also, if what I hear is true, Logan here has strong feelings for her."

Anger swelled deep within me, and it was becoming harder and harder for me to keep from showing it.

The old man smiled. "It will be good revenge for Marco's death when we kill her." He leaned in close, staring towards Felix. "I want Logan delivered to me Thursday. Understood?"

"Yes, Jefe," Felix replied.

A second later, the screen turned dark again and the muscular guy walked into view, grabbed a remote, and turned off the flat-screen. The dark room suddenly turned bright as someone switched on one of the overhead lights.

Felix ordered the others to take me into his office, which was just down the hall. Once I was there, the three guys cuffed me to a chair and left the room. Felix, who'd been only a dark figure while talking to the old guy on the monitor, moved into view and sat on a large chair across a wooden desk from me.

The first thing I noticed was a grotesque scar that stretched from his left cheek down to his neck. He had dark skin, a lean build, and piercing green eyes. He looked maybe a few years older than my thirty-two and was wearing a fancy black button-up shirt.

"Now that that bullshit's over," the man said, leaning back in his chair, "I need to talk to you, Logan Dodge."

I looked back at him, confused, as he paused for a few seconds. After clearing his throat, he reached for something behind the desk.

He smiled as he set my dagger on the desk between us. "I need to talk to you about this pirate ship you found, and this treasure."

We sat in silence for a moment. For a second, I wondered how he'd managed to learn about the treasure, then I thought about the member of Black Venom whom they'd broken out of jail and the fact that they'd had guys following us for a few days.

He leaned forward and clasped his hands together

on the desk in front of him.

"I have a proposition for you," he said. "That guy on the monitor," he added, pointing in the direction of the dark room we'd just came from, "he's the big boss. The Jefe of Black Venom. And... he wants your head on a plate." He grabbed a bottle off the desk, filled a glass, and took a few long pulls before continuing. "Well, actually he wants to torture you and then put your head on a plate. But either way, it doesn't end well for you, understand?"

I gave a slight nod and stared back into his eyes, unblinking.

"So," he said, "I could hand you over to him, and the truth is I wouldn't lose a second of sleep over it. But, I would like to offer you a means of salvation from this predicament." He poured another glass, held it in his hands for a few seconds, then stood up and began to pace around me. "You tell me where I can find this treasure and help me recover it, and in exchange, I will let you go."

He downed the glass, and again the room returned to silence for a few seconds. I had a hard time believing what I was hearing. Not only was this guy not looking to kill me, but he was offering an exchange for my release? I knew I couldn't trust him, that they were all a bunch of murdering, lying criminals. But I also knew that if I didn't play along, I'd have a much slimmer chance of escaping before being killed.

"How can I trust you to keep your word?" I said. "Even if I keep my end of the bargain, what's to stop you from still handing me over?"

The man laughed and looked off to the side.

"Nothing," he said. "But right now it's the only chance you've got, Mr. Dodge. You either take me to this treasure, or you die."

I thought it over again. Whether or not I could find the treasure, or whether it even existed at all, I needed time. The longer I was gone, the better chance I'd be giving someone to find me. Then I thought about Ange and the men the old guy had said he was sending after her.

"Okay," I said. "But on two conditions."

The man grinned and chuckled again.

"Everything I've heard about you is true," he said. "You've got balls of steel to be making demands in your current state."

"Angelina Fox," I said. "Call off the guys sent to kill her."

"I can't do that. They were sent by Jefe, and only he can call them off."

Shit, I thought as I glanced down at the floor.

"What is the second condition?"

My anger at not being able to help Ange shifted to anger of a different variety. I pictured *him* standing over me and smiling as the world went dark. My second condition related to *him*, a man I trusted, a man who would soon regret betraying me.

159

TWENTY-ONE

Angelina couldn't sleep. Her mind was far too busy as she thought about Logan, wondering what had happened and where he could be. She'd cruised all around the Lower Keys with Jack and Charles, but they hadn't found any sign of him or Ben. They'd both simply vanished without a word. She was sure that something serious had happened, and she was also sure that with every second that passed by, her chances of finding him were getting smaller and smaller.

In the early morning, she made a phone call that she knew she probably should have made the night before. Scott Cooper was one of Logan's best friends, and as a senator representing the state of Florida, he had connections that could prove useful in discovering his whereabouts.

"What do you mean, Logan's missing?" he said in a serious tone. "When was the last time you saw him?"

"Yesterday, early afternoon," she replied. "He went jet skiing with a friend and never came back."

The line went quiet for a moment. Angelina could hear him shuffling around, could hear a few keystrokes on a computer.

"Did he say where they were going?"

Angelina sighed. "Not exactly. I mean, I know they were racing on the Gulf side of the Lower Keys at first."

After another short pause, Scott said, "I got it," then paused a moment and added, "Shit."

"What's wrong?"

"Is Logan not wearing his watch?"

Angelina was surprised by the question and wondered what his watch had to do with anything.

"He is," Angelina replied with noticeable confusion.

"Well, then, he must have gotten a new one recently," Scott said. "I put a tracking device in his watch a year ago, and right now it's saying it's right at his slip at the Conch Harbor Marina. Maybe there's a problem with the tracker."

Angelina paused for a moment as she glanced down at the black-and-silver Suunto Core digital dive watch strapped around her left wrist. It had used to be Logan's, but he'd given it to her a few weeks earlier, preferring to wear the one he'd given his dad on his last birthday before he died.

"Ange? You there?"

"There's nothing wrong with the tracker," Angelina finally said. She then explained how Logan had given her the watch, so it was on her wrist and not his.

Scott sighed and said, "Well, shit. That's going to

161

make things a little more difficult."

After talking for half an hour, Scott assured her he'd do everything he could to help, and then they hung up. Ange sat out on the sunbed as the sun came up. She tried to think through the situation clearly but had a hard time keeping still. She couldn't shake the feeling that she had to move, that there was somewhere she needed to be to help Logan.

"He's a big boy," she said. "And he's a damn good fighter."

She reminded herself that Logan wasn't an ordinary guy and that it would take a well-orchestrated and executed attack to bring him down. By 0900, she was sick of sitting still and decided to take matters into her own hands.

She moved to the outdoor dinette and pulled up her laptop. Bringing up Google Maps, she searched the areas of the Lower Keys that Logan and Ben often mentioned after their trips. She started calling every marina and beachside restaurant in Big Coppitt Key, Waltz Key Basin, and the Saddlebunch Keys, asking them if they'd seen anything suspicious or any sign of Logan, Ben, or the jet skis.

She spent half the day on the phone and the other half driving around the Keys, talking to anyone and everyone she could find and looking for any sign of them. It was a long day and a long night, and she felt discouraged when she finally hit the sack. But the following morning, while continuing to make seemingly hopeless phone calls, she spoke to a waitress named Josephine at Sammy Creek Landing.

"Our dishwasher said he thought he heard gunshots yesterday afternoon," Josephine said. "He said it was hard to tell, though."

For the first time, Angelina felt like she might

actually have something.

"Okay, will he be working today?" Angelina asked.

"Gets here at eleven," she replied. "That is, if he's on time."

After ending the call, Angelina put the location into her phone, then got ready, locked up the Baia, and headed down the dock. She started up Logan's Tacoma, drove down Caroline Street, and thirty-four minutes later, she pulled off Old State Road onto a sandy driveway.

The restaurant at Sammy Creek Landing was little more than a shack, and after laying eyes on the small tiki-style hut with worn paint and a few scattered plastic tables and chairs, Angelina was surprised that they even had a phone.

There were a few people sitting along the water, eating and enjoying the quiet. The place was unique and isolated, she had to give it that. And if the food wasn't half-bad, she'd probably be back.

"Go ahead and have a seat anywhere," a young woman with short red hair said. "I'll bring you over a menu in a sec."

Ange glanced at the girl's name tag.

"Hey, Josephine," Angelina said. "We talked on the phone. Any chance I could have a word with your cook?"

"Right," Josephine said, nodding and motioning towards the restaurant. "He's just inside. I'll go and get him."

A few seconds later, she returned alongside a skinny Jamaican man wearing a black apron. He moved towards Angelina with light steps, then wiped his hands with a rag and extended his right.

"I'm Kymani," he said. "Are yuh wi duh police?"

163

Ange shook his hand, then said, "No. My name is Angelina, and I'm looking for a friend of mine that disappeared yesterday afternoon."

Kymani thought it over for a moment, then pointed towards the road.

"I wuh rite dere," he said, walking alongside Ange. "Wi kip di trash cans ova by di road an while mi did taking it out mi tink mi hear gunshots."

"Where did the sounds come from?" Angelina asked.

They stopped alongside the quiet paved road, and Kymani pointed to the other side.

"Tru dat way," he said. "Deep inna di mangroves."

Ange stared off into the thick vegetation, then said, "Is there anything over there?"

He shrugged. "Mi don't tink suh. But dere an old dirt road jus dat way."

He pointed up the road, then Angelina nodded and glanced over at the parked Tacoma.

"Thank you," Angelina said.

"No problem. Mi hope yuh find yuh bredren."

Ange stepped inside the truck, started it up and pulled back onto the main road. After less than a minute of driving east, she spotted an overgrown dirt road that looked like it hadn't been used in years. Ange didn't hesitate. She turned the wheel sharply and bounced down the sorry excuse of a road, heading through the thick mangrove forest. The road seemed to get worse the farther she went, with potholes everywhere, low spots flooded with water, and fallen branches that cracked under the Tacoma's off-road tires.

Soon the road opened up, and Ange spotted a building in the distance, along with a large dock along the waterfront. She put the truck in park along the dock, then killed the engine and stepped out. She stopped for a moment and listened, hearing only silence as she looked around, surrounded on all sides by either bay or mangroves. She grabbed her Glock from its holster on her waistband, then stepped onto the old, creaking dock.

The rotted planks creaked beneath her shoes as she moved towards the old rust-colored building with a partially caved-in roof. The place reminded her of an old mining ghost town she'd visited in Arizona while on a cross-country road trip. A place once full of people and life, and now left for nature to reclaim.

Once inside, she strode through the middle of a large open room and spotted broken bottles on top of a windowsill. As she moved towards them, she stepped on something small and hard, and glancing down, she realized that there were brass bullet casings scattered on the ground.

"Nine-millimeter," she said as she bent down and picked up one of the casings.

As she looked at the other casings, she noticed something strange about the floor. Most of it was covered in a layer of dust and dirt, but portions were wiped away. As she examined the floor closer, she realized that someone had fought and fallen to the floor. Her eyes suddenly grew wide as she spotted something else on the floor, something that pieced the entire confrontation together for her.

Reaching down, she picked up an empty tranquilizer dart and whispered, "Holy shit."

Her heart began to race, and she reached for her phone, knowing that she had to call Charles and let him know right away what she'd discovered. But before she'd pulled it from her pocket, she heard the distinct sound of a vehicle's engine growing louder just outside a broken glass window to her right.

With her Glock still clutched in her hands, she moved towards the window, looked out towards the road, and watched as a blacked-out Jeep Wrangler Renegade flew into view and parked right beside the Tacoma. Moments later, four guys stepped out wearing ski masks and carrying submachine guns. One of them said something to the others that Ange couldn't hear, then they spread out and approached the building.

Angelina's adrenaline pumped as her body instinctively went into fight mode. She crouched down, keeping her eyes trained on the four guys as she strode quietly to the other side of the building. Moving into an adjoining room, she kicked open a rusty metal door and stepped outside, keeping out of sight.

Watching her footing, she moved around the outside of the building and watched through one of the massive shattered windows as the four guys entered and searched the place. Angelina's mind went to work, going over scenarios and planning the best course of action to take them all out.

"She's here somewhere," one of the guys said in a thick Spanish accent. "Spread out and search the place."

He waved his arms, and the three other guys branched off, walking in separate directions and holding their various weapons chest height. One of the guys, a short and stocky thug wearing jeans and a black tee shirt, moved in Angelina's direction. He held a stocked Uzi in his right hand and scanned his head back and forth, his eyes peering through his ski mask.

166

Angelina moved quietly over to the metal door she'd kicked open, then holstered her Glock and crouched down. Just as the thug stepped outside, she sprang to her feet, wrapped one arm around his neck and the other around his mouth, then dragged him silently to the ground. He struggled to break free, but in just a few seconds he went limp, unconscious in her arms.

She set his body down, looked up, and heard a second thug walking with heavy steps around the outside of the building and heading straight for her. Not wanting to give her position away to the others, she kept her Glock holstered and moved swiftly toward the corner of the building.

Just as the thug rounded the corner, Angelina knocked the sawed-off shotgun out of his hands, causing it to rattle onto the old beams at their feet. Before the thug knew what was happening, Angelina punched him square in the throat, causing him to gag loudly and his head to jerk forward.

He threw a punch in retaliation, swinging wildly while struggling to breathe. Angelina stepped back, ducked down, and swung her left shin hard into the back of the thug's knee, causing his legs to sweep out from under him and his back to slam against the old wooden planks. A few of the planks shattered under his weight, and Angelina, seeing that the two other thugs had heard their confrontation, kicked the thug across his face, then stomped him in the chest. The remaining planks, which had been clinging to dear life, shattered, and the dazed thug broke through, splashing into the water below.

Angelina reached for her holstered Glock, and as she raised it to engage the remaining thugs, the loud sound of automatic gunfire erupted across the quiet afternoon air. Bullets whizzed through the air just inches over her head as she dove for cover behind the wall. They rattled relentlessly against the metal, creating a symphony of tings and loud thuds that showered sparks all around her.

Rising up into a crouched position, she moved swiftly along the wall, trying to flank the thugs, who were still firing round after round in the direction where she'd sent their buddy into the drink. She moved within a few feet of one of the thugs, who was aiming out the window above her.

She took a deep breath, and in the blink of an eye she popped to her feet, raised her Glock, and pulled the trigger twice, sending one bullet exploding into his forehead and the other into the base of his neck. Blood splattered out as his body lurched backward, twisted awkwardly, and slammed facefirst onto the old creaky floor.

The fourth and final guy took notice and had her right in his sights. Holding the trigger, he sent a stream of bullets in her direction. As fast as she could, she dropped down onto her stomach, rolled over three times to her left, then poked her Glock around the corner of a partly open doorway. Before the final thug could change his aim, Angelina fired, sending a 9mm round screaming through the air and shattering his left kneecap into pieces. His body twisted, and with his left leg out of commission, the thug fell to the ground, his right shoulder slamming hard on to the wood.

As the thug wailed violently in pain, she propped herself up onto her knee, keeping the thug right in her sights. As she stood and walked towards the guy, who was struggling in an ever-growing pool of his own blood, she watched as he reached for his revolver, which had tumbled out of his grasp when he'd fallen.

Just as his shaking hand gripped it, Angelina pulled the trigger again. This time the round struck right through the palm of the thug's right hand, causing him to yell out even louder and drop his firearm once again.

"Not so fucking fast," Angelina said as she moved up to him, her body hovering over his. "You try reaching for that piece one more time and you'll never walk again. You understand, asshole?"

She aimed at his remaining intact kneecap, and even through his wailing and agony, she saw him quickly make eye contact with her and nod. Stepping around his mangled body, she gave his revolver a kick and it slid halfway across the dirty floor.

"Alright," Angelina said, her voice a dangerous combination of anger and resolve. "Now you're gonna tell me where they've taken Logan, or not only am I gonna blow away your other kneecap, but I'm gonna rip your fingernails off one by one. Is that clear enough for you?"

TWENTY-TWO

"It's here," I said, pointing to a location on a massive high-definition display that also acted as a table. "We've found artifacts scattered all around the seafloor here."

After agreeing earlier that morning to show them the location of the wreck in exchange for my possible freedom, I'd gone to bed in a modest stateroom and been brought back to see Felix around noon. Now it wasn't only the two of us. The big guy with the tattoo around his right eye, whose name I'd learned was Cesar, was standing beside us.

"What kind of artifacts?" Felix asked.

"How much gold have you found?" Cesar added.

I took a sip of coffee using both hands, my wrists still cuffed together.

"We haven't found any gold yet," I said. They looked at each other, but before they could reply, I added, "I don't think Shadow's treasure was on his

170

ship when it sank."

Felix laughed and shook his head, his mood shifting noticeably from hopeful to agitated.

"Great," Felix said. "Then where the hell is it?"

I stared down at the large digital map that displayed all of the Florida Keys, from Dry Tortugas to Key Largo and from the Atlantic coast up to the Everglades. My gut told me that he would have buried it somewhere in the Keys, but that meant one hell of a search area.

"I don't know," I said. "Our best chance of finding it is to keep salvaging the wreck. Maybe we'll find a clue."

"Or maybe we should just forget the whole thing," Cesar said, slamming a fist into the table. "Felix, may I have a word?"

I stayed at the table, left alone as the two men stepped out of the room. My mind ran wild, wondering where the treasure could be and whether I'd ever get an opportunity to escape. I knew that these guys were criminals, murderers, and backstabbers. I knew that if I ever got an opportunity to get away, I'd have to jump on it.

The door opened behind me, and the two men returned. Felix stepped into view and looked at me with his fierce green eyes.

"Okay," he said. "We have forty-eight hours. My captain tells me that we will reach the locations you have told me in just over an hour. We have dive and salvage gear ready to go." He stepped closer to me and narrowed his gaze. "That is all, Mr. Dodge. Forty-eight hours. If we haven't found it by then"— he raised his hands into the air—"well then, there's nothing I can do for you."

I nodded and told him I understood perfectly,

then felt a pang of hunger that was followed by my stomach grumbling. How long had it been since I'd eaten? I thought back and realized that I'd gone over twenty-four hours without sustenance.

"You can stay in here until we reach the wreck," Felix said. "I'll have some food brought up. I suggest you use your time in here wisely." Felix stepped towards the door, then paused, turned back to me, and added, "By the way, if you decide to do anything stupid, just know that none of my men will hesitate to put a bullet in your leg."

I nodded and Felix stepped out, leaving just Cesar and myself still in the room.

"This laptop is for you," Cesar said, motioning towards the Toughbook on the table. "It's unable to access any email, forum, or social networking sites. In addition, our team of IT guys will be monitoring everything you do. You will research the wreck and that is all, understand?"

"Yeah."

"Good," he replied sternly.

Without another word, Cesar walked out, replaced soon after by a pair of tall, round-bellied guys that stood stoically on either side of the door and watched every move I made. Ten minutes later, a middle-aged woman with long raven-black hair and dressed in a white crew member's outfit set a tray of food in front of me with shaking hands. She didn't say a word or even make eye contact with me for an instant. She just set the food down, then walked away, her face filled with fear. Seeing her up close, I'd noticed the embroidery on her shirt pocket said *Yellow Rose*.

Once she left, I opened the tray and demolished all of the food in minutes, surprised by how good it was but knowing that I would've enjoyed anything, I was so hungry. I washed down the plate of eggs, bacon, and hash browns with orange juice and coffee, then went right back to work.

I spent my time looking over the digital map and doing intermittent searches on a laptop they'd set out. I thought back to Frank's words, how he'd told us about the engineers that had been on the *Crescent* when she'd been taken over. I agreed with the professor in that, in order for the treasure to have stayed hidden all of these years, its location must have been well thought through. Years of storms, crashing waves, and shifting tides would have revealed the treasure to human eyes years ago had Shadow simply buried it all in the sand near the shore like in the old pirate tales.

After what felt like only a few minutes, Felix returned and informed me that they were anchoring over the site. What I didn't understand was how exactly they planned to moor a massive yacht in Florida Bay and send a bunch of divers into the water to scrounge the ocean floor without expecting to draw attention. But I wasn't about to offer tips to a bunch of criminals that were just looking to use me, then, in all likelihood, hand me over to my death.

"We have the gear stowed below deck," Felix said. "And a handful of trained divers. Where are we going first?"

I finished off my coffee, then leaned over the large horizontal monitor.

"Here," I said, pointing to an area on the map we'd referred to as the Elkhorn Garden. "This is where we found a cannon a few days ago. We'll start here and dive southeast, following the trail of artifacts."

Felix nodded, then motioned towards the starboard door.

"This way."

He led me out of the dark room and into a long, bright hallway with luxury cypress hardwood floors and bright clear windows that looked out over the starboard side of the yacht. From my vantage point in the hallway, I estimated that the yacht was well over a hundred feet long and must've been worth a fortune.

We moved past two guys standing by the door, and they followed us as Felix led me down a few flights of stairs, down another hallway, and into a large open space. The port side of the room was full of all sorts of high-end scuba gear. Nitrox tanks, BCDs, first- and second-stage regulators, weights, wetsuits, and an assortment of fins and masks of various sizes. All of it looked new and was conveniently stowed.

Along the starboard bulkhead, I saw a massive fiberglass desk covered in assorted top-of-the-line underwater cameras and gear. Next to the camera gear was a table and a few sets of drawers containing underwater metal detectors, handheld sonar devices, magnetometers, sea scooters, and various other pieces of equipment that I'd never seen before.

Felix led me to the center of the room, where he lifted a lever and pressed a green button beside a large plateau that rose up a few feet from the deck. The room shook softly, and within seconds, a portion of the deck began to slide away. My eyes grew wide as the clear, tropical ocean came into view below. It was a moon pool, and one of the nicest I'd ever seen.

Felix, seeing my face light up, explained a few of the other features of the yacht and showed me the area around the opening, which was lined with cushioned seats for ease of getting in and out of gear. I couldn't help but stare in awe for a few seconds at the setup. The unfortunate situation aside, the place was a diver's paradise.

Felix then introduced me to a few of the guys I'd be diving with.

"Cesar you already know," he said. "And I understand that you met Oscar some time back."

My memory clicked in as I looked at the fat long-haired guy who I'd confronted back at Pete's place. Even without ever getting a good look at him, I could tell who he was. He shot me an evil glance as he and Cesar prepared their gear.

"And this is Antonio," Felix said. "He's a master diver and salvager."

Part of me wanted to ask what normal use Black Venom had for experienced divers, but I decided maybe another time.

Antonio barely gave me a moment's glance. He looked older than the others and was close to six and a half feet tall, though he wasn't as muscular as Felix. As I glanced Antonio's way, I watched as he grabbed a compact pistol, then made eye contact with me as he holstered it on the outside of his XXL wetsuit.

"The yacht has a crane mechanism that is stowed here," Felix said, pointing to a closed door in the bulkhead. "And we have two compressors."

"Are we getting in the water, or are we gonna talk all day?" Cesar said, adding a few weights to his weight belt.

Felix's face shifted instantaneously. He strode over to Cesar, grabbed him forcefully by the back of his neck and slammed him to the deck.

Jamming his right knee into Cesar's cheek, Felix said, "If you don't lose the fucking attitude, you'll be

175

in that water for the rest of your body's miserable existence. Understand?"

I was amazed by how fast Felix's attitude had shifted. I'd dealt with hard, crass no-bullshit-takers many times in my life, especially during SEAL training. But there was something about the way Felix spoke and the way the others reacted that made me realize that nothing he said was just a scare tactic. I knew that he was a man who could kill in a heartbeat, and that he wouldn't lose any sleep over it.

Ten minutes later we were in the water. The weather was poor for diving—overcast and windy as hell, and the current was strong. The combination stirred up silt from the ocean floor, mixing it all around us and making it difficult to navigate through the terrible visibility.

Despite the conditions, the four of us were able to set up a search pattern and use the advanced equipment to find a handful of artifacts in just the first hour of diving alone. When we returned to the yacht, we'd filled a large container with another cannonball, two broken plates, a few pirate beads with their colors somehow still intact, and the metal bore of a musket. It was during the third dive later that evening, however, that we made the greatest find of the day.

It was just after five, and after taking a break for dinner, we were preparing to drop back down beneath the waves. I shimmied into my BCD, stuck the Velcro over my abdomen, clicked the buckles, and tightened the straps. With my fins already on, I spat into my mask, wiped it away, then rinsed it in seawater. Once it was strapped over my face, I gave a thumbs-up, then held my mask and regulator in place as I dropped back into the water.

Entering negatively buoyant, I splashed and sank

a few feet underwater before letting all of the remaining air out of my BCD and descending to the bottom twenty feet below. Cesar was already at the bottom, and Antonio and Oscar came down right after me. Our plan for the dive was to search the area around the pile of ballast stones using our equipment, hoping to find something more useful than a set of antique silverware.

Just over an hour into the dive, I picked up a faint hit with my metal detector and started digging. The current had eased up a little, and the visibility was much better than it had been earlier. After five minutes of digging with a small shovel, and with my air pressure running low, I struck a hard object roughly three feet down. Kicking softly and hovering right over the hole I'd dug, I sifted my fingers through the sand and revealed a large object.

My eyes grew wide behind my mask lenses and my smile caused seawater to sneak in, forcing me to tilt my head back and exhale forcefully from my nose to clear it out. Part of me had trouble believing what I was seeing. Buried in the sand less than fifty feet from the pile of ballast stones, surrounded by patches of seagrass, were the remnants of a wooden chest.

TWENTY-THREE

Angelina had gotten everything she could out of the bleeding thug before the police cars and ambulances arrived. It had been difficult to understand him as he struggled to control himself, his hands clutching the part of his body where his healthy kneecap had once been.

"Took him… yacht…" The words struggled out of the thug as Angelina yelled at him to talk. "The… Yellow… Rose…"

He'd spoken with rushed, mumbled words and had gone into shock just as Angelina heard the sirens approaching the old structure. Paramedics provided emergency care and carried the injured thug out of the building. Of the three other thugs, only the guy who she'd kicked through the deck into the water below was still alive. Unconscious and beat up, but alive.

Sheriff Wilkes met her in the grass-infested gravel lot beside the Tacoma and the silver Jeep with tinted windows. He had a group of officers with him from the nearby Monroe County Sheriff Station on Cudjoe Key, along with a few from his department in Key West. Officers secured the area, and a few suited detectives took pictures of the scene as the ambulances blared their sirens and disappeared from view.

When detectives approached Angelina, Charles waved them off.

"I'll handle her statement," he said authoritatively.

One of the detectives, a pale-skinned guy in his early thirties, nodded and said, "It looks like a clear case of self-defense. But we'd appreciate if you sent over the statement to our department as soon as possible. The more evidence we can bring to the table, the better chance we have of locking these criminals away for a long time."

"They're with Black Venom," Angelina said, drawing the detective's undivided attention. "I'm sure they all have long criminal records."

The detective said they would take care of it, then walked away to join a group of other detectives and police officers. Once he was out of earshot, Charles ushered Angelina to the other side of the parked Tacoma.

"Are you alright?" he said.

She nodded and replied that she'd received a cut on her arm from the confrontation, but that it was minor and wouldn't require stitches. When he asked what she was doing there, she explained how she'd called around, asking if anyone had seen anything suspicious.

"The dishwasher at Sammy's," she said. "He told me he heard gunshots over this way." She took in a deep breath and let it out. "I found a tranquilizer dart, and it was clear that a scuffle had taken place before I arrived. They took Logan, Charles. Black Venom. And that thug they just took away in the ambulance said that Logan was on the *Yellow Rose*."

Charles looked back at her, surprised.

"The *Yellow Rose*?"

"Yeah. It's a yacht, supposedly."

Angelina reached for her keys and stepped towards the driver's-side door of the Tacoma.

"Wait," Charles said. "Where are you going?"

"To find the *Yellow Rose*," she fired back, unlocking and swinging open the door.

"Hold on a second. You need to calm down. We need to think this through, and whether you think it's important or not, I really need to get your statement."

"You just got it," she said, then sat down on the driver's seat and slammed the door.

Charles shook his head and leaned in through the open window.

"No, I mean a real statement. Two people are dead, Miss Fox, and two more are on the brink of it. I need you to come down to the station and—"

"Hop in," she said calmly.

Charles paused. "What?"

"Hop in and ride with me. I'll tell you everything that happened here on the way."

Charles seemed taken aback. He stepped away from the truck, thought it over for a few seconds, then looked over at a group of police officers.

"Wait here," he said sternly as he stepped towards the group.

Angelina waited impatiently, tapping her fingers against the steering wheel while watching Charles through the side and rearview mirrors. After talking

180

to them for a minute, he headed back towards the Tacoma and opened the passenger door. Just as he sat down and shut the door behind him, Angelina put the truck in drive.

She flew over what remained of the overgrown road and turned back onto Old State Road, heading west. Thirty minutes later, the tires screeched as she pulled into the Conch Harbor Marina and parked against in one of the few empty spots in the first row. On the way over, she'd gone into further detail with Charles about what had happened, and when their shoes hit the dock, she shifted the subject.

"What's the deal with Ben anyway?" she asked, anger resonating in her voice. When Charles just looked back at her, confused as hell, she continued, "Look, I'm not a detective. But whatever happened with that Black Venom guy that escaped from your station? Wasn't it Ben who was on duty that night? What did he say happened, and how was there no footage of the guys that broke him out?"

"They're professional criminals," he said. "You know that. I'm sure disarming our security system wasn't difficult for them."

"Exactly. They're professional criminals. And professional criminals don't leave things up to chance. What, you think they were just waiting at that old abandoned crap hole, hoping for the off chance that Logan would stop by?"

"What are you saying?"

"I'm saying that I think Ben had something to do with this."

Just as they were about to reach the Baia, Charles froze in place. He looked at Angelina like a priest would look at a guy who'd just cursed in the middle of a church.

"I trained Officer Kincaid," he said, stepping towards Angelina and looking her dead in the eyes. "I know his character. I don't know how this happened, alright. But I can vouch for him." He took in a deep breath and calmed himself a little. "What would he have to gain from it, anyway? You're forgetting that he was taken as well."

"Charles, you worked for the CIA for twenty years and you're seriously asking me that question?"

They walked in silence for a few moments, then both turned when they heard footsteps and saw Jack walking towards them from the *Calypso*.

Angelina took a step closer to Charles.

"I might be wrong about all of this," she said, lowering her voice. "But I don't think that I am. Either way, we know how we can find answers. We've got to find the *Yellow Rose*."

"You guys saw it too?" Jack said, cutting the tension slightly with his laid-back voice. "She was a beauty." His voice shifted and he added, "Any word on Logan?"

"What are you talking about?"

"The *Rosa Amarilla*," he said. "One of the nicest yachts I've ever seen here at the Conch. Gus even took a picture of it."

Both Charles and Angelina looked at their friend, stunned.

"You've seen it?" Angelina asked. "When?"

His demeanor changed slightly and he replied, "Last week. Why? What's going on?"

Angelina and Charles glanced at each other.

"That could be where Logan is," Charles said.

"It is where Logan is," Angelina corrected him. "That's what the cartel member told me."

Jack threw his hands in the air. "What a minute,

you ran into more of Black Venom's thugs? When did this happen?"

"Earlier today," Angelina replied. "They surrounded me over at an abandoned building near Sammy Creek Landing. The only words I got out of him were Yellow and Rose."

Jack shook his head, having a hard time believing what Angelina was saying. He sat down on the half-moon cushioned seat and stared off into space for a moment.

"That's crazy, Ange," he finally said. "I'm glad to see you're alright. Hey, Gus might be able to help us track it down. He must have some info on her. You guys call the Coasties yet?"

Charles shook his head. "This all just happened." Then he looked over his shoulder at the marina parking lot, where a police cruiser was just pulling in. "I'm gonna take off. I'll call everyone I can and see if we can find this yacht." He patted Angelina on the shoulder. "I'm glad you're alright too. But try and stay away from this. Let us do our jobs. If we learn anything, we'll let you know." He headed down the dock, then turned over his shoulder and added, "And I still need that statement."

Charles walked to the parking lot, then hopped into the passenger side and told the other officer to drive to the police station. During the short drive, he couldn't help but think about everything Angelina had said. As much as he hated to admit it, he too had a hard time believing everything that had happened involving Ben had been a coincidence. Maybe it was his nature to be too trusting of his own, but the truth was, the idea of Ben playing a role in Logan's disappearance hadn't crossed his mind until Angelina had brought it up.

Angelina and Jack watched him walk away and cruise out of the parking lot from the Baia. Both of them knew Charles hadn't really meant it when he'd told them to stay out of it. He was just doing his job, trying to save face and have them leave the law enforcing to law enforcement officers.

"We've got to find this thing," Angelina said.

Jack nodded. "I'll call around the Gulf. See if anyone I know has seen her."

Angelina looked out over the water, wishing she knew where to look.

TWENTY-FOUR

I reached down with the shovel to dig deeper, but before I could, I felt a hand grab hold of my BCD from behind and jerk me backward. I twisted my body around and saw the fat body of Oscar, his blob of a right arm pulling me back and forcing me aside. Instinctively, my right hand formed a tight fist and I wanted to give his jaw a taste of my knuckles, but I didn't. He was armed and so were the two other guys nearby. If I tried to take them out, the chances of me even making it out of the water unscathed were slim, and then what? Like a recruit, I held my temper and breathed slowly in and out of my regulator.

Oscar ripped my shovel out of my hands and finished the work I'd started, moving piles and piles of sand away from the chest. After a few minutes, the cloud of sediment had settled and most of the chest's exterior came into view. It was old, rotted, and covered in grime, barnacles, and other growths. Its metal braces were rusted and disfigured, and colored a deep dirty-red color. The chest looked like any attempt at moving it would cause it to crumble to pieces and drift away with the current, but that didn't stop Oscar.

I supported myself against the seafloor beside Oscar as he removed his fins, hunched over, dug his booties into the sand, and tried to pull the chest free. After a few unsuccessful attempts, the other guys came over, dug more sand away, and helped him pull it loose. To my astonishment, the chest held together, and within ten minutes, we had it carefully moved back to the yacht and loaded onto a mesh net.

The excitement was palpable as we broke the surface, my pressure gauge indicating a dangerously low two hundred pounds. Careful not to damage our find, we hauled it up out of the water, where it was grabbed by a few men aboard the yacht and set onto the deck.

After sliding my mask down to hang around my neck, I removed my fins, climbed out of the water, and slid out of my BCD. Within a few seconds, we crowded around the chest, our wetsuits still dripping as Felix stood beside it and looking it over.

"What's happening?" he said, taking a step back and pointing at the chest.

I moved closer and saw that the metal braces were disintegrating rapidly from the inside out.

"It's turning to orange dust," I said. "This chest has been underwater for over three hundred years. It's amazing it's managed to be in such good shape after all these years."

A few of the guys must have thought I was joking as they stared at the sorry excuse for a chest that looked like nothing more than a few pieces of dirty, rotten wood.

Cesar grabbed a crowbar from the corner of the room, his wetsuit still dripping onto the fiberglass deck as he walked over and handed it to Felix. Felix didn't hesitate. He grabbed the crowbar with one hand, wedged the end into what remained of the lock, then broke it to pieces with one strong jerk. The remnants of the lock rattled to the deck and Felix bent down and lifted the cover. The thing came off, the old hinges no longer able to hold it in place, and Felix set it aside.

We all moved closer, hoping to gaze upon the first haul of treasure from the famous pirate shipwreck. But the chest didn't contain any gold doubloons, silver bars, or rubies. The chest was completely empty aside from a rusted hunk of useless metal that had corroded to such an extent that it was impossible to tell what it originally had been.

Felix didn't say a word at first. He just bent down, grabbed the metal object, and quickly dropped it back down, his hands covered in dark gunk. Then he stood tall and gave out a frustrated sigh.

"Twenty-four hours," he said, first looking off in the distance as he wiped his hands with a towel, then turning to look at me. "And then I'm giving up this venture and handing you over. Best figure out where the pirate buried his treasure."

As Felix stormed out of the room and the group dispersed away from the chest, I moved in for a better look at the object. It was roundish and flat, and at first, I thought it was some kind of strange oval-shaped dinner plate. Holding it carefully, I did my best to wipe away the grime, but it was no use. The shit was caked on strong, and my Naval salvage training suddenly kicked in.

187

As the three other divers struggled out of their wetsuits and worked to rinse the gear, I put the strange piece in a large plastic bag, then joined them. Once I'd changed and toweled off, Oscar put my handcuffs back on, this time even tighter than before.

"Nice job, dumbass," he said. "And you looked so excited finding that thing."

The fat thug shook his head as he walked out of the room, leaving me behind with Cesar and Antonio.

"That's it for tonight," Cesar said. "We could night dive, but it seems pointless right now." He stood up alongside Antonio and motioned for me to rise. "Alright, Felix wants you back in the map room. Back to square one, I guess."

"Maybe," I said, standing beside him. "Or maybe not."

He looked visibly agitated and shook his head.

"How the fuck is this not square one?" he said, pointing at the rotted chest resting broken and lifeless beside us.

I thought for a moment, then said, "Get me a few pounds of salt, a plastic bucket, and a medium-voltage power supply and we can find out for sure."

"What are you gonna do, Navy SEAL?" he said. "Use some kind of acid to burn through your handcuffs? And then what? You realize we've got over twenty well-armed cartel members on this yacht. I mean, you seem like a confident guy, but I sure as hell wouldn't bet on your ass."

"It's not for the cuffs," I said. "It's for that."

I pointed at the bagged piece of seemingly rusted junk beside me.

Cesar laughed. "It would take a damn miracle to bring whatever the hell that thing is back to its original self."

"Not a miracle. Just science. Trust me."

"Alright, I'll talk to some of the ship staff and get you the stuff you need. But I'll be watching you, Dodge, so you don't get any ideas."

When cleaning old, encrusted metals like copper or brass, there are three main methods often used. The first is placing the item in an acid bath, usually a fifty-fifty mixture of muriatic acid and water. The downside to this common method is time, as it takes a few days for the acid to do its work and another month or so of submerging it in freshwater to remove the acid. The second is sandblasting, but since the yacht didn't have a sandblaster, that wasn't exactly an option. The third, and the method I chose to use, was electrolysis.

An hour after the dive, Cesar and a few of the ship's staff had my equipment in place up in the map room. It included a ten-gallon plastic tub, a five-pound bag of salt, a laptop charger, and a pair of large alligator clips. I put everything into the bucket as best as I could with my hands cuffed, then picked it up.

"Where are you going?" Cesar said, shaking his head.

"The fumes from the chemical reactions are toxic," I said. "I need a well-ventilated area."

Cesar nodded and walked just ahead of me, leading up to the deck. There was one more piece of equipment I would need to make it work, and as I passed a set dinner table, I picked up a big soup spoon and looked at one of the staff.

"Is this steel?"

The waiter, dressed in his all-white uniform, nodded.

"Yes, sir."

When I turned back towards Cesar, I saw that he

189

had a confused look on his face, but he just shrugged and we headed out a sliding glass door into the fresh night air. We stepped onto the basketball-court-sized deck that faced the sunset over the stern of the yacht. Moving aft, I set the bucket on a space between a fancy hot tub and two rows of luxurious outdoor furniture. After emptying the bucket, I filled it three-quarters of the way full with water using a hose that popped right out of the deck. Then, I added the salt and mixed it until most of it had dissolved into the solution.

Grabbing the big alligator clips, I used the black one to clamp the dirty object to one side of the bucket, then used the red one to clamp the big steel spoon onto the other side. I arranged them along the edge in such a way that it ensured both the spoon and the artifact were completely submerged, then reached for the laptop charger.

Usually, when I've cleaned copper pieces using electrolysis in the past, I used a simple five-volt cell phone charger. But since the piece we'd found was large, I would need a higher voltage to achieve the appropriate current in order to effectively remove all of the grime from its surface, so I'd decided on the twenty-volt laptop charger.

Once everything was in place, I plugged in the charger, then watched and waited with Cesar and two other guys hovering over me. Within just a few minutes, small white bubbles began to form around the object. The current running through the two metals and the solution causes all of the grime to be released from the copper and stick to the sacrificial piece of steel, which in this case was the spoon.

"How long does it take?" Cesar asked as he stared at the reaction.

"We'll check back in an hour," I said. "From my experience, I'd say around two hours should probably do it."

We left the bubbling bucket and headed back inside. Felix was sitting in front of the digital table when we entered the map room, and we explained to him what we were doing with the artifact.

After just over two hours, we checked the bucket a second time, and I saw that, though the object was still bubbling, it wasn't nearly as much as it had been earlier. It's amazing what just a few hours can do to reverse the effects of hundreds of years of being submerged in seawater. The grimy, dark, strange-looking object that I'd clipped into the water a few hours earlier had been revived. The grime and caked-on gunk had almost completely been transferred to the spoon, which was now a black glob instead of a shiny eating utensil.

"That's incredible," Cesar said, watching me as I de-energized the charger and lifted the object out of the water with a rubber glove.

I set it softly on a towel, then examined it with wide eyes. What had initially appeared as a rusted hunk of junk had revealed itself to be an intricately designed piece of art. It had distinctly round edges, but formed an almost triangular shape and had grooves covering the flat surfaces on both sides.

Though the electrolysis had performed its magic well, the object still had a few patches of grime and dirt. I grabbed a toothbrush and cloth and scrubbed away. After a few minutes or cleaning and rinsing, I realized that the grooves carved into its surface weren't patterns or symbols, but letters. Spanish letters.

My Spanish wasn't great, but I'd spent enough

191

time in South America working as a gun for hire that I'd learned more than enough to communicate. After reading a few of the words I motioned to Cesar, who knelt down and stared in awe.

"I'll tell Felix," he said, unable to take his eyes off the object for a few seconds before rising back to his feet.

As he left, I read the few words I could make out aloud.

"Thirty paces north of the heart. Ten fathoms down."

TWENTY-FIVE

I knew that it would take me some time to figure out what the words meant, if I even ever could. It was a riddle, secret directions to the treasure that I couldn't understand at face value. After spending eight years in Naval Special Forces and another six as a mercenary, I hadn't spent a lot of my time studying history.

When Felix walked into the room and saw me cleaning the artifact, he leaned over my shoulder, read the words, and then asked me what they meant.

"I don't know," I said as I continued to clean.

The piece was as strange as it was intricate. It looked like the artist who'd built it had dedicated many hours to it, and yet I had no idea what it was supposed to be. Carved around the words on the sides were detailed images, depictions of the ocean, palm trees, swords, skulls, and a pirate ship in the middle. Some portions of the artifact were in much better shape than others, but no matter how deep I cleaned it, the only words I could distinguish were the same ones I'd read multiple times aloud.

Thirty paces north of the heart, I thought. I wondered what it meant by *heart*, wondered whether it was a place or a metaphor of some kind. Sitting down on one of the outdoor couches and looking out over the dark ocean, I thought about Frank and wished that he was there to see the artifact and give his opinion. After all, he knew more about Shadow and his ship than anyone in the Caribbean, especially after his recent trip to the Maritime Museum in London. He was the one who'd convinced me that the treasure most likely hadn't gone down with the ship, that it had been systematically hidden by a team of some of the best engineers of the time.

It was nearly midnight when Felix and Cesar, tired of looking over maps and theorizing about the artifact, escorted me down and locked me in my cabin. Mixed emotions overtook my mind as my head rested on the plush pillow. I thought about Ange and hoped that she was still okay. I thought about the artifact, playing the words over and over again in my head. And I thought about what would happen if we didn't find the treasure the following day.

I pictured the old, gray-haired man from the television screen in my mind's eye. I'd dealt with evil men many times before, and I knew that he was right up there with the worst of them. I was sure that he had a long list of plans for me and decided that if we didn't find the treasure and we cruised across the Gulf for me to be handed over to him, I'd make my move before ever reaching land. It would be better to die fighting than at the hands of the sadistic, murdering leader of a massive cartel.

What felt like just a few seconds after my mind finally relaxed and my body fell asleep, I heard a sound that woke me up instantly. My eyes grew wide and I sprang out of the bed. Then I heard it again. It was the sound of a woman struggling and trying to scream, but her sounds were muffled by something.

I stepped towards the forward bulkhead, quieted my breathing, and listened. It came again, and I realized that the sounds were coming from the cabin right next to mine. I pressed my right ear up against the bulkhead, listening to the sound of the woman's cries and the shuffling of feet and moving of bodies. A deep, all-consuming rage took over and my feet instinctively moved me towards the door. My hands were still handcuffed and the door was locked, but I didn't care.

Knowing there was no way I could break the door off its hinges, I narrowed my gaze on the porthole style window instead. I leaned my upper body back, planted my bent left leg firmly into the deck, and forced my right foot high into the air. With all my strength, I slammed my right heel into the window and shattered it with a loud crash.

With the window in pieces, I slid the small chair across the room, stood on top of it, and reached with both hands through the porthole, extending down towards the handle and opening the door from the outside. The sharp glass remnants that remained attached to the window frame cut up my forearms, but I didn't feel any pain. My adrenaline was pumping as I pushed the chair aside, then slammed the door open and stepped out into the passageway.

Just as I stepped out, one of the guards came running around the corner holding a pistol in his hands. I pounced on him before he could level it on me, slamming his gun hand against the wall beside us. As it rattled to the floor, I grabbed hold of his shirt collar with a firm grasp, bent my knees, and hurled his body over mine. He slammed onto the deck with a loud thud, and I watched his body go motionless as he groaned in pain.

With my heart pounding in my chest, I stepped towards the door where the woman's cries had come from, wrapped my hands around the doorknob, and flung it open. The room was dark, but I could see the outline of two people on the queen-sized bed, a man on top of a woman. He was struggling to hold her down as he tried to remove her clothes, but hearing the door crash open, he jerked his head to look at me.

Even in the darkness of the room, I could tell that it was Oscar. His round build and long braided hair were unmistakable. Without thinking or hesitating for even a second, I lunged towards him, grabbed him by his leather belt, and forced him off the woman. Throwing his body with all of my strength, I slammed him into a nightstand and shattered a mirror with his head.

His large and awkward frame twisted, and he barely managed to keep himself on his feet. As I forced my right knee up towards his chest, he hit me with a quick elbow to the side of my face. Pain surged as my head whipped sideways, but I kept driving my knee up until it made contact with his abdomen. As I shook off the blow, he gave a loud grunt of air from his lungs and lurched forward.

At first, I moved around his massive body and positioned myself for a strong takedown. Then I spotted my dive knife sheathed and strapped along the side of his belt. As he struggled and threw a mean left hook at me, I dropped down and let his fist slam into the wall just over my head. Reaching for the knife, I slid it out of its sheath, rose along his right side, and accelerated the tip of the blade towards his neck in one quick motion.

The knife sliced through Oscar's soft tissue effortlessly and relentlessly. The rest of his body shook, and he gave a loud and powerful shriek as blood spewed out like water from a damaged pipe. The five-inch titanium blade had cut through to the other side, destroying his windpipe and severing an artery.

I pulled the blade free, then maneuvered around his shaking body and kicked him to the floor. He yelled violently and shook side to side with his hands pressed firmly against his neck. His dark, menacing eyes stared into mine as he tried to keep himself alive, but it was no use. In a matter of seconds, enough blood had flowed out to surround his dying body in a pool of deep red.

Just as his body stopped moving and the life drained from his eyes, Cesar ran through the doorway, followed closely behind by two more guys. He held his Desert Eagle in one hand, and his eyes were wide as they traveled from Oscar to me, and then to the young woman, who was still on the bed. She sat on the other end with her back against the port bulkhead. She covered her body with a blanket and looked scared out of her mind.

Cesar calmed himself, then slid his revolver into its holster and stared at me.

"Give me the knife," he said, holding out his right hand.

I glanced down at my dive knife in my right hand, then looked at the big dead thug at my feet. The asshole had stolen it, and sometimes karma really can be a bitch. The blade was still dripping with blood as I handed it to Cesar, handle first. After grabbing it and wiping the blade with a rag, he told the two guys behind him to deal with the body. The two thugs went to fetch a body bag, and Cesar turned back to me.

"Come with me," he said in a stern voice.

I turned and looked toward the scared woman in the corner. Focusing on the top corner of her shirt momentarily, I saw the name Penelope in black letters. I wanted to help her, to tell her that it was over and that everything would be alright.

"Don't worry about her," Cesar said, reading my mind. "She'll be fine. We need to talk to Felix and see what he wants to do about this."

Like hell she'll be fine, I thought as I glanced again at the man who only moments earlier had been trying to take her by force. Cesar grabbed my arm with his left hand while his right gravitated to his holstered Desert Eagle. He motioned towards the door. I gave one final look at the young, wide-eyed woman, mouthed that everything would be okay, then turned and followed Cesar.

Felix was sitting behind his desk. He had one leg propped up and was swirling a half-full glass of bronze liquid and ice cubes. He looked tired, his skin sagging under his green eyes as he motioned for us to come in.

"Felix, there's been an incident," Cesar said. "Oscar is dead." Felix tilted his head back, anger taking over as Cesar continued, "He was trying to rape the maid, Penelope. Logan broke out from his cabin and confronted him."

Felix looked off into the distance, then shook his head.

"Sit down, Logan," he said, looking calmly at

198

me. "That will be all, Cesar."

As Cesar left the room and shut the door behind him, Felix finished off his drink with one long pull. After setting the glass on the table, he let out a deep breath, then shook his head.

"That idiot had it coming," he said. "I told him repeatedly to leave our captives alone, but he just couldn't control himself." His words were slurred, and I was convinced that he'd probably already drunk at least five glasses of whatever his fancy was that evening. "I got another call from Jefe. He expects us in Tampico tomorrow evening."

I didn't reply. Instead, I reached up and felt a patch of blood slowly streaking down the side of my face from where Oscar had elbowed me. Felix handed me a rag, then looked off into the distance as I wiped the blood away.

"You must think I'm just a murdering bastard, huh?" he said. "Well, maybe I am." Then his eyes stared fiercely into mine, and I felt as if we were seeing each other for the first time. "But know this, everything I've done started with self-preservation." He paused a moment, then added, "Have you ever been to Tlapehuala before?"

I shook my head. "No. But I've heard about it."

"Ah, and what have you heard?"

"Nothing good."

He paused a moment, grabbed a bottle and filled his glass almost to the brim.

"It was my home, years ago. Many years ago now. Much of Black Venom's roots can be traced to a tiny village of no more than three hundred a few miles outside of the city. It was during one of the worst droughts in history and times were hard. No money. No food. No glimmer of hope." He took a drink, then continued, "Men do desperate things without hope. Terrible things. Sometimes even to their own family.

"It's kill or be killed, Mr. Dodge," he said. "Betray or be betrayed. That is how this organization operates, and it's how it has always operated. I've done what I've needed to in order to survive. And I'm not proud of it. I kept clinging to a belief that someday it would end. That I would rise high enough in the ranks to dismantle this thing from the top. To free myself and those I care about. But that will never happen."

I sat in silence, listening to his words. I didn't know how to respond, so I didn't. I wasn't sure if it was just the alcohol talking, but it felt deeper. Like it was something that had been on the hardened leader's mind for a while.

"If we find this treasure, perhaps myself, Cesar, Antonio, and a few others can escape. Perhaps one day we can even go home," he said. "Fake IDs, fake passports, fake names. We can disappear with enough cash." He took in a deep breath, then sighed. "I can only give this until tomorrow evening, Logan. If Jefe discovers what we're doing here, he will have each and every one of us killed."

His moved shifted suddenly, and anger took over. He grabbed the artifact from the desk in front of him, raised it high in the air, then slammed it onto his desk, denting the wood.

"What the fuck does this thing mean?"

TWENTY-SIX

I woke up early and headed up to the map room alongside two guards. Once there, one of the ship's staff had a full pot of coffee brought in just for me, and I wondered if it would be enough for the hours I had ahead of me. After Felix had practically passed out drunk the night before, I'd headed down to my stateroom and tried to get some sleep, only to be woken up a few hours later by a dream.

I leaned over the digital display of the table in front of me, shuffled through a few pictures of the artifact, and looked at the map of Florida Bay. My dream had been vivid and more detailed than any dream I could remember. I dreamt of Shadow, his ship, and Captain Gray, the famous pirate hunter who'd tracked him and taken him down. Upon waking up, I thought about Frank and a few of his ramblings about the Golden Age of piracy.

"Famous pirate hunters like Gray were successful

because they didn't think like normal British officers," he'd said after dinner one evening while we'd lounged about on the bridge of the *Calypso*. "They thought like pirates."

His words played over and over again in my head for what felt like an eternity. Then it hit me like a strong gust of ocean breeze against the side of my face. I shouldn't be looking for the treasure, I should be looking for Shadow. Like the great pirate hunters of the Golden Age, I too should think like a pirate. I should get myself into Shadow's mind and figure out where I would have hidden a treasure if I were him.

For a few hours before the sun came up, I read page after page about Shadow and the members of his crew. I wished for Frank's thumb drive and the records he'd found in the archives but made do by digging deep with internet searches, my every movement watched by the two big guys by the doors. At seven in the morning, Cesar came inside and told me that we were drawing anchor. Just as the words left his mouth, I heard the yacht's engines start up and felt my heart sink a few inches.

"What are you talking about?" I said. "Felix said we had until this evening."

"Relax," he said. "The damn reverse osmosis units aren't working, so we need to pull into a nearby marina and fill our freshwater tanks."

He told me to just stay in there and not leave for a few hours, then disappeared and shut the door behind him. I sat frozen for a moment as an epiphany took over my mind. *That's it. Freshwater.* A pirate ship like the *Crescent* would have had to take refuge near a freshwater source of some kind. And if I could figure out where they got their water, I was confident that the treasure would be hidden somewhere nearby.

202

I went to work, punching the keys of the laptop and searching the internet for any natural freshwater sources in the Florida Keys. I knew that it was scarce but hadn't realized just how scarce until I read a few articles. Natural freshwater sources had been almost completely nonexistent south of the Everglades. The islands were a paradise to the eyes, but a hellhole for human survival. I read stories about sailors marooned in the Keys during the dry months, about how many of them had gone crazy due to extreme dehydration and died after drinking seawater to their heart's content.

After an hour of searching, I'd found one potential freshwater source. There were only a few references to it in old maritime logs, and many people of the era had believed it didn't exist at all. In an 1820 text about the Keys, entitled "Piloting Directions for the Gulf of Mexico," it stated that there was a natural well on the north end of Old Matecumbe and that it was routinely sought out by wreckers and turtle hunters.

There was a mention of the same well by Hester Perrine when she recounted the death of her father, who was killed during the Indian Key Raid that took place August 7, 1840. Hester wrote that three days before her father's death, her father had shown her a place she referred to as the Fairy Grotto, which she described as a sparkling spring that was roughly fifteen feet across and four feet deep. Hester and her father had both been living on modern-day Lower Matecumbe Key at the time.

After reading a few more vague references to a miracle spring that saved the lives of those shipwrecked sailors fortunate enough to find it, I slid the laptop away and shifted my attention to the digital

203

map that covered the entire horizontal display of the table. I zoomed in on Lower Matecumbe Key, a stretch of land situated between Upper Matecumbe Key and Craig Key. Much of the island is covered in waterfront homes and restaurants, and I learned that all of its Indian burial grounds and its natural spring had been destroyed during the construction of the Overseas Railroad. But most of the northeast section of the island is relatively untouched, and as I looked over its satellite imagery, I concluded it to be the best place to search for a treasure. I just had to figure out what the words on the artifact meant.

I shook my head, knowing that I was betting everything on a hunch and not facts. I knew that the chances of walking onto Lower Matecumbe and stumbling onto a lost treasure were about as likely as winning the lottery two times in a row.

Soon after, I heard the engines come back to life and felt the yacht move out of whatever marina they'd decided to cruise into. Felix came in, followed by Cesar right on his heels. The Black Venom leader moved into view, then leaned against the table containing the zoomed-in map, laptop, and all the research I'd done over the past day.

"Well," Felix said, staring at me. "Where to, Dodge?"

I didn't answer for a moment, wanting to choose my words carefully. Seeing my eyes drift down to the map, Felix tapped the touchscreen a few times, then slid his fingers in different patterns, his voice visibly frustrated.

"What's the significance of this area?" he said. "And how in the hell do I get the map to flip around?"

Cesar moved in behind me, and I used my right hand to flip the map around so that it faced Felix. I was about to tell him about Lower Matecumbe and the freshwater source there, but I couldn't. Instead, my mind was entranced by an image on the screen beneath me. A shape I hadn't realized was there before.

Reaching under the table, I grabbed the artifact and held it up in front of me.

"That's it," I said, the words charging out of my mouth like a holy proclamation.

My eyes jumped back and forth between the artifact in my hands and a satellite image of a land mass that looked just like it. It was the exact same rounded triangular shape as the artifact.

Felix, seeing where I was looking, moved beside me and held out the old dagger. I realized then that the engraving beside the name and date wasn't a heart—it was the same shape as the artifact.

"What island is that?" Felix asked, staring down at the uniquely shaped piece of land.

I smiled as I thought about the island that I'd cruised by hundreds of times before, an island clearly visible from a long stretch of US-1.

"That's Lignumvitae Key," I said, and at that moment, there was a part of me that knew without a doubt that it was where Shadow had hidden his treasure.

A quick search told me that Lignumvitae, once referred to as Cayo de la Lena on Spanish charts, had the highest elevation of anywhere in the Florida Keys at nineteen feet above sea level. The island is covered in rare tropical hardwoods, the most abundant being its namesake the Hollywood Lignum Vitae, a tree that is currently endangered. The combination of the island's elevation, its close proximity to fresh water, its abundance of trees, and the shallow waters surrounding it on almost all sides, made it the perfect place for a Golden Age pirate to bury his treasure. The island would have also been concealed by Lower and Upper Matecumbe, making it ideal for keeping a ship hidden and out of sight from passing ships along the Atlantic side of the Keys.

"This is incredible," Felix said, staring down at the map. "This island is the exact same shape of the artifact. And it looks almost completely uninhabited."

"It is," I said. "It's a state park now. Its two hundred and eighty acres are mostly thick forest, with the only structures being a few houses and a dock on the east side."

Felix nodded, then grabbed the artifact and read, "Thirty paces north of the heart. Ten fathoms down."

As the words came out of his mouth, he grabbed his cell phone and called the captain, telling him to make wake for the northwestern end of Lignumvitae Key. Just as he hung up, the door flew open and Cesar ran inside.

"Felix!" he said. "We've got a problem."

TWENTY-SEVEN

I could hear the loud helicopter blades thundering through the air before I'd reached the main deck. Peering through a row of large side windows, I gazed upon the ocean dotted with specks of land surrounding us. To the north, I saw a dark blue Mil Mi-38 transport helicopter roaring towards us at its top speed of one hundred and eighty miles per hour.

Felix moved beside me, talking quickly into his cell phone and telling everyone on board to get ready. Clearly, he hadn't expected guests anytime soon.

The pilot circled the massive bird around towards the stern of the yacht, then slowed to a stop and began to descend. I watched from the main deck with two guards standing beside me as the massive main rotor blade lowered the nine-ton aircraft softly onto the helipad. The yacht swayed slightly with the added weight and shook as the rotors whooshed and slowed.

Felix ordered me to follow him as he headed out

towards the helipad. Instantly my mind went to work, assuming that the worst had happened. It had to be the old man, I thought. The one they called Jefe. No one else would make Felix act the way that he was acting and cause fear to overtake his expressions. The jig was up, the treasure had slipped away, and now I had to find a way to escape.

"Move it!" one of the big guys said as he pushed me out onto the deck.

It was loud and windy and chaotic. A few guys ran towards the helicopter to tie it down, and within a few minutes, the large side door fell open, revealing a staircase. As soon as the first guys stepped out, I knew that whatever was about to happen, it wouldn't be good. They wore dress pants and shirts and had stockless AK-47s strapped over their necks and clutched in their hands. Dark sunglasses hid their eyes as they stepped out into the tropical afternoon sun. I counted fourteen in all, and once they were away from the gusts of wind blowing down from the dying rotor above, they stood in formation in front of us.

There was nothing I could do now, no way I could escape them. I looked up towards the dark doorway leading into the helicopter and saw a figure appear. It was the old man from the video call. He was wearing a pair of silver slacks and a white dress shirt with sleeves rolled up just below his elbows. He made quick work of the stairs, which surprised me considering his age and the fact that he was carrying what looked like a cane in his right hand.

Without hesitating, he walked straight towards Felix, who stood a few paces in front of me.

"Jefe!" Felix said, holding out his arms. "I'm surprised to see you."

"I have no doubt that you are," the old man fired

back in his smooth accent.

He continued with strong strides towards Felix, who reached out to greet his leader. To my surprise, the old man greeted Felix back by rearing back his cane and slamming it across the side of his head. The sound was loud and barbaric and almost caused Felix to fall over.

As if waiting patiently for their cue, the fourteen armed men who'd arrived with Jefe aimed their weapons chest height and surrounded everyone else outside on the deck. They yelled, cursing at their fellow cartel members and ordering them to drop their weapons. Cesar and a few other guys reached for their weapons but were quickly tackled and held to the ground at gunpoint.

Felix regained his balance. He looked around briefly, then drew his gaze back at Jefe. Without hesitating, the old man grumbled, stepped towards Felix and hit him two more times, once in the side and once in the face. As Felix fell to the ground, Jefe moved in close and snatched the revolver from his chest holster.

"You fucking backstabber," Jefe said, shaking his head as he held Felix's revolver in his right hand.

He struck Felix again, this time using the handhold of his own weapon. Felix's head jerked sideways, and I could tell that he almost passed out from the blow.

"Did you really think you could pull something like this off?" Jefe continued. "Did you really think that I could be deceived so easily?" He walked around the deck, his eyes scanning over me, Cesar, and the others who'd been trying to find the treasure. "I'm insulted by your stupidity, and even more so by your lack of loyalty." He cleared his throat, then looked back at Felix, staring him straight in the eyes. "Our organization has strict laws regarding betrayal." He knelt down beside Felix. "And now I get to fucking tear you limb from limb and feed you to the sharks."

He rose back to his feet and stepped towards Cesar.

"But no," he added. "That would be letting you off too easy given the circumstances. Instead, I want you all to see your futile little plan crumble before your eyes. I want you to see me and the cartel gain from it before you meet your painful demise."

He turned towards me, then stepped closer, looking me in the eyes and trying to get a read from me. We weren't people anymore, we were mammals, and he wanted to see firsthand what kind of mammal I was. I didn't blink, didn't back down in the slightest. I was a fighter, and whether I died by his hands that day or not, he would bloody well know that much.

"So this is Logan Dodge," he said. "You're the asshole who's caused me so much trouble and, for some reason, no one can kill."

He suddenly raised the revolver, aiming it straight at my head. I didn't even flinch or shift my gaze. The samurai, some of the greatest warriors ever to walk the planet, had always believed that it was the men who were willing to die who fought the best and usually made it out of even the worst conflicts alive. It was a belief I shared, and though I loved being alive, I always tried to be prepared to die and had trained myself to no longer fear death.

With that being said, my heart still raced as I faced the barrel of his loaded weapon.

Jefe stepped towards me. "I could end you right

now. And as much as I want to, I have other, more… profitable plans for all of you."

He stepped back, lowered his revolver, and again addressed the entire group.

"Before I punish you traitors, you're going to lead me to this treasure," he said. "That's right, I know all about it. The same man within your ranks who told me that your engines were fine also told me what you were really doing here. I think Oscar deserves a promotion for that." He stepped towards Felix, who was still on the ground in pain, and added, "I think he'll have your job, Felix."

"That will never happen," I said sternly, causing Jefe to turn around in surprise.

"Oh? And why the hell is that Logan?" Jefe barked.

"Because I killed him."

His eyes grew wide in anger and he moved back towards me.

"I killed him," I said. "And I'm going to kill you as well."

Jefe froze in place, his eyes staring back at mine. He controlled his anger after a few seconds, his lips contorting to form a bone-chilling smile.

"You are exactly as I've heard you to be, Logan," he said. "It's a shame I don't have a man like you in my ranks. It's also a shame that your life will soon be no more."

He moved his face close to mine, then clenched his right hand into a fist and plowed his knuckles against the side of my face. The pain was immense, and I realized that he'd been gripping a pair of brass knuckles. I spat out a spray of blood, then looked back at him.

"You will show me where this treasure is," he

211

said, "or I will kill you right here, right now. The choice is yours."

TWENTY-EIGHT

After spending an entire day searching, calling, and brainstorming, neither Jack nor Angelina had very much to go on. The only ray of good news they'd received was from a fishing charter captain based out of Marathon who was friends with Jack. After Jack had called him, the captain had informed him that he'd spotted the *Yellow Rose* out in Florida Bay a few days earlier, while he was taking clients out for a trip. But neither Jack or Angelina saw any sign of it while cruising around the Gulf side of the Keys. The *Yellow Rose* seemed to have disappeared, and Angelina knew that it had most likely disappeared into the Gulf.

The following morning, as the sun was rising over a distant patch of thick clouds, Frank walked down the dock towards the Baia. He'd been trying to catch up on his classes at the college after taking so much time off to travel to Switzerland and to look for the treasure, but he wanted to see how the search for

213

Logan was going.

Angelina spotted him while she and Jack sat around the dinette of the Baia. They'd each only had a few hours of sleep as they continued to call around and use satellite imagery to try and locate the *Yellow Rose*. But things were looking bleak, and Angelina was ready to get back out on the water.

Frank was wearing khaki shorts, a Key West Community College tee shirt, and sunglasses with a red strap as he approached. After a quick greeting, Angelina and Jack gave him a rundown of what was happening. It didn't look good. Frank wasn't a man of action or a soldier, but he was smart and had read enough about drug operations worldwide to know that they usually handled their business brutally and hastily.

Frank sat down beside them, eager to do whatever he could to help find his friend. Ten minutes later, Angelina reached into her pocket and grabbed her cell phone as it vibrated to life. She was expecting a call back from Charles, and when she saw that it was him, she eagerly pressed the answer button and held the speaker up to her ear.

"Angelina, you're not gonna believe this," he said, his tone more energetic than usual. "The *Yellow Rose* is on its way to Tampico. They spoke to the Coast Guard yesterday as they were leaving US waters."

Angelina paused for a moment, placed a hand against her temple and shook her head.

"You're right, Sheriff," she said. "I don't believe it."

"What are you talking about? Why not? This report was made by them long before your interaction."

214

"And why in the hell would they tell the truth?"

Charles paused a moment, not knowing how to answer.

"Look, we have something," he said. "And we need to jump on it. I have the Mexican Coast Guard on alert and they will be ready in Tampico. The US Coast Guard also sent two boats into the Gulf looking for any sign of the yacht." When Angelina didn't reply, he continued, "It's all we have right now. If not in the Gulf, then where is it? If you can answer that and give me something better to go on, I'm all ears."

But Angelina couldn't. She had nothing else to go on but her common sense in dealing with criminals on a daily basis for years. The good ones never did the expected, and they rarely made stupid mistakes—and Black Venom was as good as they came.

"I'll keep you in touch," he said after a moment's pause. "Just promise me you won't do anything rash. We're handling this the best way we know how, and we'll do everything we can to find them."

"Okay," Angelina said, calming herself and knowing that anything she said would be useless at this point. After all, Charles still thought that Ben had nothing to do with Logan's capture, which gave Angelina the impression that either he was getting soft in his older years, or he was refusing to face the truth.

"I'm serious," he said. "You're not the only one who has lost someone here."

"Thank you, Sheriff," Angelina said, then they both hung up.

Angelina was so mad that she almost threw her phone over the side. She stomped towards the stern of the Baia and stared off, her heart pounding and her breathing heavy. She didn't know where the *Yellow*

Rose was or where it was going, but she sure as hell knew that it wasn't going to Tampico.

"Ange, are you okay?" Jack asked, stepping over and placing an arm on her shoulder. He'd never seen her anything but controlled and reserved before, and he did his best to comfort her. "We'll find him, alright?"

She kept her eyes peeled over the water for a few seconds.

"Why would they be in Florida Bay a day after Logan was taken?" she asked, raising her voice. "It makes no sense. Unless…"

Jack shook his head. "Unless what? What are you talking about?"

"Unless they know about the treasure," Frank said, stepping over towards them.

Angelina nodded, then grinned. "Logan's using it as a bargaining chip. It's textbook. Hostage situation 101. Find something your captors want more than you. And who wouldn't get excited about one of the largest lost pirate treasures in history?"

"We should call Charles," Jack said, grabbing his phone from the dinette.

"No!" Angelina said. "Not until we find the yacht. He probably wouldn't believe us anyway. Besides, like he said, they have their protocol. If the crew of the *Yellow Rose* said that they were heading to Tampico, that's where they've got to look for them first."

"Wait, until we find the yacht?" Jack said.

"That's right," Angelina said, jumping onto the dock and untying the lines. "We're gonna go find this *Yellow Rose*. And the first place we'll make our heading for is the wreck site."

TWENTY-NINE

When Angelina and Frank were ready, Jack started up the twin six-hundreds and eased the Baia out of Conch Harbor Marina. It was overcast but the winds were calm, creating little chop and allowing them to punch the Baia full throttle as they cruised along the Lower Keys. By the time they reached Florida Bay, it was late afternoon and they only had a few hours of daylight to search.

"Nearing the wreck site now," Jack said. "If the yacht is there, we should have our first visual any minute now."

As Jack eased back on the throttles, Angelina stepped up onto the bow with a pair of binoculars glued to her eyes. Having been boating her entire life, she kept her balance easily without swaying side to side with each slight turn or bob up and down. She was wearing a pair of black athletic shorts, and since it was colder than usual for February at sixty-three degrees, she wore a white long-sleeved tee shirt. Her feet were bare as she stepped against the railing, hoping to spot a yacht in the distance as they moved around the small island.

"Shit," she said to herself as she stared into the magnifying lenses.

She didn't see a yacht or a sign of any boat floating above the wreck site. As she continued to search, scanning around the nearby waters, she spotted only two boats, a shrimp trawler and what looked like a fishing charter. To make things worse, a thick patch of fog had rolled in, making it difficult to see more than a mile in front of her.

"See anything?" Jack said, peering through the windscreen.

"Nothing," she said.

Jack sighed. "That white curtain's gonna make seeing anything difficult. Looks like it's coming our way."

"And there's nothing that big on radar," Frank said, standing beside Jack and huddled over the instruments in the cockpit.

Jack kept the Baia just below her cruising speed of thirty knots as they cruised into the open waters of Florida Bay. In what felt like only seconds, the massive wave of fog came over them, surrounding them in a haze that made it difficult to see even a few hundred feet in any direction.

"Of course," Angelina said, stepping down into the cockpit. "The one day we need good viz on the surface and this shit happens."

Frank thought about Captain Shadow. He thought about the day the pirate had been attacked and how the accounts had described it as a foggy evening, much like the one they were experiencing. It gave him an eerie feeling that was followed by a few spine-tingling chills.

The trio was forced to rely almost solely on the radar. They cruised all around the wreck site, creating a wide arcing circle, but didn't find anything. As the evening pressed on and the fog refused to relent, Angelina began to feel like Logan was slipping away.

What are the chances that yacht is anywhere near the Keys still? Angelina thought. *If those guys were smart, and I'm betting they are, they'd be on the other side of the Gulf by now.*

The logical part of her brain fought to convince her that the chances of her ever seeing Logan again were slim to none. She'd dealt with cartels before and if there was one thing each and every one was very good at, it was making people disappear. But still, part of her believed wholeheartedly that if Logan had told them about the treasure, they would have had a hard time turning it down.

"We're gonna need fuel soon," Jack said, his voice defeated as he looked at the gauge. He glanced at the GPS monitor in front of him and added, "The Coconut Marina in Lower Matecumbe will work nicely."

Angelina didn't say anything as she looked out over the white-covered horizon surrounding them in all directions.

"How long do you think it will take to pass?" Frank said, glancing up from the radar.

Jack looked around, then checked the temperature, humidity, and wind indications on the panel in front of him. A patch of fog is difficult to predict, but he always preferred to foresee on the side of caution. He'd known too many people who'd underestimated thick fog and had paid the ultimate price for it.

"Nightfall's in an hour. It'll be here long after that," Jack said. He glanced back down at the GPS, then planned a route in his mind. "We can head east a few miles, then turn south towards Islamorada, then circle back to the marina in Lower Matecumbe. That way we can cover as much new area as possible. We'll reach Coconut's pretty low on fuel, but if we need it, I know Logan's got a spare tank down in the engine room."

Angelina didn't reply again. She just looked out over the water, seemingly lost in thought.

"That sounds good, Jack," Frank said. "We've searched all of these waters enough already," he added, pointing at the GPS, "so sweeping around to the east makes sense."

They both agreed verbally, but inside they felt like Angelina looked. Stunned and unsure what to do next. Finding the *Yellow Rose* near the wreck site was the only hope for a plan that they had. Angelina had been so confident that it would be there, and now that it wasn't, she felt a wave of disappointment that was difficult to combat.

"They could be mooring to get out of the open water and wait out the fog," Angelina said after a few minutes.

Jack and Frank were both silent, then Jack nodded and followed the course he'd laid out. As the water flapped against the bow and the thin wake trickled behind them, Angelina slumped down into the dinette and brought up the laptop. The water was eerily quiet around them. If it had been just about anyone else at the helm, both Frank and Angelina would have taken occasional glances at the GPS to make sure that they were in the right spot. But Jack knew all of the islands, cuts, and reefs in the Keys as good as anyone alive, and they trusted his sense of direction with their lives.

At just after seven, as the white glow of the sun bleeding through the fog was starting to fade away, Jack spotted a small break ahead of them. It was faint at first, then gradually the veil of powdery white slipped away, revealing a patch of light reddish sky above.

They were just north of Shell Key in only about seven feet of water when Angelina jumped to her feet and looked out over the starboard bow.

"What is it, Ange?" Jack asked, focusing in the same direction but seeing only a few patches of land dotting an empty bay.

"I don't know," Angelina said. Then she turned to Frank who was shuffling out of the dinette, and added, "Hand me the binoculars."

Once she had them, she pressed them against her eyes and focused the lenses.

"Holy shit," she said after a moment's pause.

Jack continued to look and soon spotted a large white object on the horizon. It was a few miles away and was mostly covered by a small island, but after turning and looking closer, he realized that it was a yacht.

"It's the *Rosa Amarilla*!" Angelina said, her eyes peering through the binoculars.

She brought them down and turned to look back at Jack and Frank, her face a combination of serious and excited. She handed them to Jack, who took a look as well. Right away, he spotted the distant image of a yellow rose painted onto the hull beside the name. It was the same yacht he'd seen in the Conch Harbor Marina the previous week.

221

"But why is it here and not at the wreck site?" Jack asked as he handed the binoculars to Frank.

"I don't know," Frank said. A second later, he dropped the binoculars, took a look around them to get his bearings, and added, "That's Lignumvitae, right?"

Jack nodded. "Yep. That's it alright. Makes no sense that they would drop anchor so close to the mainland." He motioned towards US-1, where portions of the road peeked through the fog just two miles to the south of them, to emphasize his point.

"There must be a reason," Angelina said. "Regardless, we need to call Charles and get ahold of the Coast Guard. They're looking for the yacht in the wrong place!"

As the words left her mouth, they heard the unmistakable sound of outboard engines coming from the stern of the Baia. Jack had the Baia's engines running at just twenty knots, making it easy for them to hear the approaching boat behind them. The three of them looked back into the thick fog, and seconds later, they saw a twenty-six-foot tan Edgewater center-console materialize as if by magic.

It didn't take Angelina long to realize that it was the same boat she'd seen earlier that day. It was the same make and model and had at least ten fishing rods attached to its stern and gunwales.

"Is it just me, or is that boat heading straight for us?" Frank said, saying what all three of them were thinking.

"Looks like a fishing charter," Jack said. "Probably out of Lower Matecumbe. I don't recognize the boat, though."

Jack and Frank glanced at Angelina, who was reaching for the loaded Glock on her hip. She didn't grab it, however. It was just a reflexive move to make sure that her handgun was still where it should be, even though she knew that it was.

"Wow, what the heck?" Frank said, glancing at her and wondering why she thought the approaching boat was a threat.

But Angelina didn't reply. She just stepped towards the stern, standing against the swim platform as the boat continued its approach. Within thirty seconds, it slowed just a few hundred feet away and Angelina could see four men standing behind the windscreen. They waved as they cruised closer and yelled towards the Baia, saying that they had an injured man aboard.

The approaching boat turned, and Angelina saw that one of the Latino guys was helping another onto his feet. Angelina surveyed the scene quickly, going over every inch of the boat. The four guys looked young, maybe late twenties, and they looked like they knew how to carry themselves. She saw no signs of weapons other than what appeared to be a few fishing knives.

"Please, my friend is hurt," one of the bigger guys said. "He was bitten by a shark as we were reeling it in. Do you have a first aid kit aboard?"

The boat was so close to the Baia now that they were almost touching, and one of the guys was holding a coiled rope, ready to throw it over once given the word. The guy who'd been bitten sat on the gunwale with his arm wrapped in a tee shirt.

Jack told Frank to take the wheel, then grabbed a first aid kit from inside the salon and moved beside Angelina. As he was about to throw it over to the other boat, the sound of another large engine roared to life, coming from the starboard side of the Baia. The

223

three looked towards the sound and saw a thirty-four-foot Baja 342, with a dark hull and silver streaks, thundering full speed straight towards them.

"Dammit!" Jack said. He threw the first aid kit to the nearby boat, then ran into the cockpit. "We need to get the hell out of here."

As Angelina turned, she saw something strange in the corner of her eye. The guy who sat on the gunwale on the boat beside them suddenly threw off the tee shirt covering his lower body, revealing a strange-looking rifle with a short, narrow barrel.

Shit, she thought as she gasped, focusing her gaze on the weapon.

She didn't have time to think things through, didn't have time to wonder who the hell they were. In a blur of swift movements, her right hand darted instinctively for her Glock 26. Grabbing hold of her pistol, she raised it in an instant and pulled the trigger just as the guy pulled the trigger of his rifle. The bullets exploded out of Angelina's Glock and struck the guy in the chest, causing him to fall backward and disappear from view.

Angelina felt a sharp pain bite deep into her side and she collapsed, taking cover and continuing to fire round after round towards the thugs on the center-console. Aside from the guy Angelina had sent to the deck, they all grabbed weapons that only moments earlier had been hidden from view. The big one with the backward hat and sunglasses suddenly leapt onto the Baia, taking cover from Angelina's assault by ducking down on the swim platform.

Jack hit the throttles, causing the Baia's engines to roar ferociously to life and propel them forward like a sprint boat after the starting pistol fires. The nylon line connecting the Baia to the small center-console went taut, causing the smaller boat to flip onto its side, knocking the three thugs into the water.

Giving Frank the wheel, Jack grabbed his dive knife from his leg, leaned over onto the sunbed, and sliced the line, allowing the Baia to accelerate without having to drag the flipped-over center-console. As the small boat tumbled over a few times in their wake, Jack dropped back down to the deck and reached for his compact Desert Eagle.

Angelina struggled to sit up. She gripped her Glock as tight as she could and tried to raise and aim it at the thug crouching aft of the transom. But its metal frame suddenly felt impossibly heavy in her hand.

What the hell was in that thing? She thought as she glanced down at the empty tranquilizer dart rocking innocently on the deck beside her. She'd experienced many kinds of sedatives before in her life, but this was something completely different. Something stronger and faster-acting than anything she'd felt before.

Her vision went and her muscles seemed to give up. She tried to keep her Glock raised but was unable to as her head began to drop back. Before Jack could draw his Desert Eagle, the thug, peeking over the transom and realizing that Angelina was in bad shape, lunged towards her. She tried to take him out, tried to muster every ounce of strength she had to raise her Glock, but couldn't. Just as she almost had the thug in her sights, the sinewy muscled man kicked her Glock free, causing it to rattle over the fiberglass and disappear into the white bubby torrent of the Baia's wake.

Angelina could feel her consciousness fading away. She could barely keep her eyes open as her vision blurred and she lost control of her body.

With Angelina down, the thug turned his gaze to Jack who'd just gripped his Desert Eagle. Jack didn't hesitate. Before the thug could take a shot at him, he fired two rounds into the guy's chest, causing him to drop his weapon and fall backward. His body hit the deck with a loud thud and he tumbled down the steps, his arms getting caught on the edge of the transom and his left leg dangling over the swim platform into the rushing water.

Jack knelt down to see if Angelina was alright, then seeing the thug try to stand, he tilted his head up towards Frank.

"Keep our speed up!" he shouted as he stood and lunged for the downed thug.

As the bloodied man tried to stand, Jack hit him with a strong front kick, sending his body flying over the stern and splashing into the water.

"Jack!" Frank yelled as the thug's body vanished under the Baia's wake.

Turning around, Jack's eyes grew wide as he realized that the speeding go-fast boat was heading straight towards the starboard bow. His heart pounded, and he knew that the two boats would collide in only a fraction of a second. With no time to turn or change speed, Jack hit the deck beside the sunbed.

"Brace!" Frank yelled as he forced the throttles to neutral, then frantically pulled Angelina's unconscious body farther forward. A moment later, the speeding boat slammed into the Baia's hull with an ear-rattling crash.

The Baia jerked violently, tilting to port in a sixty-degree list in the blink of an eye and nearly keeling over completely. The sudden shock of force caused Frank to slam against the base of the dinette and tumble onto the cushioned seat. He'd kept his body over Angelina's, causing him to take on the brunt of the damage. Jack, being farther aft, was thrown out of the Baia completely, his body launching over the port side and splashing into the water.

Frank felt a surge of pain radiate from his back and from the side of his head, which had crashed into the port windscreen. His vision was hazy for a few seconds, and he heard a ringing in his ears. The boat's momentum kept it cruising fast, and the force from the impact caused it to heel drastically back and forth.

Looking back, Frank saw no sign of Jack swimming on the surface behind them. He saw only the boat that had collided with them and watched as it cruised towards the Baia with men standing on the deck and aiming rifles in their direction.

THIRTY

The glow of the distant sun faded away through a patch of fog on the western horizon. Felix, Cesar, and myself were forced at gunpoint to climb aboard an inflatable skiff that had been lowered into the water at the stern of the *Yellow Rose*. The yacht was moored just a few hundred feet off the northwestern shore of Lignumvitae Key, and as we settled onto the wooden bench seats, one of Jefe's thugs started up the ninety-horsepower Yamaha and motored us towards the shore.

There were eight thugs in all including Jefe, who sat facing the three of us on the bow. He kept his revolver in his right hand like it was glued there, even though all three of us had our hands handcuffed behind our backs.

The vast majority of the island's two and a half miles of beachfront are covered with rocks and jungle that grows dense right up to the water line. It makes access to the island via boat difficult, and it's why a two-hundred-foot dock was constructed on the eastern shore. After cruising south for a few minutes, Jefe pointed out a small patch of white sandy beach inside a narrow inlet. It was no more than thirty feet across, but it would be plenty wide enough to accommodate the narrow dark-hulled thirty-two-foot RHIB.

A RHIB, or rigid-hull inflatable boat, is a lightweight but high-performance boat with a solid hull and pontoons around the edges that form the gunwale. They're perfect for transporting large groups quickly and in shallow waters, and I'd piloted them many times during my time in the Navy.

The pilot brought us right up to the beach, the fiberglass hull scraping against the sand as the boat slowed to a stop. He killed the engine and propped it up, protecting the prop from the shallow water beneath us. Two thugs jumped out of the boat, grabbed hold of the bow, and pulled us up onto the beach. Jefe moved with the agility of a much younger man as he climbed over the starboard pontoon and jumped onto the sand.

"Everybody off!" he said in a loud and authoritative voice. "And haul all of the gear onto the beach."

The three of us did as he said, and the others went to work unloading the piles of shovels, metal detectors, and picks. Jefe moved inland into the jungle alongside two of his men and gave the area ahead of us a quick survey before returning to the group.

Grabbing the artifact from one of his men, he held it up to the dying light and read the inscription. Then he grabbed a handheld GPS and coordinated our location relative to the center of the island.

"This way," he said, motioning forward.

He ordered everyone to leave most of the gear behind, saying that he'd have us backtrack later, once we'd reached the dig site. For the first quarter mile or so, we trekked along what looked like a rarely used footpath that cut through the island from east to west. The sandy pathway with patches of overgrown brush was much easier to navigate than the thick jungle that covered most of the island.

After five minutes, Jefe pointed north and we moved into the dense jungle. Four of Jefe's men led the way with machetes, hacking away many of the smaller branches and making it easier to navigate. It was difficult work. Lignum vitae is one of the densest hardwoods in the world. It's so hard, in fact, that it was once used to make knives and is one of the few kinds of wood dense enough to sink in water.

The men swung their machetes through the air, sweat dripping down the backs of their necks, as we pressed forward. Part of me cringed with every swing. Lignumvitae Key is a popular state park in the Keys, known for its lush botanical landscape that has remained relatively untouched for centuries. And there they were, cutting and breaking their way through its heart with reckless abandon.

Jefe raised his right hand in the air and told everyone to stop. He peered down into the GPS for a few seconds, then handed it to one of his thugs. After receiving an approving nod from the other guy, Jefe proclaimed that we'd reached the center.

"So now we dig?" one of the big guys wielding a machete said.

"Not yet," Jefe replied. He reached into a backpack and pulled out the artifact we'd found underwater in the old chest a few days earlier.

Holding the object out in front of him, he read the words aloud. "Thirty paces north of the heart. Ten fathoms down."

After a moment's pause, the big guy wielding a machete beside Jefe said, "What's the exact length of a pace?"

Jefe turned back and stared daggers at me, looking for an answer.

I sighed. I knew as well as Cesar and Felix did that helping them was our best chance at survival. The longer it took, the higher the probability they'd scratch the whole thing, riddle us with bullets, and feed us to the sharks.

"There isn't one," I said, shaking my head. "It depends on whose pace it is. But it's generally considered to be thirty inches or two and a half feet." Then I went quiet for a moment, my mind remembering a few documents I'd read. "By all accounts, Captain Shadow was above average height. Somewhere around six feet. So his pace would have probably been slightly longer, say closer three feet."

Jefe nodded, tapped the touchscreen of his GPS, and said, "So ninety feet north of the island's heart." Then he looked forward, held the device up in front of him to keep us on a perfectly straight path, and added, "Let's move."

Within minutes we reached the place, and like most of the island, it was covered in dense trees. We set what gear we'd brought with us down amongst the dirt, roots, and bushes, then headed back the way we'd come to grab more of the gear. As we went back for our second trip, I heard the sound of a pair of good-sized outboard engines puttering close by. The sounds were heading north along the island's western shore. Gazing out through the thick brush, I saw a good-sized dark-hulled go-fast boat with silver streaks. I could just make out a group of people aboard, their heads barely visible over the starboard gunwale and windscreen.

I watched it for a few moments as I wrapped my arms around a handful of shovels tied together and realized that it was heading for the *Yellow Rose*, whose stern was just barely visible.

"Hurry up!" one of Jefe's men barked as he shoved me forcefully.

I gritted my teeth as every morsel of my being wanted me to tell him to shove it and tackle to the ground. But what then? I could probably get ahold of his gun in a second or two, but then I'd still be bound, and there were seven other thugs ready to shoot me down at a moment's notice. No, the only way I'd be getting out of this alive was if I played their game, at least until the opportunity to strike revealed itself.

Less than an hour after finding the dig site, we had much of the area surrounding it cleared. Using saws, we cut away the trees, then broke ground with the picks, cutting, ripping out, and clearing away the strong and deep roots. A second boatful of men joined us from the yacht as we broke ground, digging into the dirt and rocks with our shovels.

The work was hard, long, and arduous. Only a few minutes passed before a thin layer of sweat appeared on my brow that always came right back no matter how many times I wiped it away. With nightfall came a never-ending army of tropical mosquitoes, hungry to stick their thin needles into any exposed skin and suck our blood. Not long after they appeared from the thick jungle surrounding us, Jefe and his men created a perimeter of tiki torches around our position, deterring most of the savage insects from coming close. They also set up nearly silent running generators and work lights, allowing us to see what we were doing as we dug deeper into the earth.

The hole was roughly ten feet across, allowing a handful of us to climb down and dig while the rest moved dirt on the surface or took a much-needed rest filled with intermittent gulps of water. The going was painstakingly slow in the moment, but as the hours wore on, our progress became more and more apparent. By midnight, we'd reached five feet down on all corners of the hole.

Less than an hour later, Jefe left, leaving the three of us under the watchful eyes of twelve of his thugs. The night was quiet and calm, the only sounds being the rhythmic crashing of our pointed shovels through the dirt, followed by a cascading thud as we threw the pile up onto the flat ground above. A few of the thugs took intermittent puffs of their Marlboros. They complained about the work, feeling the aches and pains of the long hours of manual labor take over. I was feeling it too and wished that we had an excavator.

By four in the morning, we'd reached ten feet and had to use a long metal ladder to climb in and out. After taking a break and heading back down into the hole, I struck my shovel into the dirt near the middle, expecting it to slice through the soil. But it didn't. The blade pushed only a few inches down. I raised it back up, then struck down again, this time with more force. But again the shovel stopped, and this time I heard the distinct ting of the cutting edge colliding with a piece of rock.

I'd encountered a few large rocks over the course of the evening, so I had no expectations as I dropped down and dug through the dirt. But after brushing the soil away, I saw that there was something different about that rock. It was flat, unnaturally flat, and was so wide that even after digging for a few minutes I couldn't find the end of it.

"I think I have something here," I said, my breathing labored as I continued to dig around the rock.

Soon I reached the edges of a flat, square piece of stone and found that there were more of them in place beside it.

"Holy shit!" Cesar said as he leaned over me. "That sure as hell looks man-made."

"It has to be," one of Jefe's thugs said as he motioned for more men to come over and help dig the area out. He knelt down, grazing a hand over the stone, and added, "Doesn't feel like limestone."

"It's flagstone," a voice said from the top of the hole.

It was a familiar voice. A voice I knew well but had never expected to hear at that moment. For a second, I thought my tired mind was playing tricks on me. We'd been up all night, working tirelessly without any sleep, and I knew what kind of effect that could have on your mind. It can play with you, make you feel like you're hearing and seeing things that aren't actually real. But as I turned my aching body around, I saw him standing high above, near the rim of the hole.

"Frank?" I said, squinting my eyes to get a better look.

He nodded.

"Professor Murchison was snooping around near the island yesterday," Jefe said in a sinister voice. "I was going to just kill him but decided that we could use a mind like his in this endeavor."

My heart sank in my chest as I looked up, still unable to believe what I was seeing. He must have been looking for me and been captured, and I couldn't help but wonder who else he'd been with, even though deep down I already knew the answer to that.

"Are you alright?" I asked, noticing that he had a cut on his forehead.

"Never better," he said.

"Oh, the professor here is fine," Jefe said, raising his voice and patting Frank on the back. "It's Miss Fox who I would be more concerned about."

"Where is she?" I said, my voice loud and powerful.

I looked up at Jefe, staring at him and narrowing my gaze like a carnivore eyeing its prey. For a moment, I forgot about the situation. I forgot about myself entirely and instinctively took a step closer to the thug beside me and the handgun holstered to his right leg.

Jefe, seeing that he'd struck a chord, tried to pour salt in the wound by shooting back an evil smile followed by a coarse laugh. I didn't hesitate to reply with an action of my own. In a flash of movement, I reached to the thug beside me and snatched the tan Beretta from his holster. As he tried to grab me I swung my right leg, slamming it hard into his calf muscles and causing his lower body to buckle and collapse under his weight.

A fraction of a second later, I shifted my aim up towards Jefe. His eyes grew wide and his arrogant smile left only for a moment. Just as I was about to press the trigger and send hot lead surging through his arrogant face, I heard a loud explosion followed by a slamming pain as a high-velocity beanbag freight-trained into my left pectoral muscle. It hit my body with such force that it knocked the air out of my lungs and caused my body to spin. It was a relentless and jarring pain that radiated across my chest and almost knocked me to the ground.

Before I could regain myself and take aim a second time, three thugs grabbed hold of me and forced me sternly into the dirt. I punched one of them across the face, breaking his nose as they slammed their knees into my body and ripped the Beretta out of my hands. With hands still cuffed and my face shoved in the dirt, I struggled to breathe as the pain continued, then cursed at the thugs holding me down.

As I went quiet, I heard only the thundering of my heart beating deep in my chest. As it subsided, I heard a slow and ominous clap echo down from the top of the hole. Through a dirty haze, I saw Jefe staring down at me. He'd stepped closer into the light, allowing me to see his black slacks, rolled-up dress shirt, and the half-burned cigarette sticking out of his mouth.

"A brave attempt, Mr. Dodge," he said, giving one final clap. "But too rash. If you had let me finish, I was about to tell you that she's still alive. For now, anyway." Then he looked up, raising his voice as he addressed Felix and Cesar. "But if you don't find this treasure soon, the only thing you will have accomplished this evening will be digging your own graves."

THIRTY-ONE

As the pain in my chest slowly abated, I labored to my feet with the barrels of three different guns aimed at me. I chastised myself for acting out based on my emotions and for my inability to practice self-control. For years I'd learned to take charge of such impulses, to push them aside and to listen to the voice of reason instead. I guess the days of being a captive, the long night of work, and the mention of Angelina had combined to tip me over the edge. I found myself caring and worrying about her like I'd never done for anyone before, even though I knew that she could take care of herself as well as anybody alive.

"You make a move like that again," Jefe barked as I stood tall, "and I'll personally fill your body with lead. Understand?"

I nodded my dirt-covered forehead, then turned around and stepped towards the low spot where I'd discovered the flat stones. Dropping down, I grabbed my shovel, then struck its worn cutting edge in between two of the stones. With weary arms and calloused hands, I pried up one of the flagstones, then dug my fingers under and pulled it up out of its place. It was heavy, but I made quick work of it with my adrenaline still pumping after the confrontation. I set it aside with a thud, and to my astonishment, I gazed upon a dark open space beneath where the stone had been.

I grabbed a nearby flashlight and shined it into the space. I felt like I was looking through a window into another world as I gazed into the illuminated darkness. I saw that the space below opened up much wider than I'd originally thought. Just a few feet beneath me, I saw what appeared to be an old stone staircase that led down into the darkness.

"What is it, dammit?" Jefe said, his voice a combination of agitated and intrigued.

I moved back from the opening and wiped the sweat from my brow with the top of my forearm.

I let out a deep breath and said, "It's a staircase."

I moved back as Jefe climbed down the ladder and had a look for himself. A smile came over his face as he shined his flashlight into the opening, then he glanced down at his watch. I knew that it had to be around five in the morning and that daybreak would come soon. The island wasn't exactly the biggest tourist attraction in the Keys, but it still attracted a lot of people who were interested in its history and plant life. The chances of someone wandering off on a guided tour and finding our operation was slim, but that didn't make it impossible.

"Back to work," Jefe said as he stepped away from the opening and reached for the rungs of the ladder. "I want all of these stones removed an hour

238

ago."

With aching, tired bodies, we all went back to work, digging and pulling up the flagstones one at a time and hoisting them out of the hole. After nearly an hour of sweaty, backbreaking work, we'd removed enough of the stones to climb down onto the stairs below.

"That's enough," Jefe said, shining his high-powered flashlight down into the opening we'd created.

The sun had already begun to rise, giving off an ever-brightening glow that allowed us to switch off our work lights. Jefe climbed down the ladder to the bottom of the hole alongside six armed thugs. Most of the thugs that had climbed down looked alike, and the only one that caught my eye was a monstrosity of a man who looked like Andre the Giant. I wondered if he'd even be able to fit inside he was so big.

"You first," he said, pointing a finger at me. "I may need the professor, and I want you two traitors to see this treasure before I kill you."

He motioned to Felix and Cesar, who stood beside me, then urged me forward. Clasping a flashlight awkwardly with my hands bound in front of me, I shined the light down over the ominous stone stairway. Under other circumstances, I would have been excited. Finding a long-lost pirate's treasure trove is a fantasy most everyone probably has at least some point in their life. I know I had. But something about having my hands bound, guns aimed at my back, and people I cared about in harm's way brought the thrill factor down a few pegs.

As I took my first slow step down into the darkness, Frank moved in behind me.

"Be careful," he said. "And move slow. Pirates

were notorious for leaving booby traps."

"Booby traps?" Jefe said, listening to Frank and shaking his head. "What the hell kind of traps could these guys have constructed that would last for hundreds of years and still work?"

Jefe laughed, and he was quickly joined in by a few of his men.

"I guess we'll find out," Frank said flatly. As the thugs went quiet, he looked at me and added, "Just watch your step."

I proceeded down with caution. If Frank said there would most likely be booby traps, then I knew that it was probably true. The fact that Shadow had also had a group of highly trained engineers wiggled its way into my mind too. The artifact had clearly said ten fathoms down, and we were not even half that far down. If the ten feet of dirt and thousands of pounds of flagstones were any indication of things to come, we still had a long way ahead of us.

I moved down slowly into the darkness, checking the ground and walls ahead of me before each step. The air was stale after having been stagnant for over three hundred years, and the stone steps were covered in dirt and rocks that had crumbled down while we'd dug out the stones. Frank and Jefe were right on my heels, followed closely by Cesar, Felix, and the six armed thugs.

"Looks like limestone," Frank said, shining his light on the walls. "And it appears as though they used some kind of local concrete mixture to hold them in place."

The walls looked well made, and aside from a few jutting edges and broken portions, they had remained relatively smooth even through the years. I shined my beam of light ahead and saw that the stairs

240

flattened out a short ways down, leading into what looked like a corridor of some kind.

The rubber soles of my shoes made quiet contact with the coarse stone as I reached the bottom step and looked forward. The long passageway ahead of me appeared to dead-end about fifty feet away. As I moved forward, stepping down the long corridor, Frank suddenly grabbed my shirt from behind.

"What is it?" I said, glancing over my shoulder at him. Then I motioned towards the empty tunnel ahead of us and added, "There's nothing here."

"That's what worries me," Frank said, his eyes scanning over every inch of the corridor.

"What's the holdup?" Jefe said, moving up behind me and shining his light over my shoulder. Upon seeing that the coast was clear, he added, "Come on, Dodge! Move your ass."

Frank and I ignored him, and we continued to examine the ground. In a flash of realization, he stood up tall and glanced at me.

"It's really something," he said, and I sensed that there was a part of him that was excited, even given the circumstances. "The architecture is amazing if it's true."

"If what's true?" Jefe barked. "What the hell is the holdup?"

"There are traps," Frank fired back. "Portions of the ground ahead will give way under our weight."

I kept my light forward, kept scanning over the ground until I saw it too. Some of the stones looked slightly different than the others. The variations were subtle, only noticeable upon careful examination, but they were there.

"What in the hell are you two talking about?" Jefe said, shaking his head.

I scanned my eyes over the ground ahead of us a few seconds longer, then said, "We need to bring down one of the flagstones." Before Jefe could reply, I turned back to him and added, "We need to figure out where we can and can't walk."

Jefe paused a moment, then rushed alongside us and stared down the corridor. He looked at both of us like we were crazy, then cast his gaze to the ground. After looking it over, he ordered a few of his men to head back up and grab one of the stones. When they returned a few minutes later, they handed it to me and I muscled it up against my chest.

"If you cause this place to collapse, I'm going to kill you," Jefe said.

"Right there," Frank said, pointing at a portion of the ground in the middle that I too had noticed was strange.

I grunted, and with all of my strength, I hurled the stone. Moments later it crashed into the ground, shattered the stones beneath it, and crashed into a dark pit, disappearing from view. The ground crumbled free from one side all the way to the other, and Frank and I had to step back to avoid falling into it.

The heavy stones smashed and crumbled far below us, leaving a gap in the floor. Cautiously, Frank and I stepped towards the edge of the pit. As dust settled around us, I shined my flashlight down and saw rows of menacing wooden spikes extending up like the mouth of a hungry beast roughly twenty feet below us.

"Holy shit," Jefe said, glancing over our shoulders.

After shining his light over the spikes and seeing that we still had a long ways to go to get to the end of the corridor, he turned and ordered a few of his men to bring back more of the stones. One by one, I hurled more stones as far as I could down the tunnel, revealing two more traps along the way. The pits were wide, and in order to take on the first one, I got a running start, dug my right leg hard into the ground, and hurled my body through the dark air. I landed softly on a ledge between two of the pits, my momentum nearly causing me to fall off the other side. My body leaned over the side as I tried to regain my balance. My eyes grew big as I gazed down at the sharpened points of splintered wood that waited patiently for someone to drop down and be brutally impaled.

Once I'd recovered, I did my best to help the others. The group followed behind me, making the leaps and bounds with a few close calls, but no casualties. Once we'd reached the end of the corridor, I saw that what had looked like a dead end was really a fork, with dark, narrow passageways leading both to the left and to the right. I shined my light both ways, but they looked the same to me. They each branched out for about twenty feet, then cut at a ninety-degree angle back to the north.

Jefe took charge, pushing me aside and looking in each direction.

"One of them must be a trap," one of Jefe's thugs said.

"No shit," Jefe replied. "The only question is, which one?"

He looked at Frank, expecting an answer. Frank examined both ways carefully, looking over the walls and hoping to find any kind of clue. But there was nothing.

"We can't know for sure," Frank said, feeling the

walls with his hands as he looked back and forth. "My gut tells me we should go right. Most people are right-handed, including Shadow, and a right turn in a space as narrow as this would allow them to better fight off any attackers if they were ambushed inside."

Jefe laughed and shook his head. "Well, there is one way to know for sure." He took a step back, grabbed Cesar forcefully by his handcuffs, and pushed him down the right side. "You go right, and Logan will go left." Then he paused a moment and added, "It's pirate roulette."

I faced down the corridor, shining my flashlight all around me. I didn't relish the idea of walking right into an unknown pirate booby trap but fought to keep my sense about me. I'd been in dangerous situations many times before. I'd been beaten, outnumbered, and forced to defy all odds in order to make it out alive. Calming my breath and narrowing my gaze, I stepped forward.

"Emilio," Jefe said. "Go with Logan."

The guy built like Andre the Giant strode over beside me. I nodded at Cesar, then turned, shined my light ahead, and stepped into the darkness. I felt like a mouse stepping onto the wooden portions of a trap, knowing it was likely only a matter of time before I hit the trigger and ended up at the mercy of whatever cruel device Shadow and his crew had whipped up.

The passageway was narrower than the one we'd came from, and Emilio barely managed to fit as he lumbered with loud steps behind me. When I reached the turn, I shined my flashlight around the corner and saw that the way ahead of us shot upward at a ninety-degree angle roughly twenty feet away. There appeared to be indentations carved into the stone, and as they took shape, they revealed themselves to be a makeshift ladder of some kind.

Halfway down the corridor, I stepped onto a stone that surprised me when it displaced under my weight. I pulled my leg back, but it was too late. The stone sank into the ground six inches or so, causing my senses to go on the alert and my heart to race. I heard a sound up ahead in the darkness, and just as I shined my flashlight ahead, my eyes grew wide as I saw a large dark object with spikes rocketing towards me.

In the blink of an eye, I dropped to the ground, my body sprawling out as flat as possible just as the object accelerated and whooshed right over my head. The sound of tensioned old rope and creaking timbers was quickly replaced by the loud groans of the man behind me as the object crashed into his chest. His massive body hadn't reacted as quickly as mine, and twisting my head back, I watched from just a few feet away as wooden spikes drove through his chest and slammed him against the wall behind us. His groans went quiet in an instant and his body went lifeless. Blood flowed down and pooled beneath his feet as I slowly rose from my position, scanning the light around me to make sure that that was the only trap.

Jefe called out from down the other corridor and I heard footsteps moving in my direction. I looked at the large object closely for the first time and realized that it was a wooden log, probably part of a ship's mast, with sharp wooden spikes sticking out of it in all directions. The log was attached to old ropes that extended up and out of sight around the corner, making the trap invisible from our angle as we approached.

I moved back towards the group just as they arrived and gazed upon the horrific scene.

"Well, I guess we know which is the right way now," Jefe said in a hard and unaffected tone. Then he motioned to me and added, "You're leading the way again."

I stepped through the narrow space between the bloodied dead guy and the wall, then moved past the group. Frank was looking at the corpse and the device that had killed him in amazement. I too was hard-pressed to believe that such a trap, built hundreds of years ago, would still spring today and function as it was intended to.

Heading in the other direction, I noticed a few differences to the corridor on the other side. The main one was that it was slightly wider and, once I made the turn around the corner, I saw that the way led down another set of steps instead of up. I moved slowly through the dark chamber that was quickly becoming a house of horrors. With light steps, I headed down the small staircase that only had four steps. At the bottom, the space opened up into a room with skeletons sprawled out at the corners and strange paintings on the walls. On one of the walls, the word *Traitors* was written in big black letters.

At the far end, there was a massive stone wall with a small space to the right of it. As we approached the wall, it quickly became clear that it was a door of some kind and that it sat loose from the rest of the structures around it. I stepped towards the space, which was only about six inches wide, and shined my light through.

"What's in there?" Jefe barked as he moved up right behind me.

I didn't reply. Instead, I just stared in amazement at the piles of old wooden chests stacked on top of each other against a far wall. Part of me couldn't believe what I was seeing. There had to be at least a hundred of them and they were each just as large as the one I'd pulled out of the seafloor a few days earlier.

Jefe pushed me aside and looked through. A smile came across his face as he shined his light back and forth, gazing upon the riches of Captain Shadow.

THIRTY-TWO

Angelina woke up on a bed in a small dark room with her hands cuffed behind her back. The mattress was soft and the room was quiet. Once the hint of grogginess faded from her mind, her eyes went big and she sat up instantly.

Where am I? she thought as she took a look around the room.

There wasn't much to it, just the bed she was on, a curtain covered window to her right, and two shut wooden doors.

Shifting her legs around, she scooted off the bed and came to her feet. The last thing she could remember was being chased on the Baia by a boat full of thugs. *And the dart*, she thought, pausing a moment as she remembered being struck by a high-speed tranquilizer dart shot from the rifle one of the thugs had been carrying.

Rage burned within her as she tried each of the

doorknobs, knowing that the doors would be locked before she'd even grabbed hold of them. When she found herself unable to turn the knobs, Angelina took a moment to think through her situation. She was on the *Yellow Rose*. She had no doubt about that, and she was being held hostage by Black Venom, one of the most notoriously ruthless drug cartels in the world. *Logan is probably close by*, she thought, *and the others as well*.

If they aren't already dead, she thought, reminding herself of the dark but highly probable possibility.

She had to move; she couldn't stay there and just wait like a useless captive or damsel in distress. The old stories she'd read as a child where the girl gets rescued by the prince had always made her mad. The girl just sitting by and waiting to be saved usually caused her to throw the book across the room, and it was a mentality she'd never had. No, Angelina was usually the one doing the saving, and the last thing she was going to do was just sit by and wait for something to happen.

She turned her attention to the two doors, and once she'd decided which door led into the passageway instead of a head, she went to work. It was a well-constructed one-and-three-quarter-inch-thick maple door, with a steel handle and locking device, as well as steel hinges that allowed the door to swing inward. She wouldn't be able to kick it open, and the handle design meant that picking the outside lock was out of the question. But grazing her hands over the metal plate holding the handle in place, she got an idea.

Turning around, she scanned the dark room and spotted a few drawers built into the nightstand beside the bed. After searching through them, she found a stack of hairpins, grabbed one, and moved back to the door. She bent the small piece of metal then stuck it into the grooves of the Phillips head and began to twist.

The first few movements were the hardest, but once it started to go, the screw revolved easily out of place. It was slow and difficult with her hands bound behind her back, but one by one, she removed all of the screws, gathered them up, and put them in the drawer beside the rest of the hairpins.

She then jimmied off the cover plate and wedged one of its edges into the deadbolt mechanism. Leaning her weight against the plate, she forced the deadbolt loose, then slid it out of the door frame. Setting the plate aside, she listened quietly, then slowly opened the door.

She peeked through at a dimly lit hallway and then pulled the door open just enough to fit through. She stepped out, and a second later, she paused as she spotted a guy standing and leaning against the port hallway paneling. He had a revolver strapped to his waist. His arms were crossed in front of him, and his eyes were closed, with his head bent sideways.

Angelina didn't hesitate. With light steps, she strode towards him. She'd fought with her hands bound behind her back before. It wasn't easy, but as with all fights, she knew that the key was to strike first and disable your opponent as quickly as possible.

Twisting her body, she threw her bound hands over the unsuspecting thug's head, then bent her elbows with all her strength, squeezing his neck tightly. Just as the thug woke up and realized he was in a fight, Angelina bent her knees, jerked her body sideways, and slammed his head into the deck. He grunted in pain, dazed from the hard hit to his head, then gagged and struggled to free himself as Angelina flexed her arms wrapped around his neck.

Within a few seconds, his struggling stopped and he lay motionless beside her. Knowing their scuffle would have undoubtedly drawn the attention of other nearby thugs, Angelina quickly rose to her feet and pulled his body through the open doorway, into the room she'd come from. Moments later, as if her intuition had summoned them, she heard heavy footsteps moving quickly down the passageway just forward of her cabin.

She dragged the big thug around the bed, where he could be relatively out of sight, then snatched his revolver and crawled on top of the messy bed. When the two guys reached her cabin, they examined the open door momentarily, then stepped inside. Both of them were surprised when all they saw was Angelina lying on her back with her eyes closed, appearing to be sound asleep.

"Where the fuck is Jose?" one of the guys said to the other.

The other guy didn't reply. He could sense that something strange was going on, and he reached for the Beretta holstered to his waist and held it out in front of him. He moved in towards the bed, hovering over Angelina as her chest moved slowly up and down. When he was just a few feet above her, she made her move.

In a flash of movement, she shot her legs into the air and wrapped them forcefully around the guy's neck. Before the thug could do anything but gasp, she jerked her legs hard in opposite directions, causing his neck to crack, then flung him as hard as she could sideways into the window beside her.

Thug number two reached for his piece. Angelina, still gripping the revolver in her right hand, turned her body around and fired two rounds into his chest before his fingers had even reached the handgrip of his weapon. Blood splattered out from his shirt, and his body lurched backward, collapsing and slamming into the far wall.

With both thugs down for the count, Angelina slid off the bed and jumped to her feet. The two loud explosions of gunpowder had shaken the cabin and adjoining passageway to life, and she knew that she only had a short window to act before another handful of thugs descended upon her.

As quickly as she could, Angelina searched the corpses and found a jingling set of keys in the front pants pocket of the guy she'd filled with lead. She recognized instantly the type of key she wanted, grabbed hold of it, and freed herself from the handcuffs. Then she snatched the Beretta from the thug whose neck she'd snapped with both hands and moved towards the cabin door.

Hearing footsteps grow louder as they moved in her direction down the hallway, she waited in the dark shadows behind the door frame. An Uzi appeared first through the door, and she kicked the arm holding it. The thug held down the trigger, sending a stream of bullets into the ceiling as Angelina moved into view, held the thug's hand up with hers, and sent a bullet exploding into his face. His life vanished in a mess of blood and bone, and Angelina used him as a human shield as she stepped into the passageway.

The two other thugs running towards her opened fire, shooting rounds into their dead buddy as Angelina snuck her Beretta around his body and pulled the trigger. She hit the first guy in the hip, causing him to tumble over awkwardly and slam into the ground near her feet. She hit the second guy in the shoulder, causing his body to spin, then shot him again in the back.

Letting go of the dead guy in her arms and allowing his body to collapse beside her, she finished off the other two, then bent down, grabbed a full magazine, and quickly exchanged it with the one in her Beretta that was almost spent. Once locked and loaded, she ran for a set of stairs at the end of the passageway. Her heart was pounding, her adrenaline surging. She had no way of knowing how many more cartel were on board or where they were keeping Logan. She just knew that she had to find him, Frank, and Jack at all costs.

She approached the stairs slowly and with the Beretta gripped with two hands in front of her. She made quick work of the steps, and when she reached the top, she gasped as she took aim at a shadowy figure that stood just a few feet in front of her. She didn't know how one of the thugs had managed to sneak up on her, but she didn't have time to ponder the situation.

As she raised her Beretta towards the cartel, he suddenly sprang towards her. Before she could pull the trigger, he slid to the side and knocked the weapon from her hands with a strong left hook. As it rattled to the floor, Angelina retaliated by planting her left foot and swinging her right leg into the air towards her opponent. He tried to move, but her leg jammed hard into his side and caused him to grunt quietly.

The man kept his balance, grabbed her by the leg, and hurled her to the floor. Her blood boiling and her anger rising, she brought her right arm back, preparing to slam her fist into the face of the guy, who'd clearly had much more hand-to-hand combat training than she'd initially expected. But before throwing her fist, she saw the guy's face for the first time through the light bleeding through a nearby window curtain.

"Ange?" he said, gasping for air as his arm muscles still held her down.

For a moment, she thought her mind was playing tricks on her.

"Scott?" she said, shaking her head. He loosened his grip, kneeling on the deck beside her as she sat up. "What are you doing here?"

He rose to his feet, then held out a hand to help her up as well. He looked back and forth, making sure there weren't any other cartel nearby. He was wearing a pair of black tactical pants, a dark gray long-sleeved shirt, and a bulletproof vest. His short dark hair was wet, and he had a thin layer of black paint over his face.

"I'm here for you guys," he said in his serious and authoritative voice. "When Pete called and told me you, Jack, and Frank had been taken too, I knew I had to come down and help out."

She stared at him, still in disbelief.

"But how did you find us?"

He smiled slightly and pointed at the watch strapped to her left wrist.

"I told you," he said. "I put a tracker in it a year ago."

She glanced down at her black-and-silver Suunto Core digital dive watch, then smiled. She'd completely forgotten about her conversation with him back when Logan had first disappeared.

"Where are the others?" Scott asked, glancing at

the stairs behind Angelina. "I only saw Black Venom up here."

Angelina shrugged. "I don't know. I just woke up a few minutes ago." She looked beyond the former Naval officer and saw a cluster of bodies sprawled out on the deck behind him. "Jeez, how many guys did you take out?"

He blew off her question and said, "We need to find them. Let's search all of the rooms and then head to shore."

She looked back at him, confused. "Shore? Wait, is this still moored alongside Lignumvitae Key?"

"Yep. And a helicopter took off just a few minutes ago when I arrived, heading for the island. The yacht's skiff is missing as well. Any idea what they're doing here?"

Angelina shook her head and said, "No." Then she thought it over a moment and added, "Unless…"

"Unless what?"

She paused a moment, staring down the hallway, lost in thought.

"You remember that pirate treasure we told you about?" she said a few seconds later.

"Yeah, why?"

She looked back at him, waiting for it to click. When it did, his eyes grew wide and he motioned down the stairs.

"We need to move!" he said, striding alongside her with his Glock raised chest height.

THIRTY-THREE

My excitement upon seeing Shadow's lost treasure for the first time was trumped by the voice in the back of my mind, reminding me that we were captives. Now that we'd found the treasure, I knew that there would no longer be any reason for Jefe to keep us alive. I watched him closely as he peered through the opening in the stone and shined his light upon the stacks of wooden chests, ready to make my move at a moment's notice if necessary.

He turned back to us, tongued a wad of dip from the corner of his cheek, and spat it into the corner beside him. He had a stern and all-business air to him as he stepped towards us.

"Shove that wall aside," he said to no one in particular.

A few of his big thugs stepped forward, but before they'd reached the wall, Frank sprang towards them and said, "Wait!" The two thugs froze in their tracks as Frank moved beside them. "There's markings on the wall here." He pointed to parts of the wall that were covered in strange dark symbols, and part of the wall that was carved out.

"What the fuck do I care about symbols?" Jefe barked. "Look, Professor, we found the treasure. You can just can it with all the history crap now, 'cause we don't need it."

Frank ignored him as he looked over the wall, scanning his flashlight as he moved his way down to the other side of it. Jefe, growing frustrated, ordered his men to move the wall.

"It's load-bearing," Frank said. "If you move that wall, then the ceiling will cave in on us. It's another trap."

Reluctantly, Jefe called off his men and moved over beside Frank.

"See?" Frank said. "There are handholds carved in here. It was a final attempt to keep outsiders from reaching the treasure."

Reluctantly, Jefe conceded and ordered his men to push the wall in the other direction. His thugs stepped over and, grabbing hold of the wall, slowly slid it over to the right. It took a while to get it going, but once the space was large enough, we all moved in and helped push it out of the way. Frank had been right. Despite a few disconcerting shakes and crumbles of dirt and rock, the ceiling hadn't budged. With the wall pushed aside, we now had a four-foot-wide opening leading into the treasure room.

Jefe stepped in first, shining his light around the room. Even he wasn't able to keep his excitement from showing. It was a large space, roughly thirty feet wide, fifty feet deep, and ten feet tall. Most of it was covered with stacks of old chests, ranging in style and size.

I was amazed at how, after all these years, the room had managed to remain so intact. There were a few areas where the stones had crumbled loose or water had seeped in and mildewed, but for the most part, I imagined that the room looked much like it had back when it was constructed.

Jefe and his thugs gravitated towards the chests as if possessed. The leader of Black Venom slid his hands over one of the larger ones, then lifted its old squeaky lid, revealing a massive pile of gold and silver coins mixed with uncut rubies and emeralds. His face contorted into a smile as he grabbed a handful of the treasure, then slowly let the pieces fall from his hand and jingle against each other. I reasoned that in that one chest alone, there was probably over ten million dollars' worth of treasure. Looking around the room, I couldn't tell how many chests there were but estimated close to fifty.

It was a bittersweet moment. Finding Shadow's long-lost treasure should have been one of the most exciting moments of my life, but our present circumstance cast a dark cloud over it all, and all I could think about was how and when to make our move. Timing is key in any skirmish, especially one where your enemy has you severely outnumbered and outgunned.

Felix and Cesar had both been uncharacteristically quiet ever since we'd entered the structure. Felix was still banged up from his confrontation with Jefe. He had cuts across his face and moved with painful, labored steps. Cesar too had been beaten up pretty bad when Jefe had first arrived. Backstabbing in the notorious drug cartel is an unforgivable crime, almost always punished with a painful death. They looked defeated, and I knew that if Frank and I were going to have any chance of getting out of this, we'd need their help.

We stood in silence as Jefe and his thugs went through the chests, then gazed in awe at the rest of the room. After spending less than a minute admiring what we'd found, Jefe turned back to us and ordered that the treasure be loaded up into the helicopter. He was a hard man who didn't mess around and didn't like wasting time. He put us into groups, with Frank and me carrying chests back and forth together, and Felix and Cesar doing the same. We were escorted by two thugs each, and the rest of the thugs joined in the work.

It was difficult, tiresome, and slow going. The chests had to weigh over a hundred pounds each, and navigating along the corridors and up the old stairs wasn't easy. Jefe had called more of his thugs to help with the load. They tied a handful of metal rung ladders across the main long corridor, allowing us to traverse its dangerous surface without falling through and becoming human kabobs.

My calloused hands and my weary muscles screamed in pain, but I pushed through it as Frank and I carried the first chest up into the light of the hole we'd dug. The sun had risen fully off to the east, its light glowing through the overcast sky and allowing us to see a group of Jefe's thugs and the dark blue Mil Mi-38 transport helicopter parked above with its large side door wide open.

They used ropes to bring up the chest the rest of the way, then ordered us to go back down for another. Slowly and carefully, Frank and I made our way back towards the treasure room, avoiding the other groups as they labored by along the way. As we stepped across the ladders, Frank moved close behind me.

"Please tell me you have a plan here?" he whispered as we creaked from rung to rung like mountaineers traversing an icefall.

"Making it up as I go along," I said. "But I'm open to ideas."

Frank went quiet for a moment, then, when we reached the end of the final ladder he said, "I may have something. But it's reckless, and the odds of its success rival a game of roulette."

I laughed softly, though only for a moment. The two thugs Jefe had ordered to follow us were watching us like hawks. They were some of the best fighters in Black Venom, Jefe's personal guards, and I knew that they meant business. A confrontation with any of them would take more than just a few strong blows, and I knew that they were the type of hardened men who would capitalize on any mistake we made.

"I love it," I said when we reached the fork and turned right.

Frank and I continued our quiet and concise conversation while hauling the rest of the chests back and forth. We all knew that the helicopter wouldn't be able to carry all of it along with his men, but no one questioned Jefe. He had evil in his eyes, cruelty in his heart, and a short temper. A particularly dangerous combination of traits.

Frank and I moved our fatigued bodies into the treasure chamber and stepped towards one of the last remaining chests. Over the past half hour, we'd been able to pass along a few words to both Felix and Cesar about our plan, but neither of them had given more than a simple nod in return. I didn't know what they were going through or if they were with us, but regardless if they were or not, one thing was certain: I sure as hell wasn't about to be murdered by a bunch of thugs without putting up a fight. And I didn't care how high the odds were stacked against us.

Jefe was still standing stoically in the chamber, barking out orders and yelling at us to go faster. We kept our eyes forward as we moved to opposite sides of a chest that was slightly larger and had a drastically different color than the rest. Instead of dark wood with aged iron hasps, the chest had a lighter color and was adorned with diamonds. It was also resting on top of a large flagstone that only Frank had initially noticed. It was difficult to distinguish it from the floor surrounding it, but once Frank had pointed it out, it became obvious what it was.

"Stop!" Jefe yelled, causing Frank and me to freeze in place.

He then ordered us to move along the far wall, away from the chests. I shot a glance at Frank, knowing that whether intentionally or not, Jefe was throwing a wrench into our plans. We'd just placed our hands on the chest, but as Jefe eyed us, we let go and did as he said. My mind went to work, strategizing and trying to figure out what we should do. Striking fast and hard would be key. Trying to take them by surprise would be vital to our success.

"My men will take it from here," Jefe continued in a hard, arrogant tone. "You guys have been a lot of help."

He laughed as Felix and Cesar labored into the chamber. Aiming his revolver at them, he forced them to stand beside us. Jefe and eight of his thugs stood across from us, and for a second I thought that he was going to try and kill us all by firing squad.

"As much as I would like to take you down one by one right now," Jefe said, "I have a different fate in mind." He panned his revolver slowly back and forth, then added, "Like Shadow's traitors who he left behind, you too shall remain here forever." He stepped towards us, then trained his revolver on Felix. "Felix Callejo. One of my oldest and most trusted companions. A man I first met as a boy in Tlapehuala." He moved right into Felix's face. "I saved your life back then, and this is how you repay me?"

I saw emotion on Felix's face for the first time since we'd arrived on the island. A sudden and powerful rage took over. His eyes narrowed, his jaw clenched, and a vein pulsed visibly on his forehead.

"You saved me?" Felix said, still gasping for air from the long hours of heavy labor. "You murdered my entire family," he continued, raising his voice. "You killed them right in front of me, and you threatened to do the same to me if I didn't join in."

"And you didn't!" Jefe barked. "It was your initiation and you failed. You should have died that day in the mud right alongside them. I'm the only reason you were spared."

"You're a monster," Felix fired back. "You're a fucking—"

Felix was interrupted by an ear-rattling explosion and a hot rocket of lead that struck him right in the chest. His body lurched backward, and he grunted in pain as the .44 Magnum round exploded out the back of his body in a large spray of blood. He fell to the ground, overtaken with pain, and I knew that, in all likelihood, he only had a couple seconds of life left.

Anger swelled within me as I watched him. I looked at Jefe, who still had his smoking revolver raised at Felix. He showed no emotion except a sadistic satisfaction.

With an evil smile on his face, Jefe said, "That's what you deserve, Felix. To die here painfully in this dark cave that has become all of your tombs."

He turned to his thugs and ordered that the two remaining chests be carried out and loaded into the helicopter. Time slowed as they reached down to grab the large chest Frank and I had gone for before. My eyes went from Felix to Jefe, and to Frank as two thugs grabbed its handholds. I didn't know what was going to happen, and neither did Frank. He only knew that it was a final booby trap, Shadow's last effort to rain down retribution from the grave upon anyone who tried to steal his treasure.

Without the slightest inkling of what they were doing, the two thugs lifted the chest from its place. For a split second, nothing happened. I wondered if maybe we'd been wrong, but my thoughts were instantly silenced when the large, flat flagstone the chest had been resting on moments before began to move.

Everyone in the chamber froze and turned their attention to the movement and sound. Even the two thugs who'd lifted the chest froze and stared as the stone shook and then began to rise up out of the floor. Its movements were slow at first but gradually sped up until we realized that the stone was a long, wide pillar instead of a normal part of the floor.

"What the fuck is happening?" Jefe barked as he stared at the rising slab of rock.

As Jefe and his thugs stood frozen and stared as if entranced by the movement, Frank and I glanced at each other, then stepped towards a pair of Jefe's thugs that had their backs to us. Part of me wanted to kneel down and help Felix. He had his head down and was struggling to breathe and move. But I knew that if we didn't act now, we'd end up just like him. Cesar, seeing what we were doing, moved in as well, trying to flank them from behind.

I glanced in amazement as the stone continued to rise. It was sticking out over three feet and moving faster and faster with each passing second. Just as I reached within arm's length of one of the thugs, the silence and anticipation inside the chamber shattered in an instant. A loud and powerful hissing sound filled the air as if a large water pipe had spontaneously ruptured. My eyes darted over to the pillar of rock, focusing on a spray of water bursting out from its edges and splashing into the walls and the thugs beside it.

My mind raced, reminding me that we were probably sixty feet underground on an island that is nineteen feet above sea level. The rock was still moving, the water gushing out intensely, and the realization came over everyone in the chamber that we'd all soon be underwater if we didn't get the hell out of there. With my hands still bound behind me and with all of the thugs focused on the spraying water, I made my move.

Stepping towards the nearest thug, I snatched the Taurus 9mm from his hip holster, then planted my right foot, spun around quickly and kicked him in the neck. His head whipped forward and his eyes bulged while his body flew backward and slammed into the ground. Just as he hit the ground, I took aim with the Taurus, firing two rounds into the second thug beside me and sending him screaming to the ground.

For a fraction of a second, I glanced over at Frank and Cesar, who'd sprung into action just after I had. They each managed to take down a thug as well, leaving four not including Jefe. Upon seeing what was happening and hearing the gunshots over the loud spraying water, Jefe made a break for the opening leading out of the chamber. Time slowed as Jefe's remaining thugs ran behind their leader, trying to escape the room, which already had over two feet of water. They turned back occasionally, sending bullets flying wildly in our direction.

Aiming the Taurus as best as I could with my hands bound behind me, I fired off a few shots into the swarm of thugs running through the narrow opening, then dove for cover. My body splashed into the warm seawater, and I crawled as fast as I could toward Felix, who was still lying motionless. Bullets rang out from all directions as Jefe and his thugs opened fire, then disappeared from view. Frank and Cesar managed to take a few more out as I brought my cuffed hands under my feet to the front of my body and helped Felix. He was still breathing, but in erratic and short gasps. Blood dripped out from his chest as I helped him to his feet, then forced him to move as fast as he could towards the opening.

The pillar stopped suddenly and the large spray of water turned into a row of open fire hydrants, causing the water to rise expeditiously. I held on to Felix, helping him splash through the water beside me as the water level rose up around us. It was just above our waists by the time we reached the opening alongside Frank and Cesar.

Once out of the treasure chamber and into the adjacent room, we glanced around momentarily for any sign of Jefe or his thugs. We couldn't see anyone and couldn't hear anything over the sound of the roaring waters behind us. Holding tight to our weapons and helping Felix to stay on his feet, we moved as fast as we could away from the water and towards the small set of stairs on the other side of the room.

By the time we reached it, the water almost overtook us completely. For a moment I thought we'd have to swim out of the tunnels, then the sole of my shoes struck the first step and the four of us heaved up away from the water.

As we lumbered up the steps, the rising water slowed behind us. When we reached the top step, we were able to catch our breath for the first time. Looking forward, we still saw no sign of Jefe or any of his men. Looking back, we saw that, though its ferocity had died a little, the water would still overtake us in a matter of seconds if we didn't move.

With soaked clothes and weary bodies, we used the surge of adrenaline to press on through the tunnels. When we reached the fork, I spotted movement up ahead. It was one of Jefe's thugs and he was running towards the long corridor, about to disappear from view. I didn't hesitate. Still gripping the Taurus, I raised it and fired off two rounds as fast as I could. The bullets struck the running thug in the leg and the side of his chest, causing him to yell in pain as he tumbled forward and collapsed onto the ground just out of our view around the corner.

I led the way, keeping my Taurus locked in as I moved around the edge of the rock. The distant rushing water made it difficult to hear anything going on up ahead, so I wanted to be prepared for the worst.

My eyes grew wide as the long corridor came into view. Less than twenty feet in front of me, I saw two big thugs facing me with their weapons raised. I only had a fraction of a second to react, and in that time I squeezed the trigger over and over, sending a series of bullets straight towards them as I yelled for the others to stop and dove to the ground for cover. They pulled their triggers as well just as the rounds struck their bodies. The long dark corridor came to life with loud, pounding automatic gunfire. Bullets streaked through the air just over my head, ricocheting against the tunnel wall behind me.

I landed hard on the rock and contorted my body into a roll before hitting the side of the tunnel. Keeping my eyes trained forward, I watched as both thugs fell backward, still holding the triggers and sending streams of bullets across the ceiling as they slammed into the ground and went motionless. I could hear my heart pounding in my chest as I scanned over the rest of the corridor, ready for more stragglers to appear.

When I turned back to look at the others, my eyes grew wide as I saw dark figures reveal themselves from the shadows. With all of my attention drawn forward, I hadn't even looked down the other side of the fork, where the swinging log full of spikes had ended the massive thug's life less than an hour before. There, out of the darkness, appeared Jefe alongside three of his men.

In an instant, his three men sprang out and grabbed hold of Frank and Cesar, catching us all off guard. With Felix struggling to stay on his feet right behind me, I spun to aim my Taurus at Jefe, knowing that I only had one round left and I needed to make it count. But before I could take him out, he fired, sending a round into the rock wall just inches over my head.

"Drop the fucking gun!" Jefe shouted while aiming his Magnum straight at my head.

I froze in place, staring back into his eyes and contemplating whether to take my chances and try and take him out.

Seeing me pause momentarily, he stepped closer and repeated the order. His thugs held tightly to Frank and Cesar and ripped the weapons from their hands. We were caught off guard, and my mind went to work, trying to think of a way out of it.

I watched closely as Jefe's finger moved slightly, starting to squeeze the trigger of his Magnum, which was still locked on to my head. With a slow movement, I released the Taurus, letting it drop and clatter against the flat rock at my feet. Felix collapsed to the ground in front of me. He was so weak and disoriented from the loss of blood that Jefe didn't bother to have anyone grab hold of him.

Jefe shot me an evil smile as he glanced at the Taurus at my feet.

"You're a bunch of reckless fools," he said sternly. "Well, before you all die, just know that you handed us a treasure on a silver plate. The treasure is ours, and now... now it's time for you all to die."

Time slowed as I debated what to do next. I had to do something, I convinced myself. Jefe would kill us all, and I wasn't about to go down without a fight.

I bent my knees slightly, preparing to dive to the side in order to avoid Jefe's round. But, catching me by surprise, he suddenly pulled the trigger. Keeping my eyes trained forward, I realized that Felix had positioned himself in front of me. As the dark air shook and the loud explosion overtook my senses, Felix sprang forward, rotating his body around and blocking the line of sight between Jefe and me.

The bullets struck Felix's torso as I dove to the right. I didn't have time to wonder why he'd done it. No, he'd surprised everyone and given me an opportunity I wasn't about to waste. Jefe continued to pull the trigger like a madman as I landed into a somersault, then twisted my body around in a flash and slammed my leg into his hands. The loud, repetitive gunpowder explosions ceased as his Magnum flew into the air and rattled onto the ground over near the edge of one of the pits. Sliding my left leg around, I hit him hard in the calf, causing his body to collapse backward and hit the ground with a loud thud.

Before I could rise to my feet, the thug beside him lunged towards me and wrapped his meaty hands around my neck. Grabbing hold of his wrists, I jerked my body back, dug my heels into his chest and hurled him over me. His massive frame flew through the air and crashed onto the ground, causing him to grunt loudly as he tumbled, barely able to stop his momentum from hurtling him over the edge and to a painful death at the bottom of the pit.

I glanced over at Frank and Cesar, watching as they fought to overtake the two men who had been holding them in place moments earlier. I wanted to help them but didn't have time as Jefe jumped to his feet and sprinted towards his Magnum on the ground.

I ran after him, reaching his back just as he bent down to grab the weapon. Without hesitating, I grabbed him forcefully by the collar of his dirty black dress shirt, jerked him back, and slammed him into the wall beside us. He grunted in pain, twisted his body around, and threw a strong fist through the air. I moved sideways, narrowly escaping the path of knuckles and rage. As I turned to send a punch myself, he transitioned quickly and struck me in the side with his knee.

It hurt bad, but I didn't show it or pause for a second. Instead, I forced myself behind him, dropped down, and lifted him over my head like he was a barbell and I was going for a heavy squat. Before he knew what was happening, I bent forward and slammed him hard into the ground like a WWE wrestler. It felt good to bring pain to such an evil guy, and moments after he landed, I kicked him across the face, causing his nose to crack and splatter blood over the stone floor.

With the cartel leader struggling in pain at my feet, I looked up just in time to see the big guy I'd kicked across the room as he sprinted straight towards me. I had only a brief moment to brace for impact before he ran into me like a freight train. Tackling me at full speed, he knocked the air out of my lungs as I flew backward in a haze. Tumbling onto the hard ground, I pressed my hands beneath me and struggled to stop myself before reaching the edge.

Before I could blink, he was on top of me, rearing his massive arms back and pounding them towards my face. The first blow skinned the side of my cheek, and the second I was able to fully deflect, causing his knuckles to grind into the stone less than an inch away from my left ear. As his body shifted sideways, I held his arm in place then jammed my left hand into his neck. His head jerked forward and the air burst free from his lungs. With all of my strength, I forced him off me, grabbed a nearby loose stone, and slammed it across his head. His body went motionless beside me, right on the edge of the trap.

As I turned to look for the others, I saw Jefe reach down and grab hold of his Magnum just a few feet away from me. I saw Jefe's face in the darkness. His eyes were narrowed, his jaw clenched, and there was blood dripping down from his broken nose. For the first time since I'd met him, his lips didn't bow to

270

form their typical evil smile. Instead, he looked only pissed off beyond belief as he raised his piece towards me. I knew that if he managed to get a shot off, the force from the blow alone would knock me over the edge, which was just inches behind my heels.

Fractions of a second stretched thin as I quickly reared back the rock that I'd used to take out the big guy resting in a heap of blood beside me. It was my only chance. But before I could hurl it towards the cartel leader, I saw his right index finger begin to flex.

As fast as I could, I shifted my upper body to the left, trying desperately to avoid the bullet's path of destruction. The loud, shaking sound of a gunshot filled the air and I expected my life to end there in a flash of bright light in the dark corridor. As I landed on my side I heard a painful yell and realized that I hadn't been hit. Jefe still stood beside me, but his revolver rattled to his feet as he stared at his bloody, mangled hands.

My eyes darted towards the back of the corridor, where I saw two figures walking out from the shadows. Cesar stepped into the light of one of the flashlights that had fallen to the ground, followed closely behind by Frank. I hadn't been able to help them since the start of the fight, but clearly they'd been able to take down the two cartels they'd been with without too much trouble.

As they stepped towards us, Jefe's face filled with rage. He shouted violently and pressed his hands against his chest as blood continued to flow out from under them. Since we hadn't moved far down the tunnel, the inrushing water grew louder just behind us. I could tell it was about to reach Felix and Frank and watched as they turned slightly to see the water

271

reach their feet.

Suddenly, Jefe snapped his head up to look at me. Channeling every ounce of strength and anger he had left, he dove towards me. I only had a split second to prepare myself before he crashed into me, tackling me onto the hard ground and causing my body to tumble over the edge. With the corner pressed against my chest, I was barely able to stop myself from falling to my death.

Jefe yelled at me, cursed at me as I tried to stay up. As I deflected one of his punches, I saw the faint glimmer of metal peeking out from his waistband. I knew what it was and reached for it as Jefe transformed into a mass of personified rage. Wrapping my right hand around the handle, I snatched the old dagger, brought it back a few inches, and stabbed it as hard as I could into his neck.

Blood gushed out, and his eyes grew wide as the blade sliced all the way through to the other side. With all of my remaining strength, I pulled myself up onto the ledge, rose to my feet, then grabbed ahold of his bloodied body. He made eye contact with me, and I could see the life draining out of him by the light of Frank's flashlight.

Tilting my head in closer, I said, "Black Venom is over."

Before he could struggle to get out a reply, I dug my heels into the stone, gripped his body tightly and hurled him over the edge. His wails and gagging lasted only a moment longer before being silenced forever as his body was pierced by rows of scattered wooden spikes.

With my gaze drawn to the edge of the trap and my right hand wrapped around the handle of the dagger, which dripped with Jefe's blood, I gave out a brief sigh of relief.

"We've got to get out of here," Frank said, running up beside me and placing a hand on my shoulder.

He held a set of keys in his left hand, and less than a minute later he used it to remove all three of our handcuffs. I wrapped my hands around my wrists, happy to finally have them free after so many hours bound together.

Bending down, I grabbed a flashlight from the ground, then scanned it around until I found Jefe's revolver. Moving over to it, I gripped it with one hand and joined the others. As we walked over the first creaky metal ladder, I shined the beam of the flashlight downward. Twenty feet below me, I saw the bodies of Jefe, Felix, and the three other thugs. I was relieved to see that Jefe had finally met his end but felt an unusual pang of sadness upon seeing Felix. Though only days earlier he'd been my captor, a man who I would have killed without a moment's pause, he had become something more.

When we reached the end of the corridor and took the first few steps, our eyes grew wide as we heard the sound of gunshots echoing from up ahead. The three of us glanced at each other, then picked up the pace, taking the old stairs three at a time before coming to a stop and peeking through the opening above.

We switched our flashlights off and stealthily crawled out through the opening in the flagstone and into the dirt. The gunshots persisted, rattling over the morning air as we glanced up at the top of the hole. When we didn't see anyone, we turned and strode for the ladder. I reached it first, grabbing the rungs and moving up as quickly and quietly as I could. Still holding Jefe's revolver in my right hand, I reached the top and aimed it over the edge, ready to fire at a moment's notice. My eyes darted back and forth, and I saw a handful of Jefe's thugs lying dead in the dirt surrounding the same dark blue Mil Mi-38 transport helicopter Jefe had arrived on the previous day.

I watched as the few remaining thugs still on their feet ran for cover, only to be struck down by their unknown enemies in the dense jungle surrounding them. Bullets struck them from all directions, and within seconds they were all gone. The scene turned ghostly quiet as I kept to cover at the edge of the hole. I felt uneasy coming out and letting my guard down with so many unknown soldiers surrounding me.

My trepidations were quelled in an instant as I saw the figure of a woman appear from the jungle, followed closely behind by two men. Even from so far away, I could tell instantly that it was Ange, Scott, and Jack.

For the first time in what felt like ages, a smile came over my face. I grabbed onto the top rungs and stepped up onto the dirt-covered surface. After a quick look around to make sure they'd taken down all of the bad guys, I dropped my revolver to the dirt and ran over to Ange. She ran as well, her face lighting up like the fireworks we'd watched while moored beside Islamorada on New Year's Eve.

My heart pounded in excitement as she jumped into my arms. I held her close, wrapping my dirty arms around her lower body and propping her in the air. Even tired and covered in sweat, she looked amazing, and I didn't waste a second before I locked my lips to hers. For a few seconds, the whole world faded and it was just the two of us in all of existence.

I reveled in the passion of the moment and the warmth of her body against mine.

I didn't know how much time had passed when I finally lowered her back to the ground. She shifted her head back, slid a few stray strands of blond hair from her tanned face, and looked up at me with her beautiful blue eyes.

"That's the last time I'll ever leave you alone again," she said, smiling playfully.

She was joking, I knew. But there was something in her eyes, something in her mannerisms and tone of voice that made me realize there was a deeper meaning to her words. In the heat of the moment, I didn't know what to say back, so I smiled back at her and wrapped my arms around her lean, sexy frame.

THIRTY-FOUR

It wasn't until late afternoon that I was finally able to get away and get some rest. I was tired. More tired than I'd been since my adrenaline-filled rampage on Loggerhead Key last August. With the Baia in the boatyard for repairs, I rode in the passenger seat of my Tacoma as Ange drove us over to my house on Palmetto Street.

Turning into the gravel driveway, she parked under the stilted light gray house with white trim, and we both stepped out. Heading up the stairs on the right side, we reached the wraparound porch, and I took a quick peek out the back, making sure that everything was in order and nothing looked unusual before I disengaged the security system and we stepped inside.

I felt like I hadn't been home in forever. I realized that it had been a few weeks, since I'd spent every night on either the Baia or the *Calypso* while looking for the pirate wreck before being taken by Black Venom. The house always felt bigger than its seventeen hundred square feet. It had a large, open living room with floor-to-ceiling windows that looked out over the palm trees, green grass, and the channel in my backyard. Glancing through the windows, I scanned over a covered boat lift that housed my twenty-two-foot Robalo center-console.

As I headed for the kitchen, Ange placed a hand on my chest and said, "Oh, no, you don't." She grabbed me softly by my shirt, steered me towards the master bedroom, and playfully pushed me between the shoulder blades. "You shower and change and I'll make food. Just don't fall asleep in the shower." I mumbled a few incoherent words and she spoke over them, adding, "And if you have any regard for my sense of smell, you'll throw that tee shirt in the trash."

The hot water cascading down over my sore, tired body felt amazing. After spending what felt like an eternity washing off the dirt and grime, I turned off the water, then toweled off. After a quick and much-needed shave, I felt refreshed as I stepped out into my walk-in closet and picked out a pair of comfortable workout shorts and a cutoff Dive Curaçao shirt. The unmistakable smell of grilled lobster and shrimp wafted down the hall and into my nostrils. My legs guided the rest of my body towards the smell instinctively, and I arrived back in the kitchen just as Ange plated the food.

After stuffing my stomach full of delicious seafood, I hit the sack and didn't stir until just after sunrise the following morning. There was a lot I had to do. I knew that the aftermath of what had happened on Lignumvitae Key and on the *Yellow Rose* would drag on for months. Thankfully, I had Scott and

Charles to back me up and help me sift through all of the government protocols. I spent an entire week giving statements and helping with the recovery and exploration of Shadow's treasure trove. I'd never much cared for dealing with the government, and to the surprise of most everyone I met, I didn't care about the treasure. The truth was, I'd searched for the wreck and treasure out of pure excitement. The thrill of the discovery and the history behind it all were what interested me most. I harbored no hopes of obtaining any monetary gain, and thankfully, from what I'd received for finding the Aztec treasure and from my years of working as an expensive gun for hire, I didn't really need it.

Luckily Frank stepped in and took over the project on Lignumvitae, allowing me to get back to at least a somewhat normal routine. Ange and I ran every morning, usually making a loop through downtown and around Fort Zachary Taylor State Park before heading back to the house. I fished with Jack a few times a week. Ange and I went diving every other day. And we spent much of our time hanging out with Pete over at his restaurant and entertaining him with stories about my capture, Ange's search, and our discovery of the treasure trove.

The *Yellow Rose*, it turned out, was privately owned outright by members of Black Venom. The beautiful yacht was confiscated by Uncle Sam and taken to a shipyard up near Fort Myers. As for the treasure, it was claimed by the United States, Spain, and England, each nation making the argument that it belonged to them. I stayed clear of the fight and wished only for a few coins from the treasure for my own personal humble collection of trinkets.

In March, a few weeks after the events on

Lignumvitae, I was sitting on my backyard patio on a warm Sunday afternoon. Jimmy Buffett filled the air as I sat on a wicker chair cleaning my Sig, MP5N, and Lapua sniper rifle. Ange was in the yard doing a long series of difficult yoga poses when she was disturbed by my favorite neighbor.

"Atticus!" she said, dropping softly to the grass and wrapping her hands around the ears of the energetic yellow Lab.

He sprawled out on the grass beside her, rolled onto his side, and enjoyed the scratches. After a minute with Ange, he rose to his feet, trotted over to me, and dropped the tennis ball from his mouth onto the ground beside my chair. Setting my Lapua and cleaning rag on the wicker table beside me, I snatched the tennis ball. I tried to fake him out a few times, pretending to throw it left and then right, but like the fictional character for whom he was named, Atticus was smart. He didn't budge. The only parts of his body that moved were his eyes as they tracked the bright yellow ball with fighter pilot precision.

Bringing it back, I tossed the ball far into my backyard towards the channel. It bounced twice before ricocheting off the wooden barrier along the edge of the channel beside my boat shed. Just before the rubber ball rolled to a stop on the grass, Atticus engulfed it in his mouth, then performed a somewhat graceful U-turn and ran triumphantly back towards me, his slobbery prize barely visible behind his lips and canines.

Dropping the soaked ball at my feet, he looked up and gave me an *is that the best you got?* look.

I grinned back at him. Atticus had been coming over to my yard every day I was home since my neighbor had gotten him five months earlier. I looked forward to his visits, and I was always amazed by how well behaved he was for such a young dog. My neighbor had told me he wasn't even a year old yet. Just a puppy.

I shook my head at him and performed a few full-range-of-motion circles with my right shoulder, loosening it up a bit. He dropped his upper body down, bent his hind legs, and looked up eagerly, ready to bolt at a moment's notice. Bending over, I grabbed the ball with a four-seam fastball grip, reared it back, and chucked it as far as I could from a seated position. The ball rocketed through the air, flying right over the channel wall and splashing into the water over fifty feet beyond it.

Ange, who'd been watching with a craned neck from her upward dog position, laughed as Atticus sprinted across my yard. As he neared the wall, he didn't slow or hesitate for a second. With reckless abandon, he hurled himself over the wall and disappeared from my view. A second later, I heard a splash as he hit the water five feet below.

"Logan!" Ange said playfully as she smiled at me.

I raised a hand and chuckled. "He's fine."

Fortunately there weren't any boats motoring in or out of the channel, something I should have checked before throwing it. A minute later, I heard his paws on the metal steps that led down to my boat below. He appeared, soaked, and ran across the grass back towards me. Before he'd gotten halfway there, I called his name and told him to dry off out there. Somehow he understood, and instead of showering me with drops of water like most wet dogs do to their owners, he listened and took a few moments to shake off what he could.

After half an hour of playing, I filled a bowl with water and set it on the grass beside me. Atticus drank half of it, then sprawled out on his belly beside me. He looked relaxed and content, his ears and head only rising when he heard footsteps approach from the direction of my neighbor's house.

An average-height man wearing tan slacks and a gray button-up who looked about my age walked with a smooth gait around the blue fence and hedges, heading straight towards me. He had curly black hair and skin paler than a piece of printer paper. Before he was halfway across my lawn, he waved.

Atticus jumped to his feet and ran towards the guy, stopping at his feet to be petted.

"Hey, boy," the guy said. Then he looked up at me. "Logan Dodge?" he said, continuing to walk towards me. He carried himself well and spoke articulately.

I rose from my chair.

Before I replied, he added, "I'm Josh Peterson. Whit's son."

Whit Peterson had lived next door since I'd bought the place almost a year earlier. And though we didn't know each other well, all of our interactions had been good, and of course I always enjoyed having his dog come over.

I extended my hand. "It's good to meet you. This is Angelina Fox." I motioned towards her, and she smiled and nodded at him. "How's Whit? I haven't seen him around town much lately. Heard he's visiting up north for some reason."

Josh nodded. "He came up to Cincinnati to see me and…" He paused for a moment. "And to get better treatment."

"I didn't know that he was sick," I said, shifting

my tone.

"Cancer," Josh said. "Dad didn't like to draw attention, though. It was much worse than he let on." There was a short moment of silence as he looked down at Atticus, then sighed. "He passed away a few days ago. I'm here to take care of his things. I'm his only child, and he didn't have any living siblings, so it's gonna take me a few days to get his affairs in order."

"I'm sorry to hear that," I said. "He was a good man. Let me know if there's anything I can help you with."

He smiled softly. "Maybe there is something you can do." I shrugged and he added, "I live in a high-rise condo in the city and work long hours at a hospital." Then he glanced back at Atticus. "He really seems to like you."

After another twenty minutes of talking, I told Josh that if he needed anything else, I was willing to help, and then he walked back around the hedges. I placed a hand on Atticus's still-damp head. For the first time in my life, I was a dog owner. For some reason, the feeling of settling down hit me even harder than when I'd bought the house. But as I watched Ange play with Atticus in the yard, I knew that my adventures were far from being over.

When I sat back down in my chair, my iPhone indicated that I'd received a message. I hadn't heard any word from Cesar or his men since they'd disappeared into the Gulf, but when I read the text, I knew instantly who it was from.

"We found him," was all it said.

EPILOGUE

Koh Samui, Thailand
Two Weeks Later

I stepped out of the soft crashing waves and onto a sandy beach lined with palm trees. It was just past twenty-one hundred, and Thailand's second-largest island was cast with a degree of darkness that only a new moon can provide. I slogged up onto a narrow shoreline and used the cover of the trees to change out of my dry suit, stow it in a black leather shoulder bag, and towel off my hair. I was wearing a gray suit underneath with a white button-up. The place I was going had a dress code, and I wanted to look the part. After sliding into a pair of black loafers, I clipped a ballpoint pen Ange had given me into my breast pocket, then grabbed my leather bag and headed south along the beach.

After a few short strides, I saw lights bleeding

283

through the palm leaves and heard voices not far off. Rounding a particularly large palm, I stepped onto a wide-open section of beach with a few scattered tables right by the surf. They were covered in white tablecloths, lit by strands of romantic outdoor lighting, and arranged among blooming flowers and elegant fountains in the distance.

Without hesitating, I moved towards the table closest to the beach, which had the only empty seat in the place. Grabbing hold of the wooden seat, I dragged it back a few inches through the fine white sand. Ben Kincaid sat in the other chair. He was wearing a black button-up with silver slacks, and his blond hair was slicked back. As I stepped around the chair, set my leather bag on the sand beside me, and sat down, we made eye contact for the first time. In an instant, he went from being relaxed and happy to looking like he'd just seen a ghost.

"What the hell?" was all his vocal cords could muster as his right hand gravitated to something near his waist. A second later, after blinking a few times and realizing that he wasn't in a dream, he added, "You're... you're alive. How in the hell are you alive?"

I pressed my heels into the sand, sat up slightly, and nudged the chair in closer to the table. Leaning back, I kept myself cool and composed, while my old friend looked like a spooked animal. I knew that he had a hand on some kind of weapon, but my Sig was holstered out of sight near my right hip, and I knew that I could put a bullet in his chest in half a second if I needed to.

"Wine, sir?" the waiter said as he moved in beside me. He was a Thai man. He spoke elegantly, wore a black suit, and had great posture.

I glanced at the bottle of Dom Perignon that had a vintage date of 1998 and would probably set Ben back over four hundred bucks.

"No," Ben spat. "He isn't staying. I have company arriving any minute now."

"The plans have changed," I said. "Miss Ankana will not be coming tonight. And I'd love a glass."

Ben looked furious, but the waiter nodded, grabbed the bottle, and filled the champagne glass resting on the table in front of me. As the waiter walked off, I casually grabbed the glass and took a sip. I'd never been a big fan of wine, but I actually enjoyed its sleek, mouthwatering flavor.

"I have people here," Ben said, narrowing his gaze. "People I've hired to protect me."

I grinned. "You have me just drowning in fear." Taking another sip, I added, "Something tells me your people won't be coming to your rescue anytime soon."

His eyes grew wide as I set the glass on the table.

"I'm just curious about one thing," I said. "How much money did they give you, anyway?"

He smiled arrogantly. "Two million."

I shook my head. "So that's the cost of your integrity." I grabbed the glass, raised it in the air, and said, "To protecting and serving."

He sat frozen as I finished off the champagne. Then, leaning over the table, he said, "You're not going to kill me."

Time slowed as his eyes revealed his next move. His right hand twitched, and I leaned towards him. In a flash of movement, his hand appeared above the table, his fingers wrapped tightly around the handle of a six-inch tanto knife. He stabbed the blade towards the side of my face, and just before being impaled, I snatched his wrist and redirected his strength. The sharp steel drove into the wooden table in front of me, causing the glasses and silverware to chime. Before Ben could retaliate, I leaned to my right, snatched a pair of handcuffs from the front flap of my leather bag, and locked one of the cuffs around his left ankle. The ratchet teeth clicked as it tightened, cutting off his circulation.

Ben dislodged his knife, looked at me furiously, then scanned over the table and looked towards our feet.

"What the fuck," he said, shaking his leg and clanging the metal. "One handcuff, Logan, really?"

He brought the knife back and for a second he thought about trying to stab me again. Then he froze and cocked his head.

"You're right, Ben," I said, seeing his expression shift from pissed off to confused. "I'm not going to kill you." I paused for a moment and glanced over my right shoulder, looking out towards the dark ocean beside us. "But they might."

His eyes grew wide as he kept his gaze directed towards the sand around our feet. For the first time, he realized that the other handcuff had a thin line tied to it. Following the line with his eyes, he saw that it disappeared into the dark ocean.

A pair of outboard motors suddenly roared to life far in the distance. Ben looked up at me for only a moment, his face filled with rage, then the high-strength fishing line went taut. He grunted an incoherent chaos of curses as his body jerked horizontally. He slid helplessly along the sand for a brief second before splashing into the surf. In a blur of splashes and screams, he vanished into the night. After a few seconds, his sounds and the sounds of the distant boat were silenced. All that was left behind was a trail in the sand leading from our table to the ocean.

The other patrons were in shock. A few of them spoke, wondering what was going on, but most just sat quiet, stunned and in disbelief.

I grabbed my wallet, slid out five hundred-dollar bills, and set them on the table next to the gash Ben's blade had cut in the tablecloth. Then, with my bag in my right hand and the bottle of champagne in my left, I walked casually down the beach, heading in the opposite direction of where I'd come from. Just a few hundred feet beyond the restaurant, I came to a secluded section of beach that jutted inland to form a cove.

Just down the beach, I spotted a boat with its bow carved slightly into the sand. The water was calm, and the black-and-white-hulled Monterey 270 CR barely rocked at all. Angelina sat up on the bow with one leg hanging over, toes touching the water, and the other curled up on the deck. She was wearing a pink dress and had a local white flower over her right ear. I smiled as I stepped towards her and noticed three guys tied up to a palm tree down the beach. *Ben's security.* I smiled even bigger.

"That was crazy," she said, setting a pair of binoculars on the deck beside her.

When I reached the boat we'd rented on the mainland earlier that day, I set my black leather bag in the cockpit and handed Ange the bottle of Dom Perignon. Grabbing hold of the railing, I lifted myself up and pressed my lips to hers. After a few seconds, I dropped back down onto the sand.

She smiled. "From here, it looked like an angry titan decided to use him as a skipping rock. Be honest, how close were you to wringing his neck?"

I pressed my hands into the bow, dug my feet into the sand, and pushed the boat out towards the water. Then, to avoid getting my shoes wet, I pulled myself up over the railing at the last second and plopped down beside Ange.

"I was tempted, but I'm confident that Felix and his boys will take care of him."

I rose to my feet and offered my right hand to her. After I pulled her up beside me, we stepped down into the cockpit and I started up the Volvo 425-hp engine. As I pulled us out of the cove, Ange stepped out from the galley, holding a glass of wine in each hand. She squeezed onto the pilot's seat alongside me, and I wrapped an arm around her.

"Let's go home," I said, kissing her on the cheek.

I took a few sips, savoring the flavor, then quickly brought us up on plane, cruising out into the open water of the Chumphon Archipelago. The engine roared as we skirted across the dark water. Behind us, the lights indicating Koh Samui dimmed as the distance between us grew, and the island soon disappeared altogether.

THE END

Logan Dodge Adventures

Gold in the Keys
(Florida Keys Adventure Series Book 1)

Hunted in the Keys
(Florida Keys Adventure Series Book 2)

Revenge in the Keys
(Florida Keys Adventure Series Book 3)

Betrayed in the Keys
(Florida Keys Adventure Series Book 4)

If you're interested in receiving my newsletter for updates on my upcoming books, you can sign up on my website:

matthewrief.com

About the Author

Matthew has a deep-rooted love for adventure and the ocean. He loves traveling, diving, rock climbing and writing adventure novels. Though he grew up in the Pacific Northwest, he currently lives in Virginia Beach with his wife, Jenny.

Made in the USA
Columbia, SC
04 August 2023

21273120R00174